EyeCue Productions
Presents

DUNCAN P. BRADSHAW

Second Edition
Class Three First Published in 2014

Published by EyeCue Productions

Cover design by Mike McGee.

ISBN 978-0993279300

ACKNOWLEDGEMENTS

George A. Romero for Dawn of the Dead, the inspiration for my zombies.

The Somerset Horror Cabal in its initial guise for giving me the final push to do this.

Ash and Greg for being the first 'outsiders' to read it and give me some feedback, cheers.

Stuart Park for suddenly trawling through the early draft and pointing out my writer foibles, thanks. Suddenly.

Defective Assembly for use of the song lyrics.

Mike McGee for the most excellent cover.

DEDICATION

For Debbie, my wonderful wife.

Mum, dad and Stu, finally something that I've seen all the
way through, only taken thirty odd years!

My friends and family, who get to put up with
my……unique personality, thank you.

Finally, to you, I hope you enjoy what lies within, I've been
obsessed with zombies for years, this is my initial offering
to the genre, let's begin…

ZOMBIE OUTBREAK CLASSIFICATION

Class One - Low-level outbreak, usually Third world or rural First world, numbers of infected range from one to fifty. Time of infection before 'correction' is between 24 and 48 hours

Class Two - Urban or densely populated area infection, numbers between twenty and one hundred. Casualties could reach around seven hundred. Time elapsed can be about the same as a Class One outbreak.

Class Three - Zombies measure in the thousands and infection could last several months if not dealt with immediately.

Class Four - The undead now rule the world. Society and civilisation has collapsed, humans are scattered to the wind. Survival is the only option.

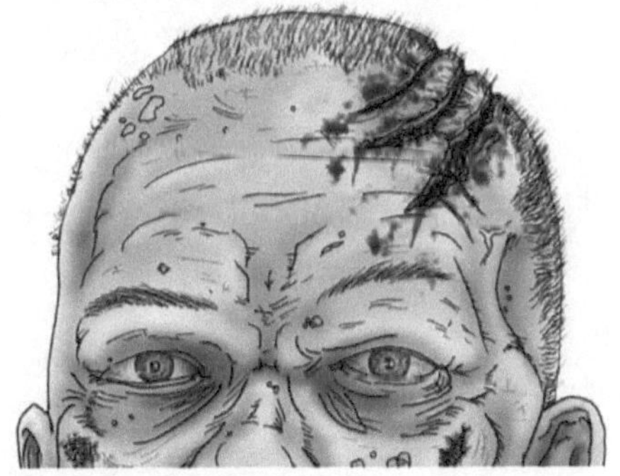

CHAPTER I

"Who do you think they were?" Francine asked, gently squeezing Colin's hand as it rested on top of the gearstick. She could feel that his heart rate was still raised, his pupils like black saucers taking in as much of the familiar surroundings as possible.

"No idea, just glad we got away from them, think they were the ones the Jefferson's talked about taking up residence at Lawn Farm," Colin replied, his voice thick with trepidation.

The Volvo estate turned left, leaving the main road and crawling slowly up a bone-dry dirt track. It kicked up a small dust cloud in its wake as it made its way towards a solitary cottage, surrounded by fields.

He relaxed slightly, the car approached the cottage and headed towards a small exposed carport on the side of the house. He looked across at Francine, "It will be okay, there's no way they could know where we are heading, let's get the food inside and we'll batten down the hatches. Have you managed to get hold of them yet?"

She raised her hand and stroked his age-worn face gently, "No, haven't managed to get a signal, I'm sure they're alright."

Colin looked across at his wife, and smiled, "Ha, the eternal optimist, glad one of us is."

The car came to a halt under the carport, they retrieved

the shopping from the boot and entered through a side door into the house. Colin manfully carried the heaviest ones, the ends of his fingers going white from the strain.

They entered the kitchen, placed the bags on the worktop and looked at each other. Francine ran a wrinkled hand through her short grey hair, "Did you manage to catch anything they said?" she enquired.

Colin cradled the back of his head with his hands, "Nothing that made sense, the only word I could make out was rapture, the tall one said it a number of times."

Francine took a couple of steps forward and closed the distance to Colin, pulling him into a tight hug, which he gladly reciprocated. The universe seemed to blink out of existence for the briefest of moments, leaving them to feel like the only two people in all of creation.

"Let's get this lot away," she whispered and squeezed his bum, before walking over to a radio resting on the windowsill and turning it on.

A squall of static erupted from the open mouth grille, she turned the dial until the white noise broke and an authoritative voice boomed out "...right now we have nothing further to add. Our advice to the public remains the same. Stay in your homes. We are preparing sites in every county should the need arise to evacuate any heavily built up areas, but right now we need everyone to stay calm."

Colin pursed his lips and raised his hand to them, absorbing every morsel of information.

"If you come across any of these individuals, we ask you to not approach them as they are extremely dangerous. If you do encounter any of them, please contact your local authority using the numbers provided on the Health Protection Agency website, or our Freephone number 08000 111555," a radio unfriendly pause took hold, it seemed louder than any words.

"In order to deal with these terrible events, we need the streets clear so we can do what is required, to protect the citizens of the United Kingdom, thank you," a cluster of frenzied voices asked multiple questions at once, none of which were discernible.

"So there you have Captain Henry Rhodes asking for…." Francine turned the volume down, and looked over at Colin, still lost in his introspection.

"Let's do what the good man says, stay at home," making a bottle of Bordeaux appear from one of the carrier bags.

Colin looked across and smiled, "It would be rude not to my love," and started packing away the shopping.

Francine stood in the living room, cradling a glass of wine and looking through the large bay window onto the field which was their front garden, a vegetable patch lay to one side, reminding her that she needed to tend to it in the next few days.

The television was on mute, the 24 hour news channel recycling the same events, quickly cutting to shaky cameras in different towns and cities, across the world, all relaying the same message.

Death and panic.

Whilst the reports differed in location and language, they all reported the same eerie tale. People being attacked by others, some by strangers, some by people they knew, other wilder reports even held tales of cannibalism.

Reams of text scrolled across with reports of a power station on the verge of going critical in Germany, of contact numbers and advice from numerous government agencies.

"Still all seems like some kind of nightmare-" Colin said distractedly, he was sat in his armchair which faced the window, "-that at any moment, I'll wake up and everything will be okay," he finished. He took a sip of wine and rested the glass on a slate coaster.

Francine turned to him and smiled, "Everything is okay, we're home and safe, and we have each other," he returned her smile and relaxed slightly.

"I was thinking about that trip we took to the Isle of Wight a few years back," Colin reclined a little in his chair and gazed at her. "We went to the zoo, remember the snake?" he asked, suppressing a smile.

She smiled, "Oh, this story again."

Colin laughed and continued "Yep, that keeper was trying for ages to get you to hold that bloody thing, after fifteen minutes, you finally relented."

"I was scared stiff, never liked them, never trust an animal with no legs," Francine added, shuddering at the memory.

"So he wraps it around you, you look down and then…" Colin began to say.

"…it pissed all over the zoo-keepers shirt," Francine finished, laughing loudly, "Never realised how much wee and shit something like that could keep in!" Colin laughed with her, smudging away a tear of laughter from the corner of his eye.

"Speaking of which, time to syphon my python," he said still wiping his eye, Colin hauled himself out of his chair, walked over to his wife and kissed her on the top of her head.

"It's no python my love," she replied, jabbing him playfully in the ribs.

"Yeah, yeah…" Colin walked out of the living room and into the toilet opposite.

Francine turned back to the window and raised the glass to her mouth allowing the wine to flow down her throat.

She hadn't drunk alcohol this early in the morning since her early twenties, but with everything that had happened since the previous night, it helped to steady her nerves.

As she rested the glass in her hand, she caught a glimmer in the distance, by the wall in front of the main road, a small burst of prism-like light.

She walked to the window, and peered closer, she

could make out something sat on top of the wall, but from this distance it could be anything, a bird or a squirrel perhaps.

Colin flushed the toilet and started to wash his hands, whistling some non-existent song. He dried his hands and opened the door, heading towards the living room opposite, crossing a small hallway which ran the width of the house, leading to the front and back doors.

He stood in the living room doorway and looked across to his wife, "Franny, what's up?" he asked, seeing that she was intently staring towards the main road.

"Nothing, just thought I saw…." her brain barely had time to register the muzzle flash or the bang before the .308 round corkscrewed through the living room window and through her skull, she crumpled like a collapsing deck chair and sank onto the floor, the glass of wine falling and weeping onto the pale blue carpet.

Colin shutdown temporarily, trying to comprehend what had just happened, he flung himself to the floor and crawled to her prone body. He gently put an arm under her neck, raising her head slightly.

He looked down at the face of the woman he had spent the last thirty-seven years of his life with and wept. Tears of sorrow rolled off his face and landed on hers, some running down her forehead and into the small bloody hole above her left eye, her entire body was loose and heavy.

He held her for what seemed like an eternity, before he could hear the sounds of people trudging up the path to the front door, heavy booted feet thudding against the dried mud path.

He laid Francine down reverently, into a small puddle of ruby red liquid, a mix of blood and wine, all life extinguished, wiped the tears from his eyes and scuttled across to the living room doorway.

He stayed hunched down, looking at the front door, the sound of voices were easily heard close by. He could make out at least two or three different voices, a few sounded local, their West Country timbre floating on the morning air.

Then silence.

He peeked round the corner of the door frame and watched as a large round hole suddenly appeared where the lock was, quickly followed by the unmistakable sound of a shotgun blast, the door resisted for a moment before creaking open.

It revealed a tall man covered in a hooded white robe, small patches of mud and grass stains were dotted here and there, a flash of black cordite smeared on one arm.

He held a double barreled shotgun easily in his hands, smoke fell lazily from one of the barrels, his face half covered with a brown scarf.

The door had given up the ghost and now continued to open, watching the scene unfold, "I don't understand," Colin said, leaning further out of the doorway, hands raised "Why are you doing this?" he asked, his voice wavering with barely checked fear.

The man stopped, his robe gently swaying in the mild morning air, "My child, it's the end of days, we gave you the chance to repent earlier, which you ungraciously declined."

Colin could tell that he wasn't a local, his accent was southern but of no identifiable region. The robed man raised the shotgun slightly, aiming it at Colin, "This is your Rapture."

The shot struck Colin on the right side of his chest, red hot pellets tearing through clothes, skin, bone and charging through his lung. The force knocked him back against the frame, his head lolled down taking in the devastation wrought by the close range blast. His breathing was wet and ragged, every pull of breath filled him with pain and heat.

As he sat slumped, another robed figure appeared from behind him, stepped over his agonised form, and walked over to Francine's body.

"You fucking idiot Billy, you shot this bitch in the head, she ain't gonna ascend now," he shouted at an unseen figure beyond the window.

The tall robed man turned his head to the sound of his accomplices voice, "No matter, Her flock will still be swollen before this day is through," and looked back at Colin who was clutching his ravaged form.

He could feel his heart pumping blood to veins that no longer existed, which in turn was seeping into his grey shirt and brown trousers. He looked up to see the tall man peering at him, head cocked to one side.

"Be at peace my child, we've spared you from the horrors that are yet to come, you are soon to be one of the Ascended." He turned, his robe billowing out behind him as the shotgun was cast onto a shoulder like a toy soldier, before he walked out of the house. Colin was left sitting in an ever increasing pool of sticky blood.

He took in another breath of pained air, slumped and was still.

CHAPTER II

Fourteen hours earlier....

"It's not me, it's you."

The words bowled across the small dining table and struck Jim square in the face. The piece of spaghetti he had spent the last thirty seconds trying to cajole into his mouth now swung like a grandfather clock pendulum, dripping globules of tomato sauce onto the white tablecloth.

Suddenly his brain rebooted, and in one movement sucked the rogue spaghetti into his mouth and picked up the full glass of wine.

Ordinarily, Jim would savour red wine, but operating in default mode he simply chinned it in one. He ran the sleeve of his white shirt across his mouth, leaving a red go faster stripe.

Sophie stared at him across the pockmarked table, her blue-eyed gaze steely and determined, no sign of emotion or regret. Jim's brain struggled to find words to form into a sentence, to try and ascertain how a quiet meal out at Il Maestoso Salmone had descended into an episode of Jerry Springer.

Jim had researched the venue on the internet before booking, it was rated 17th best on Trip Advisor, how could such callous evil exist here?

"Erm, what? Me?"

Nice work stud, obviously upon reboot, his brain had decided to just repeat the bleeding obvious. Sophie visibly sagged as if the one thing she had wanted from her bombshell had failed to materialise.

"You know what, I'm going, I can't even be in the same room as you right now," she said angrily, looking into her handbag, rooting around for her phone.

"Wh…" Jim's words had barely formed in the air, when Sophie suddenly locked onto his face, her brown, shiny hair bounced like a coiled spring, eyes like laser beams narrowed on his reddening face.

"When was the last time we went out, just you and I?" she demanded, Jim instinctively paused, his brain, now fuelled by a large glass of wine floundered in the face of such an obvious question.

"Erm….about…" again he had hardly birthed the words into reality before Sophie leant forward, like a cobra preparing to attack.

Here it comes.

"My birthday-" she uttered through a clenched jaw.

That's not bad.

"-three years ago," she quickly followed up with.

Balls.

"Well, we've been busy, doing…" he trailed off, *why can I not remember what we've been doing*, her eyebrow arched.

Oh god, not the eyebrow.

"Yes. We've been busy doing what?" she half-said, half-snarled.

"There was……" Jim trailed off, it was at this point his mental faculties, in a sign of protest and disgust at his complete lack of action, decided it was better spent playing the intro from Dangermouse in lieu of any face-saving words.

She edged further into the tables no-man's land, where only breadcrumbs and a now extinguished tea light existed. "Three whole FUCKING YEARS AGO," she blasted, her usually dignified exterior was replaced with that of a banshee.

Nearby restaurant-dwellers now quelled their own conversations and cautiously looked across to the domestic that was going on in their midst.

"We've been together for five years, but the last three and a half has just seen us existing together, not being together," her demeanour had calmed, her initial poise had returned.

Sophie carefully moved a gently curled section of hair from her eyes and sighed. "We used to go out, have fun, do things for each other, but now we're just like those miserable bastards we used to take the piss out of, the ones who sit in each other's company and just look at their phones."

Sophie withdrew her hands to her lap, carefully extricating the napkin, she gently dabbed her lips, and placed it next to her pappardelle con pollo, which was completely untouched, save for a fork embedded in its side like a food voodoo doll.

She stood up, the chair squawking and grinding against the tiled floor, piercing the already sterile, hushed atmosphere.

By now Jim had been reduced to pure autonomic responses, his eyes ran over her outline. *That's the dress she wore at her mates wedding,* he recalled spending the day sullen and morose, attempting to ingratiate himself with people he neither knew nor wanted to know.

He stared at her as she retrieved her coat from the back of her chair, shoulder length hair gently rolled over her shoulders, *she doesn't look a day older than when we first got together,* yet the energy and heat from that time was now so evidently missing.

"I'm going to stay at my mum's for a bit, we'll sort out what to do with the house in a few days once I've had a chance to work out what I'm going to do," Sophie turned from the table and took a step towards the door, the restaurant clientele in rapture to her every move.

She stopped, looked back and said "Don't call or text me, I want a few days where you fail to exist to me," the final barb was delivered in her usual softly spoken tone.

Her work done, she turned and walked to the door, exchanging stares with people as she left, each of which sunk back into their respective worlds, as if she had just disconnected their life-support.

The door closed with a click and Jim was left sitting there, fixated on the Sophie-shaped hole in his visage.

DO SOMETHING MAN, his brain demanded.

He reached out for Sophie's wine glass, peered inside its inky depths and sunk it.

Idiot.

"Excuse me sir, would you like anything else?" the waiter had asked the same question to Jim seven times now, he slowly stirred from his stupor.

"Erm, the bill please." Operating on pure instinct, he made a mental checklist of his next steps;

1 - Pay the bill

2 - Stand up and leave without falling over

3 - Head next door to the Randy Dog and have a pint to settle his shattered world

4 - Phone his brother and get him to drop him home into a pit of wallowing and self-loathing

Encumbered by the half bottle of red wine he had recently consumed, he knew each step was now filled with mild peril.

The waiter returned with a folded piece of paper on a small silver tray, a mint imperial acting as its paperweight. With a gentle cough he placed the tray on the table amongst the food debris, took a step back and looked at Jim expectantly.

Forgetting temporarily what the waiter's part in life's current theatre production was, Jim looked at him, and half-smiled.

Teeth stained with red wine and glazed with fragments of herb changed the waiter's disposition to one of annoyance. "Sir," he said insistently, his only agenda now was to get this half-cut dumpee out of his establishment without violence or vomit.

He got half his wish.

Jim ran a hand through his closely cropped hair, the taste of vomit was all pervading, but he had somehow managed to traverse the fifty feet between his seat in the restaurant to the closest stool in the Randy Dog.

His travels had not been without incident, but having paid for both dinner and a donation to the waiter's dry cleaning bill, the process of putting one foot in front of the other had gone surprisingly well.

His head was resting gently on the bar, he looked down at his boots, now speckled with stomach lining, spaghetti and red wine and wondered where it had all gone wrong.

Unable to process this, he forced his heavy head to look at the bar and focus on the banality of real life to steady the ship.

The Randy Dog was a pub time capsule, a hark back to the age of bars with a separate lounge and saloon, where the floral carpet, which despite many years of drunken footfall, still displayed intricately looping plants, leaves and stems.

It was the kind of place where even after the smoking ban had been introduced nearly a decade ago, still reeked of ingrained smoke and damp dog, as if the fibre of the building had incorporated it into it's very being, refusing to accept that times had changed and it should smell solely of spilt beer and misery.

The bar had time-dulled horse brasses hanging from it, with photos of long-forgotten parties of long-forgotten people looking as though it was the last place they wanted to be. Their frozen faces of forced revelry stared back, in-between knock-off bottles of spirits and card holders clutching bags of dry roasted nuts and scampi fries.

In front of him, on an old Badger Brewery beer towel sat his pint of Guinness, untouched, with the worst attempt at a four leafed clover on top.

Is that a swastika?

His mind rebelled between the primal urge to consume more alcohol to purge the evening's events, to one of sobriety and self-preservation.

So far tonight, he'd been dumped, had his brain fail on a whole new level, thrown up over a waiter and been subject to public humiliation. The only way things were going to improve in the short-term would be if Valhalla itself claimed him to its bosom.

He waited.

Nothing.

Balls.

Glancing around at his fellow patrons, he was met with a smorgasbord of incest, decrepitude, desperation and a hint of casual racism.

Nowhere was that epitomised more, than by the barman, Ted, he had introduced himself the minute Jim had climbed the south face of the bar stool, and sat triumphantly on its summit.

Ted had a lived in face, worn and leathered, heavily lined and creased like a sad puppet. A stained nineties lime green t-shirt hung over his generously proportioned beer gut, creating a fabric overhang almost lending an air of mystery, to which his equally stained grey trousers then removed. A mop of grey and black hair sat atop his Costa del Sol-tanned head, awkwardly positioned as if it had been put there as a joke.

"It's a bird ain't it?" Ted gruffly asked as he dried chunky glass tankards with a towel so dirty that no light could cling to its surface.

He was automaton-like in his task, pick glass up, peer into it, plunge the filth-towel into its bowels, twist, retract the towel, peer again, shrug and then place the glass in its place on the respective shelf.

Jim offered no answer except an almost imperceptible shrug. Ted, trained in the art of the barman, read this in an instant. "Knew it, minute I saw you stumble through the front door, bird I said, clear as day," Ted offered, "What was it, another fella? You been dipping your fingers into other pies? Heard it all mate, I always say the same thing."

Ted temporarily paused in his duties, the towel appearing as a macabre skull like image through the glass. "You can live with 'em, you can love 'em, hell you can even marry 'em, but you ain't never gonna figure 'em out," Ted leant back, resuming cleaning duties, happy with his little morsel of life-advice.

Jim picked up his pint, determined to at least break the surface and distort the now elongated swastika etched into the white froth. He took a few sips and placed the glass back on the towel.

How have I come to this?

Stirred into life by the disturbingly warm Guinness, Jim decided that it was finally time to try and piece together what had happened for his life to be so completely and utterly turned upside down.

Right, the facts, yes, they used to go out all the time when they first got together, but didn't everyone? Hardly much of a story for the kids "Oh me and your mum met at Spar, and spent our days locked in a vicious cycle of dinner from the chippie and small talk about our latest medical condition."

And yes, Sophie was right, it had been a while since they had gone out for a meal, but three years? He attempted to work out where they had gone the last time and when it was.

Damn, it was that long ago.

Okay, so that's not ideal, but there must be a reason for it, some important quest perchance or business of high worth which he........no, none of that. The reason was simple.

He sank more of the Guinness, the warmth made him dry-wretch.

Life. That was the reason. Well, that and his insatiable desire to climb the greasy pole at Warchucks Pharmaceutical Supplies.

He realised that the apparent neglect of his relationship with Sophie had coincided with the time he had started work in the Finance Department at Warchucks, with the promise of quick promotions and heady bonuses, neither of which had been forthcoming.

Instead he had endured a mind-numbingly tedious process of watching other people, those he deemed less capable, being given the more important and noteworthy tasks.

Had he really spent three years trying to get promoted in a job where even Stella, graced with the personality of a genital crab and the intelligence of an Opal Fruit, had somehow managed to get a better position than him?

And why tonight? Why had he decided to break his restaurant fast tonight? It wasn't anyone's birthday, it was mid-May, so quasi-religious festivals were ruled out.

His mind struggled to reveal the motives for booking a restaurant bettered only by sixteen other eateries in Monroe.

And then he remembered, *she* had suggested it. He groped around in his trouser pocket for his phone, clumsily slid it out of its leather case, and encountered another issue in a night chock full of unbridled problems.

WHAT WAS THE FUDGING UNLOCK CODE.

Imagine you've lost your keys.

Jim slugged back another mouthful of the warm liquid purporting to be Guinness. He wondered if the devils towel was responsible for the quite unique aftertaste of mackerel and lemon.

Imagine you've lost your keys and you need to find them, like right fiddling now.

From nowhere, The Heretic Anthem by Slipknot

played in the darkest recesses of his skull.

5-5-5-6-6-6

The lock screen disappeared and Jim quickly dove into the messages, trying to focus on the impossibly small writing. *Here it is.* From a week ago;

SOPHIE: Let's go out next week, like PROPERLY, for food, and not Pret a fucking Manger x

JIM: OK babe, I can only do Wednesday as Stella wants me to get those damn month end accounts done :-o xx

SOPHIE: Fine, just make sure you do, don't forget I'm late home tonight as it's the gym x

As Jim read the messages, synapses fired in his alcohol addled brain, about a warning from the past and something he had forgotten to do.

Phone Philip.

Separated by thirteen months, Philip was Jim's older brother, or as Jim knew him for the first twelve years of life, the tormentor.

It wasn't in a bullying way, but in the atypical older sibling way. Using his size and added nous, a series of Chinese burns, petrol pumps and nipple cripples had been the staple diet of growing up for Jim. Once in a while he managed to get a small amount of retribution when one of their parents witnessed it, but if they had been in prison, he'd have been Philip's bitch.

Despite sharing certain habits and mannerisms which only exist between siblings, similar laughs, gaits etc, they were polar opposites on so many things.

In place of Jim's logical approach to situations, Philip operated on instinct, where Jim repressed his emotions, Philip wore his on his sleeve, for every list Jim made,

Philip was already halfway through winging it. They infuriated and complemented each other in equal measure, but every time either hit rock bottom, they were always there for each other.

Jim knew exactly what Philip was going to say, he'd ventured his opinion prior to heading out this evening. He breathed in a lungful of stale pub air, found Phil in the contacts and hit the dial button.

"What in the name of fuckery do you want rent boy?" Philip shouted down the phone, his voice half-muffled.

"Evening Phil, how you doing?" Jim knew it was pointless to delay his request, but thinking clearly was not on the agenda this evening.

"I'm cool bro, you know, chillin' and ting, how's it going on your little tete a tete?" Philip sounded distracted, Jim could detect a TV or something on in the background, dividing his attention.

Jim sighed, much like ripping a plaster from a hairy arm, he had to just get it done "I think it's over mate, she pretty much said as much."

Silence.

It seemed as though some unseen viewer had paused the tape of his life and gone to the toilet. Ted appeared caught in motion, nose embedded in a large jar of pickled eggs, his face a mix of revulsion and pleasure. "Phil?" Jim asked, almost pleading for some kind of proof of life.

"I FUCKING TOLD YOU, YOU KNOBBER," Philip bellowed down the phone.

Jim knew this was coming, if there was one thing his brother loved, aside from liberally swearing, it was being right, even more so when Jim had sworn that there would be no way on earth that he would be, this time.

"She fucking ambushed ya, you set it up, walked in and tucked yourself right up didn't you? Man, I knew it, public place so even if you stirred from your android state, she knew you wouldn't do anything. No-one can stand seeing a bloke cry in public, or taking a shit, but that was never likely," Philip wooted.

Silence.

"You didn't take a shit in public did you Jimmy?"

Silence.

Jim held his phone to his face, he mused on the possibility of some great conspiracy, a giant galactic joke where he was the punchline.

"Dude, I'm sorry, just I did fucking tell you," Philip interjected, for all his matter-of-factness, he didn't want his brother suffering.

"So, I'm guessing you didn't call for my witty banter, what can I do for ya?" he enquired.

"Just wondered, well, hoped, you could come and pick me up, I've already had too much to drink and can't face a taxi," Jim said, an air of resignation seeping into his voice.

"You're joking aren't ya? I'm literally chasing Defalt through the streets of Chicago now man, the slippery bastard nearly lost me, even with the cars handling like milk floats on acid, I have got this motherfucker," Philip replied with no sense of realisation of the actual words he was saying.

Jim's eye twitched, the vein on his temple inflated ever so slightly, the bar turned into a long tunnel, as he started to feel something he hadn't for a long time. Anger.

"You're not coming to help your only brother out cos you want to finish off Watch Dogs, have you gone simple? All the times I spent with you when you and Helen split…"

Jim had barely started his rant when Philip interrupted "WOAH, calm down dude, I can do this later, where you at? I can take a hint that you're at DefCon One, you know I'll be there for ya."

Jim exhaled, "The Randy Dog, you know it?" the phone from Philip's end crackled for a few seconds, emitted a shriek then broke back into life.

"…where it is, been there a few times, which side you in?"

CLASS THREE

Jim was unsure if it was the phone or merely his own head that had caused the interference. "No idea dude, all I know is that I'm here and Ted the landlord owns what appears to be the largest individual collection of pickled goods known to man."

"No worries, gimme fifteen minutes to stow my shit and I'll be with you, and Jim?"

"Yeah?"

"Smells," and with that the phone went dead.

Throughout their entire lives, every time it was revealed they were brothers, everyone always said the same thing, "But you two look nothing alike."

Although similar in height, that was the closest it got, Philip had gone grey in his late twenties, but still persisted in keeping Just For Men in business, even with his short hair.

Philip was follically challenged whilst Jim had almost persistent stubble. It mirrored many parts of their personality were one physical trait was almost completely reversed in the other.

He found Jim perched precariously on a stool in the saloon bar, staring into space, a half full pint of Guinness sat expectantly within Jim's reach, though for some reason, he made no intention to drink from it.

"Howdy pard'ner," Philip said in his best cowboy drawl, making guns with his fingers and pretending to shoot them at his brother.

Jim turned to face him, partially sobered up, but still pissed on the monumental catastrophe that had befallen him in the preceding hours.

"Fuck, you look like Lord Satan himself has crapped you out," Philip said, recoiling slightly at his brother's image.

"It's true, I've had better evenings than this one, like when my appendix burst and I nearly died," Jim replied, looking utterly defeated.

"Well, it's your old roister doister here to come and

save the day, huh? Drive you off into the sunset and to a land of bounty and wonder." Philip painted out a huge horizon with his arms as if imagining the open road which lay before them.

Jim slouched forward on the stool, his feet locked into the bottom foot-rest, looking like a baroque gargoyle leering at the world.

"Bounty," he mused, "Wonder?" momentum lurched him forward and in a heartbeat he had unfurled his feet from the stool and stood before Philip, the gracefulness a marked contrast to his bedraggled appearance.

As quickly as his composure had been regained, he was returned to his half-drunken state, like a suddenly paralysed marionette. Jolted back to life he staggered past Philip towards the door and opened it with his head.

"Ow."

Philip stood facing the bar, as if savouring the last bastion of the Great British pub, an institution dating back centuries, which had provided a haven for the downtrodden, a port in the storm for the meek, a barrel of fish for the libidinally driven, an ember of respite in the world when all other outlets were closed, out of bounds or illegal.

"Is that a swastika in your pint?"

Jim had barely made three steps outside before he seemed to be held in place by an invisible force, his head tilted upwards, mouth agape, looking at the sky.

"Why is the sky red? Like, proper red." he slurred.

Philip stood behind him "Red sky at night..." he started.

"...yes, barn on fire, but that's like proper red, like blood red," Jim finished.

"Some probe carrying meteor stuff exploded on re-entry they're saying. I bet you explode on re-entry next time too," he nudged Jim in the ribs, causing him to flinch automatically to one side.

Philip walked down the pavement towards the solitary

car parked a few feet down the road, almost oblivious to the tumult in the sky above him.

Jim's mind swam with the vision of Hades above him, like some murderous Rorschach test, or a petri dish virulent with disease.

"Doesn't that seem a bit odd to you?" he spoke, expecting Philip to be stood in close proximity. Only when he got no reply did he climb back into the real world and scan the streets for his brother, upon seeing him he tottered towards him.

"Eh?" Philip called, already pressing the door release button on his key, one muffled clunk was followed by another as the doors retracted their hold on the frame.

"I said, doesn't the sky seem a bit odd to you?" Jim asked again. Philip half-opened the door, looked at his brother shuffling towards him and then up at the sky.

It had a strange iridescence, the clouds maintained their usual white-grey mottling, but even at this time of night, when it would certainly have been starting to get dark, the red sky shimmered gently between light and dark, never too bright, but a gentle glow like a flickering candle burning in the heavens.

"I guess, wasn't as bad as this when I left to come and get you," Philip replied flatly.

It was like a paintbrush laden with red paint had been dipped into the top of the world, and the colour was bleeding out to the edges.

Just as his eyes got drawn to this spectacular if not unnerving view he heard the sound of wretching and liquid spilling onto the floor, he sighed.

"You better not get any on my car, or I'll use you to clean it off," Philip said, annoyed, turning round to see Jim bent over by the car boot, he formed a near perfect right angle to the road as a small, but spreading puddle of reddish vomit oozed out from ground zero.

"Good, once you're done, jump in, it's still early, I wanna get back and get some more gaming in before the nights out," Philip said as he climbed into the driver's seat.

The drive back to Jim's house took less than ten minutes, Jim was too fixated on trying not to invoke upchuck, Philip too intent on getting back to what was left of his evening.

The sky itself appeared to have settled, as the unseemly red sky now intermingled with the natural dark blue of the late spring evening, turning it into a giant deep purple bruise from horizon to horizon.

Jim's place was two thirds down a row of Victorian terraced houses, all identical except for different colour doors or window dressings.

Parking outside usually presented the biggest issue, but as fortune would have it, an adequate space was available a few doors down from Jim's front door. Philip reversed his worn Corsa into the spot, checked he wasn't too close to the kerb, and killed the lights and ignition.

Jim was leaning forward, just enough for the seatbelt lock to have kicked in and suspend him forwards in the passenger seat.

In the half light of amber streetlights and the purple haze from above, he took on an almost comic book like appearance.

"Oi, bummer, we're home," Philip prodded Jim in the upper arm in a crude attempt to inject life into his brother.

"Great, can't wait, you can get back to your X-Box now then," Jim mumbled, not quite able to work out why he wasn't able to move forwards in the chair, as the seatbelt still held him in its caress.

Philip sighed, "Cool, c'mon bro, let's get you indoors and settled," he observed his brother trying to work out which of the three seatbelt buckles were real. Opting to put him out of his misery he pressed the button which set Jim into freefall against the dashboard.

"Ow."

"Sorry dude."

By the time Philip had walked round to the passenger

door, Jim had already managed to open the door and stand unaided, "Good work Jimbo, you really are a Larry Lightweight when it comes to booze," Philip changed course and headed down the street towards Jim's front door.

Due to their construct, the houses in Jim's street had no front gardens, both the front door that opened straight onto the pavement and the living room window which peered out onto it, were easily susceptible to the noises of passers-by.

As Philip approached his brother's front door, he glanced sideways at his neighbours window, where an old woman's stern face manifested through the net curtains.

"Fucking hell Skeletor, you scared the crap out of me," he shouted, almost jumping back into a parked car.

Jim's slow trudge had caught his brother up, he turned to the old lady glaring at the pair through the window and said "Evening Mrs Lundy, you're looking lovely this evening," enunciating every word as if she was deaf.

He gave her an enthusiastic thumbs up, at which point she shook her head and disappeared back into the confines of her house, leaving no sign of her appearance other than a gently swaying net curtain.

"Dude, see Dignitas still haven't started home-visits then," Philip muttered, regaining his composure. Jim lumbered to his front door, wrestled around in his trouser pocket determined on liberating his keys, before then fumbling them into the lock. He half-opened, half-fell through the door into the awaiting gloom of the living room.

As Philip walked through the door and closed it, the house was instantaneously bathed in light, Jim appeared from the other end of the living room, "Taa-daa! Let there be light," happy with his work, he then turned to walk through a doorway into the adjoining kitchen/dining room, before stopping, his body slightly deflated.

"She's not going to come back is she Phil?" he asked

sullenly, eyes fixed on a nondescript piece of kitchen floor tile.

Philip walked through the clean and tidy living room, noting that no mess existed except for a side table next to one half of the sofa, obviously where his brother took up residence in the evenings.

He put an arm around Jim, who sagged further, before he pulled him in close for a monumental bear hug. The pressure of which pulled Jim's body right up to Philip's whilst simultaneously pushing his arms outwards like a star on a Christmas tree.

"Shhh, it'll be alright mate, you just need to sober up and work out what you want to do," Philip uttered into Jim's ear, though at such close proximity it turned his whisper into a boom.

Jim patted his brother on the back like a wrestler yielding, and Philip gently released him, as he did so he noticed that Jim's eyes were red and welling up.

"Fuck a sock, the Tin-man has a heart after all," Philip blurted out.

Jim looked up at him "Tact and subtlety were never your strongpoint huh Phil?"

Philip looked back and half-smiled "Fuck no, I left all that to you and mum, you two were always the closed books, you know what you get with me, like it or lump it."

Philip stood back, "Fine, there's only one thing that will help right now, a cup of tea and a biscuit," he stepped past Jim into the slowly brightening kitchen, "You sit yourself down, chuck some tunes on and I'll rustle us up a brew," his voice trailed off as his head disappeared into a cupboard hunting for teabags.

Jim sighed, and sloped off to the sideboard where his MP3 player was resting in its dock, *what possible music could fit an occasion such as this?*

He could barely focus on the list of scrolling album names, before accidentally hitting play on Stone Sour's 'Get Inside' at full volume. A sonic blast akin to a plane taking off ripped through the living room, before Jim came to his senses and hit pause.

Silence.

"Oops."

Philip appeared from the kitchen, "Fucking hell man, you nearly gave me a heart attack!," before disappearing back into the kitchen on his scavenging hunt.

Jim heard a faint thud from next door, "Sorry Mrs Lundy," before settling on Hoobastanks 'Every Man For Himself'.

It had been so long since he had experienced a break-up that he instinctively fell back to what he had listened to the last time he'd been heartbroken.

As the drill sergeant intro started, Jim plopped himself into the space on his side of the sofa, pulled his phone out of his pocket and checked to see if he had any messages.

None.

His resistance now plummeted and he realised that it had not been some horrible nightmare. His bottom lip started to wobble.

No. Not yet.

Jim's apparent lack of emotion was something he learned from his teens, always too trusting and accepting of people at face value. By the umpteenth time he'd been hurt, he decided enough was enough, he had to protect himself, to build a wall around his inner self, never let anyone in again.

Except he had let Sophie in, and in the process of losing her tonight, something inside had come loose. A faulty connection, where once there was a uniform function and purpose, now there was a break, missing code, none of which he knew would be repaired with ease.

"Here you go bumder," Philip said as he placed the mug of tea on the side table next to Jim. He grunted in acknowledgement and sat up.

"She said it was me, not her, but surely it's both of us? There are two people in a relationship, it's not down to one party to do all the work," Jim said, almost as if to no-one but himself.

"Mate, I'm not going to pretend for one minute I know what in the name of fuck goes on between you two, you want my opinion?" Philip asked.

"Yeah."

Philip took a sip of tea, and squeezed halfway down an already open packet of orange chocolate digestives, "Man, I fucking love these, good work bro," he shoved the entire biscuit sideways into his mouth and before biting down, looked like a cartoon snake who had swallowed a plate.

There followed an awkward lull as Philip hurriedly chewed the biscuit with Jim looking on, finally finishing, he took another sip of tea, and turned to his brother.

"Every time I saw you guys together, you looked kinda made for each other, but the last time I saw you both, you could see that she wasn't entirely happy. Remember mum and dad's wedding anniversary?" Philip asked, looking at him straight in the eyes.

Jim attempted to recall the event, it was at the end of last year, Phil was still with Helen, and all six of them had gone out to the Bridge Brasserie in town for a meal, from what he remembered it was a perfectly normal evening. "What of it?" he could feel himself move onto the defensive.

"We were all chatting away, and mum, as she always does when we go out with them and our partners, started the usual questioning about when you guys were gonna get married, have kids and all the jazz." Philip stopped, put his mug down and started to excavate nuggets of biscuit from his back teeth with his fingers. Jim could still not recall anything of note.

Satisfied with his haul, Philip continued "Sophie did what she always did, be non-committal, except she was staring at you the entire time, not in a malicious way, but in an inquisitive way, trying to gauge something from your demeanour."

His intrigue piqued, Jim asked "What was I doing?"

Philip was looking distractedly at the packet of biscuits on the sofa, "You looked up from your phone, apologised, said it was work and then asked what everyone was talking about. Remember Sophie looking away, looked a bit crestfallen to be honest," Philip replied. "These biscuits are well nice mate, you should tuck in before I destroy them all,"

"You reckon she wants all that then?" Jim asked.

"How the fuck should I know brainiac, you're the one who has lived with her for the past god knows how many years, haven't you talked about this with her?" Philip pulled another biscuit from the packet and shoved it in his mouth.

"We did, a few times, but not for ages, seems like a common theme huh? Man, how did I let this get so messed up?" Jim muttered, looking down at his stained and creased clothes.

"Dude, best thing you can do right now, is get some kip, then wake up tomorrow and work out what you want. This might not be gone completely yet, you might be able to do something about it, but you have to know yourself what the hell is important to you." Philip picked up his mug of tea and glugged it down in one, took a biscuit and stood up.

"Mate, I gotta go, do what you think is best, I'm not exactly the relationship guru here, look at my history, hardly spectacular. Life might be better off without her, this could be a blessing in disguise."

"Or the biggest mistake I've made," Jim countered.

"Yeah, or that, anyway, it don't matter really, what's happened has happened, no point worrying about what ifs or maybes, deal with the reality. That's what you always used to say wasn't it?" Philip said, a subtle dig buried in his words.

Something inside Jim clicked back into place, some familiar setting was switched back to 'Standby'. "You're right. For once," Jim smirked and held his hand out.

Philip reciprocated in a bro-shake, "You know I'm always right you nonce, now, I really am going."

Philip stood up, shaking crumbs onto the floor, Jim prised himself from the sofa and stood up slowly, he could feel his life force returning, like the opportunity for redemption had offered itself to him.

Philip opened the front door and stepped into the pavement, he looked back at Jim standing in the doorway holding the door open, using it as a crutch to remain vertical.

"Cheers Phil, for everything, it's appreciated."

"Think nothing of it Jimbo, it's what family is for huh?" Philip looked up at the raisin coloured sky, then back at Jim, "Besides, not as if it's the end of the world huh?"

CHAPTER III

PHIL: It's the end of the world!!!!

Jim glared at the text again, as if some hidden meaning would become apparent if he stared at it more intently. He glanced around and realised he hadn't made it to his bed, instead he had passed out on the sofa.

He rubbed the sleep from his eyes and looked at his phone again. It was clear that Philip had tried to call him a number of times in the morning, the text message was timed at 09:35.

It was then reality hit him square in the face like a prize-fighter taking on a busboy. He wasn't just late for work, he was monumentally late for work, he looked at the time, and it almost laughed back at him;

10:01.

Balls.

He was always at his desk by 8, a gurgling emanated from his stomach as he reassembled his skeletal frame into action after sleeping sat up.

He mentally triaged what basic acts of sanitation he could get away with and headed towards the stairs. Climbing them as fast as his one dead leg would allow, he quickly entered the bathroom and began the morning ritual of ablutions, cleaning his teeth and washing his face, before lurching into the bedroom and opening the wardrobe.

Where are her clothes?

She had obviously packed prior to their dinner date the evening before, she had evidently put some thought into what was going to happen.

He allowed himself a brief minute to catch his thoughts before remembering his prime directive involved getting to work before Stella decided to tear him a new one.

Moments later he was by the front door, dressed, and carrying out the last minute departure checks before leaving his house.

"Work pass, yep," he patted his shirt pocket.

"Wallet, yeah," slapping his back trouser pocket.

"MP3 player to drown out the world, a-ffirmative," holding it aloft to see that some travelling music by Enter Shikari was playing next.

"Keys and bag, right let's roll," he shook his keys like maracas and picked up his bag.

Luckily, work was a ten minute stroll away, he was confident that even in his drowsy state he could be there in five.

As he closed the door and put his MP3 player on he noticed that the world seemed slightly off this morning.

He didn't live on a busy road, but there were more people than usual on the streets, all moving with purpose and a degree of controlled panic.

He paid them no heed and turned down the pavement, when he caught something out of the corner of his eye. "WAAAHHH!" he shouted as something slammed against the inside of Mrs Lundy's living room window.

He removed his earphones and looked closer, it looked like Mrs Lundy, but whatever stared back at him was almost like a facsimile of her.

She was always immaculately presented, never a hair pin or button out of place, but it looked as though she too had spent the night on the sofa as she was still wearing the same clothes as the previous night.

"I'm sorry about last night," Jim half-shouted, half-mimed at the old lady transfixed on him through the net curtain and double glazed window.

She paid his words no heed and appeared to be trying to say something, her mouth was moving up and down as if in conversation, but no words were coming out.

He looked closer, what the hell was up with her eyes? Two milky white marbles with small black dots peered back, registering him only on the basest of levels.

"I think you need to go to the opticians Mrs Lundy," he shouted, emphasising every word as if she had suffered some kind of brain trauma.

Without warning, Mrs Lundy jolted forwards battering her forehead into the window, her teeth gnashing against the net curtain and glass, looking as though she was trying to chew her way through to Jim.

Jim looked at her again, she wasn't bleeding, and aside from adding glass chewing to her CV of being the world's most miserable hag, she seemed otherwise okay.

"Look, I've got to get to work Mrs Lundy, I'll pop round and see you later," he shouted, before turning away and putting his earphones in.

Looks like her daughter will be putting her in that home sooner rather than later.

The Warchucks building was in a small retail park on the edge of town, easily reached via back streets from where Jim lived. The buildings were all alike, small self-contained two storey red bricked units, housing various local businesses and operations. On a normal day, the roads would have cars and vans parked up and down like some giant game of dominos, but not today it would seem.

Is it a bank holiday or something?

The vehicles that were parked seemed to have been put there in haste, many still had their engines running. Jim removed his earphones and could hear distant sirens, and a crackling sound, like popcorn being born in tin foil on the hob.

He scanned the horizon and could see a small pall of smoke coming from the approximate direction of his office. He picked up his pace and jogged, all the time, people were spilling out of buildings, clutching personal possessions, such as golf trophies and picture frames. One person was even carrying a small beer fridge out of a solicitors at the entrance to the cul de sac, oblivious to anyone else.

I am definitely missing something this morning.

As he approached the small car park directly outside Warchucks he saw Stella standing in an empty parking bay. She was looking at the building which had a small stack of smoke emanating from the far corner.

He heard behind him the sound of an over-revved car, "Stella!" Jim yelled, as she turned, the world descended into time lapse photography. From his left hand side, a hatchback car careened past him, not travelling fast, but quick enough to know that it wasn't under control.

As the car flew past, his main vision saw Stella turn to the sound of her name being called. Her tied back ginger hair swivelled to reveal her stern alabaster white face, thick black rimmed glasses staring at Jim, she was clutching a fire extinguisher to her chest. Her expression changed from one of consternation to that of surprise as she saw the car heading right for her.

Time suddenly accelerated back to normal speed again, and in one motion, the car hit Stella square on, bunting her forward like a pinball flipper, turning her into a human Catherine Wheel.

She flew backwards from the impact until she hit the front wall of the office, the car, only slowed slightly by the collision, continued its way forward, until it had also hit the office wall, and loomed over Stella's prone body.

Jim stood still momentarily, trying to process the many events which had unfurled in the space of a few seconds.

He came to and ran over to the car, where Stella lay. As he got closer he could see that the car had hit the building on its front left corner and was partially lodged in the brickwork. The engine still revved loudly and he looked inside to see a middle aged man slumped over the wheel, wearing what appeared to be a hospital gown. His liver-spotted back a contrast to the striped gown now hanging off his thin frail body.

He opened the driver's door and turned the ignition off, the whining ceased instantly as the engine spluttered and died. The man was propped against the steering wheel, a large growing purple bruise started to swell across the expanse of his forehead from the impact with the dashboard. His arms were limp and hung to each side like an ape, Jim felt the man's pulse and waited.

Nothing.

He held on, perhaps he wasn't doing it right, he slid his fingers up and down the man's wrist.

Nothing.

The man's skin felt clammy and rubbery like it was some kind of prosthesis. He leant forward, moving his ear in the direction of the man's open mouth, he couldn't hear anything.

"Sugarpops, he's dead."

Jim had never seen a dead body before, he froze, pulled back from the open door and just stood there.

"Heeellpp me Jiiimmmm…." said a hushed, raspy voice, formed from words and the sound of gargling.

He turned towards the sound and saw Stella lying on the floor, the front right corner of the car which hadn't embedded itself in the building instead existed in the same place as the bottom half of Stella's body.

At the front of each building was a small grass verge edged by kerb stones, the car wheel was firmly pressed up against the kerb stone and Stella's pelvis. Her legs appeared from either side of the centre of the tyre, and it looked for a brief moment like they were growing out of the ground.

Her body was half sat up against the kerb stone, looking over Stella's body he saw her back had been brutally snapped back onto the grass verge, she looked as though she was an art installation, some kind of broken doll. Her glasses had come off during the impact, and her ivory face was flecked with blood, small clumps of her hair stuck to larger congealed splatters of fluid.

Jim almost didn't know where to look, such was her ruin, her head was resting on the concrete step to the front door, a puddle of sticky ichor slowly spread under her matted hair. The fire extinguisher lay off to one side by her left arm, it was her only arm that was visible and it was clearly broken.

Smaller scratches and contusions seemed to hint that the appendage could be saved, until Jim looked at where her elbow should be and saw beneath the skin broken pieces of bone were frozen in time like falling Jenga.

"Heeelllpppp meeee yoouuuu fuuucccckkkkiinnnngg diiicccckkk," she gasped, sounding like a drowning Dalek. Blood trickled from the corner of her mouth, even in her demolished state, with her only saviour at hand, she still could've done with the Customer Care Course provided by Warchucks.

Jim knelt down by her face, not knowing what he should do, "It'll be alright," he said, not even believing the words himself.

"Phhooonneee thhheee ammbbbuullllllaaaannnnccccceeee yoooo moorrrooo….." the lisping, wet words drifted off, her eyes rolled back in her head, the parts of her body still connected to her central nervous system shuddered and then stopped.

Her decimated body settled into the shape of the floor she had been smashed into, looking like a blood-drenched human welcome mat stretched over the grass and concrete.

Jim could feel his heart beating in his brain, thudding like a low powered jackhammer. Finally, he pulled the phone out of his pocket and dialled 999.

"This is the Emergency Services, unfortunately due to

exceedingly high call volumes, we are unable to connect your call right now. Please stay on the line and you will be connected as soon as one of our operators is free…" there followed a pause and then a tinny instrumental rendition of 'Message in a Bottle'.

Jim looked at his phone dumbstruck, *this has got to be some kind of joke or messed up dream.*

He ended the call, and redialled, "This is the Emer…" he ended the call again.

What is happening here?

Still kneeling, he looked at Stella's face, he had never seen her so calm and peaceful. Humanity washed over him, he brushed the hair from her face and closed her eyelids, he had no idea why, but they did it on every film he had seen where someone had died.

"Sleep tight Stella, may you find peace in death that you never found in-" suddenly her eyelids rolled open and two milky white orbs stared back, punctuated only by a black dot in the middle.

"-life?" Jim gasped, going all high-pitched.

"Stella! You're alive! Stay with me, I'll go and get help," Jim said, barely believing that anyone could have survived.

"Man, you really are one tough son of a-" he stopped as Stella started to try to move forwards, towards him.

"-bitch."

Her smashed upper arm suddenly jerked towards him, the lower half of her arm a mere jumble of broken bones contained within a sack of skin. Unable to get much momentum with her arm, she began trying to reach for him, which just made her lower arm swing like a bag of marbles. It hit him gently on the face, the grinding crunch of bones intermingled with a slapping sound.

Her head tilted forward as much as it could, given that her lower back was completely contorted against the kerb.

The sound of small bones breaking and straining were drowned out by the chomping of Stella's mouth, furiously moving as if chewing on an impossibly tough bit of steak.

Jim fell onto his backside, not quite believing what he was seeing, this broken machine had come back to life intent on doing anything possible to get at him.

The thing formerly known as Stella appeared to realise he was out of reach, the gnashing of teeth stopped, and a low-end moan wailed from her open mouth. From nowhere, it was joined by another, Jim looked to his left and saw the man in the car looking at him, his eyes the same balls of nothingness, arms outstretched, reaching for Jim like a crane, his mouth wide open, a moan like a detuned bullhorn centred onto Jim's location.

His mind sent conflicting messages, both of these people were dead, he knew that, yet here they were as clear as day moving. Not just moving, but trying to get to *him*. He pedalled backwards along the floor, scuttling like an insect, the hypothalamus had spoken, flight took effect.

His motion was abruptly stopped as he felt himself nuzzle up against someone's feet and legs. The legs were immovable and firm, he put his hands behind him and they rested on two well-built boots, his mind told him not to do so, but he instinctively looked up.

A head silhouetted by the sun looked down at him, and took a step back, Jim completed his fall backwards, and was now lying completely prone on the floor, the sound of moaning seemed to disappear as the person bent down towards him.

A face materialised out of the bright light, piercing eyes looked directly into his, seemingly satisfied with what they saw, the person stood up to full height and held out a hand, "Hey buddy."

Jim was yanked to his feet by an arm made of pure sinew and muscle, as he drew level with his saviours face, he looked at the man's features. He looked in his forties, taut skin held over a square skull, with a thick brown moustache bristling with intent.

The receding hairline gave him the appearance of a Californian cop, as did his uniform, all black, smartly pressed, with flecks of dried blood now engrained within its surface. Jim looked down to a shiny metal badge on the man's broad cliff-face of a chest, 'SECURITY'.

He was about to thank his rescuer, when he was unceremoniously shoved behind his hulking frame. He could make out that his liberator was carrying something in his left hand. The hulk now turned his gaze to the man draped in the hospital gown, heaving his way out of the driver's seat.

It was apparent that he too had broken his legs or worse, as he was unable to walk. He poured out of the car like a human waterfall, the gown parting as he did to reveal a naked arse.

"Pilgrim, you could at least have wiped," said Jim's protector, he took one pace towards the man and raised his arm. Now he was a few steps back, with the sun behind him he could at last make out what the man was carrying. It was a wooden baseball bat, blood-stained, with several twelve inch nails punched through its head, some bent and buckled. In one simple movement the bat arced down at the half naked man sprawled on the floor, who was still clawing his way along the tarmac towards them both.

A dull thud rumbled through Jim's feet as the bat connected with the back of the man's skull and the road. The security guard huffed once, and started to retract his swing, ready to strike again. As he raised the bat, it was clear that the bat and its hat of nails had got stuck in the back of the man's head.

"Shit," he muttered, "Thought those damn nails would help, oh well, know for next time," and he stomped down on the impaled skull, sending it bouncing off the grey road.

The man had stopped moaning, and either side of where his face now lay were fragments of teeth and blood.

The guard took a step back, and hit the bat against the road, bending over the nails, he swung up and down again like an oil pump jack, this time it connected with the base of the skull where it meets the neck and an almighty crack sounded out.

The guard huffed again and sent down another pile driver, hitting the skull in the same place, it carried on its course and hit tarmac, sending bone and brain matter in a 360 degree arc. The gowned man's appendages sprawled like a cross, twitched once as if electricity coursed through them, and were then still.

Momentarily expended from the effort, the guard stood, the bat resting from his hands into the cracked skull. He hefted the bat onto his shoulder, turned to Jim and said coolly "The names Francis, what's yours?" As he spoke he pulled a pack of cigarettes from his trouser pocket, pulled one out and put it in his mouth.

"Francis, isn't that a girl's name?" Jim replied, on autopilot.

Francis was in the process of applying flame to cigarette, when he stopped and cocked a sideways glance at Jim. He paused, lit the cigarette, took a drag and then put the lighter back in his pocket.

Jim realised what he had just said and gulped. "Erm, I mean…." but was greeted by the sound of rumbling laughter.

"I like you, you're funny. Now what are you doing here?" Francis asked, still smiling.

"I work here, well, worked here. Excuse me for asking but what is going on? Why did they come back to life? Why did you smack him till his skull split open and when will my damn hands stop shaking?" Jim blurted out.

The two men looked at each other, "Excuse me a minute' Francis said, and he walked off to the front of the car. Jim fell back into reality and could hear the moaning again, coming from where Stella lay, "Wait a minute!" he said and headed towards Francis, side-stepping the scatterings of head offal and bone laying strewn around the hospital patients body.

They stood over Stella, still unable to free herself from the car, she was trying to jab at them with her broken arm, which was still swinging round like a skeletal swing ball set. Whatever was left of the woman he had worked with for the past two years now seemed gone. She had been replaced by some *thing* whose sole duty was to get to them.

"You know her?" Francis asked, taking another pull from the cigarette.

"Yeah, I know, knew her…." Jim corrected himself, the guard took another drag from the cigarette, holding it in longer than before.

"Best I can figure it, if you die, you come back as that," Francis pointed at the Stella abomination with the bat, small pieces of bloodied tissue falling from the end onto the ground.

"You mean?" Jim started to ask.

"Yep, it's the goddamn zombie apocalypse," Francis replied, raising the bat skywards.

"WAIT," Jim demanded, "I think I should do it, you know, kinda like a dry run."

Francis took another long drag, and exhaled the smoke in front of Jim, causing him to cough. "Ha, I do like you, be my guest slim," he stood back and offered Jim the bat.

Jim shook his head and picked up the fire extinguisher. Francis stood back, and gave Jim some space to work in. Jim moved forward, looking down at what remained of the woman who had delighted in bossing him around.

"Stella, you're fired," he brought the fire extinguisher down on her head like a rock crusher. It instantly sank through her forehead, dividing her head in two, the main bulk of the skull and her facial features now existing as separate entities. He raised it again and brought it down hard, easily pulverising the exposed soft tissue of the frontal lobes. He released it and looked down. Before turning his head sideways and throwing up.

Francis allowed him time to finish vomiting and placed a fatherly hand on Jim's back, "Okay son, good work, we best be going now though."

Jim wiped his mouth clean of sick and looked up at

Francis. "Fire extinguisher, you're fired, do you get it?" he asked.

"Ha, yes kid, very witty, you're like Arnie out of Commando." The bromance was interrupted by the muffled sound of the Grand Theft Auto 3 Mission Complete ringtone.

"Phil."

"Jimbo!"

"Zombies."

"Yeah, I hate those guys, where you at, I'll come get you, we got plans to make."

Jim looked down at the remains of his boss, the fire extinguisher cemented upright in the remains of her head, "I'm outside work, I just punched out."

Philip pulled up outside Warchucks with as much gusto as the 1.2 engine would allow, the traffic on the streets was getting worse, with people deciding it was time to get out of Dodge.

He turned off the engine, opened the door and left the car, walking over to where his brother and a burly man were sat on a car bonnet, a short distance from a car attempting to mate with an office wall.

As he got closer he could see two bodies, one was a half-naked man in a backless gown, mooning the sky, with his head now a bowl of chunks of brain and pieces of bone. The other was a woman, or so he guessed, it was difficult to make out the bodies features as it was bent and twisted in unnatural ways. Where its head should have been stood a blood-caked fire extinguisher, acting as a memorial to the violence that had gone on there.

Philip deviated from course at the last moment, walking past his brother to the scene of brutality. As he got closer, he pulled out a notebook from a bag slung around his shoulder, and started writing furiously. The flurry of writing ceased as quickly as it started, he put the notebook back into the bag and looked over at the two protagonists.

"Wow, you've been busy," Philip said, "You are?" he

extended his hand to the moustachioed stranger, smoking a cigarette and shouldering a baseball bat.

"Francis, I pulled security on this estate, you must be James' brother, pleased to meet ya slim." He took Phil's hand and shook it, it was a solid grip, two firm shakes and was then released, before retrieving the cigarette from his mouth and blowing out smoke.

"Francis? Isn't that a girl's name?" Philip said dead-pan, he clapped his hands together excitedly, then stopped, "Oh wait, I had something then, it'll come back to me."

Francis rolled his eyes and nodded, "I get that a lot."

"You weren't joking earlier with your text Phil, you got any idea how bad it is?" Jim glared maniacally at his brother, eyes aflame with adrenaline as if he'd been up for three days straight on an MDMA and ketamine binge.

"Well, it's difficult to say, think we should head back to mine, get sorted and work out what the fuck we're going to do. Reports are coming in from all over the shop, whatever it is, it's global, and it's nasty, real nasty," Philip replied, attempting to equal the masculinity exuding from Francis.

Francis slid off the bonnet and turned to the pair, flicking the cigarette on the floor, he looked up "Well fella's, it's been emotional, but I better make tracks, gonna be a lot of folks in need of help right now, and I best do what I can."

"Cissy! That's it!" Philip shouted, the memory returned. Francis looked him square in the eyes, the stare a question in itself. "Erm, Cissy is short for Francis....okay, moving on."

Jim sighed and tried to slide off the car, but with the blood still congealing on his trousers, he remained rooted to the spot like a child stuck on a wet slide.

Philip looked across and smiled, "You got any family to see, anyone to get Francis?" For the first time since meeting Jim, Francis looked vulnerable, for the briefest of minutes he could see thoughts racing through his head.

"Nope, not anymore," his poise returned, "You two take it easy, look after each other and get out of the cities, in a few days it's going to be overrun with these things, you mark my words."

He gave them a salute and walked away.

"Where the fuck did you find him?" Philip asked with a hint of jealousy, watching as Francis made his way out of the estate.

In the distance he could see people running, whilst closer to hand, others still retrieved items from buildings.

"He saved me Phil, came out of nowhere when Mr Naked Ass man and Stella tried to get me," he had now managed to climb off the car bonnet, and was trying to take stock of the situation.

"Well, let's get back to mine and get organised, it's time to invoke. *The Plan,*" Philip said, staring at Jim expectantly.

"The plan?"

"Yeah, the motherfucking plan, you know, the one that we made for this exact same motherfucking situation. You know. THE. MOTHER. FUCKING. PLAN." Philip replied, looking annoyed.

"I have no idea what you're on about, let's go, you can remind me on the way," Jim turned towards Philip's car and headed off.

Philip looked to the ground and shook his head, mumbling to himself "Dude can't even remember the motherfucking plan."

CHAPTER IV

"We can't stay here forever love, everything's gone to pot," she said, running a hand through her daughter's hair, still drying from a hasty shower.

Sophie pulled her legs up to her chest and hugged them, "I know mum, just not sure what we should do right now, I think we should listen to what they're saying on the telly and just stay put for now, he…" she drifted off.

"Isn't coming, you told him not to contact you remember? I think that ship has not only sailed but it's over the horizon and probably considering alternative harbours," her mother finished curtly.

Aside from the ruby red sky, the hour long journey back to her mum's house had been uneventful. The familiar route was well travelled over the years, whether from university or when she had met Jim and they'd moved in together.

Lugging the suitcase from the boot and walking through the front door, the same smell had greeted her, the one that had been there in that house since she could remember, the smell of home.

Her mother pulled the lid off a large metal tin and slid it across the table, "Go on love, have a biscuit, I'll put the kettle on, we can have a look on the internets and see what we should do."

Sophie smiled, "It's the inter*net* mum, there's not more

than one of it," she reached into the pile of biscuits and pulled out a custard cream.

She unfurled her legs and reached into her vacuous handbag, rooting around in its depths before pulling out an iPad covered in a pink floral cover and browsed to the BBC News website.

Every headline on the front page was related in one way or another, it was mostly reports from the UK. It seemed the island of the United Kingdom had been cut adrift, largely due to the global communication networks being overloaded.

"They're saying London is a complete no-go now, advising people to not even bother trying to get in. Some Captain Rhodes saying that the military will be heading there as a matter of priority," Sophie reported.

Her mum poked her head round the kitchen door, "Still one sugar love?" Sophie and her latest failed fad diet glared back at her, "Fine, fine, one it is," and she disappeared back into the kitchen.

"Something here saying that the Prime Minister hasn't been seen since first thing this morning," she clicked on the story, the progress bar appeared at the top of the screen, barely even visible and not moving. "For fucks sake," she muttered, and pressed the cross to cancel it.

She scrolled down the page, past a headline from Germany, "Shit, some nuclear power place in Germany has gone haywire, sending some blokes in to try and stem the worst of it," she shook her head, "Poor bastards, just like that Fukishima place, doubt they'll be getting out of that in one piece."

She continued to scan the headlines, most seemed to report the same thing, gangs of cannibals attacking people up and down the land, even some preposterous reports of the dead coming back to life.

"Ooh, look, some stupid football man has decided to stop playing for someone, how does that qualify as news when all this other stuff is going on?" her mum appeared from the kitchen, clutching two huge mugs of tea.

"What's that dear?" she asked, completely oblivious.

"Nothing mum, here you go, 'Advice from the Department of Health', good job you made the tea, this could take a while loading up," Sophie set the iPad down onto the table.

Her mum sat opposite, straightening out the tablecloth, "So…how do you feel about it all now, in the cold light of day?" blowing into the top of her tea, sending steam curling into the air.

Sophie seemed distracted, caught in a world of her own, "Not sure, I'd been thinking about it for so long, that it doesn't feel real, part of me is glad I did it, the other thinks I should've gone about it differently, tried to make it work somehow."

Her mother put her mug down and walked over to a low chest of drawers, opening the top drawer, she dug around for a while and then pulled something out, closing the drawer behind her softly. "Do you remember when this was taken?" she held out a picture frame, a young couple cradled a small child at the seaside, in the background children played in seaweed infested water.

"Ha, yes, just, that was at Studland, our first proper holiday, it was just before dad…" Sophie stopped.

"Before he sodded off! Going out for a paper my arse, the coward didn't even have the balls to tell me it was over, open the frame up Soph," her face struggling to hold back decades of bitterness.

Sophie turned the frame over and unclipped the back, inside lay a yellowed postcard of Tucktonia, showing children in hideous brown shorts and knitted jumpers from the seventies, looking in awe at model replicas of famous landmarks.

"I remember Tucktonia, I loved the mini Eiffel Tower, walking round there made me feel like a giant, we went there just before…." Sophie turned the postcard over, her mum's address was written in big letters, on the other side were three large words;

SORRY

LOVE, PETE

She re-read it, and then looked at her mum, puzzled. "That was the sum total of what he told me. The only thing I've ever had from him since was the divorce papers off his solicitor a few months later." Her mum retrieved the postcard from Sophie and studied it again, even though she knew every centimetre of it.

"You never talked about him, y'know, when I was growing up, just said that he had gone, and that he was never coming back. I asked for ages, but you never said anything, in the end I just stopped asking," Sophie reached out a hand and placed it on top of her mothers.

"As you can see, there wasn't a great deal I could tell you, even if I wanted to! A few years back I ran into his sister when I was on holiday in Cornwall. She said that he had married again to a butcher up near Leeds, she hardly saw him, but said that he seemed happy enough," she clutched Sophie's hand, before roughly rubbing an invisible tear from the corner of her eye, "Bastard."

She looked at her daughter, "Ha, listen to me, didn't mean to go on, just-" She inhaled deeply, "-I never got a chance to find out why he left or if there was anything I could've done to stop him. Hell, after all these years and all the things I've done, I don't even want to know what I would be now if I had." She turned the postcard over, tracing a line over the mini tower bridge on the front.

"Only you know if you've made the right choice, whether you think it is worth working at or worth saving, he always seemed like a nice boy, just a little quiet," her mother said, picking her mug up and resuming the cooling process. "Plus, with everything that's going on, is it even practical, you couldn't get there easily now and I've tried calling your aunt today and had no luck."

Sophie looked at the photo, its appearance seemed to have distorted and altered following her mother's revelation. She looked closely at her father and saw that the grin was forced, eyes she assumed were full of love for his family now showed that he seemed distracted, he already looked out of place.

"You're right, Jim can wait for now, we just need to focus on what we should do, everything else will sort itself out," Sophie said, her mind made up. "Finally," she added, and picked up the iPad to see what nuggets of information the DoH had for them.

"Stay indoors. Keep pets indoors. Don't approach strangers," Sophie read some of the choice phrases aloud.

"Don't approach strangers? So we should stay away from Henry next door then!" her mum said, followed by a giggle.

Sophie skim-read the page, feeling more indignant and patronised the more she read. "Says here that they are looking to set up some safe zones in each county soon, so how can we stay indoors and get to these safe zones?"

Sophie's mum caught something out of the corner of her eye, "About bloody time, gimme a moment love," and walked into the hallway, beyond the frosted glass was an outline of someone in a blue uniform, with a splash of red over their shoulder.

She pulled the door open "Been waiting for you all bloody morning, you're normally here by half nine, what's kept ya postie?" a postman stood with his back to her, looking at the house opposite swaying gently.

"Have you been drinking? Is that why you're late? Been tucking into a Weatherspoon's breakfast and a cheeky Tuborg before work? No matter, just need me passport, only a week till Mykonos," she said, hands on hips.

She tutted and put her hand on his shoulder, turning him to face her, "I said…" before stopping dead. A head wrapped in grey skin turned to regard her, where his nose should be was now an upside down heart of cartilage and bone, blood had seeped from the wound and now created a dark crimson crusty goatee.

"What useless wankers, 'go and check on your neighbours if they are elderly or infirm' again what boffin comes up with this shit?" Sophie was nearing the bottom of the page when she heard a yelp from the hallway, "Mum?" she shouted.

The yelp turned into "WHAT-THE-BLOODY-HELL-ARE-YOU-DOING-GET-OFF-OF-ME," Sophie stood up and walked over to the hallway door, "Mum, you alright?"

As she got to the doorway Sophie could see her mum appearing to struggle with the postman. "Mum you daft beggar, you're not that desperate are ya?"

Sophie started to turn away, as she did so her mum yelled "It's one of them Soph, one of those cannibals off the telly, bloody twat him will ya!" she shouted desperately, still holding the proboscis-challenged postman at bay, his jaws snapped at her incessantly, chewing on thin air.

Sophie turned back, and looked at his face, "Bloody hell!" and ran to her mum's aid, as she did, her mother took a step back just as the postman shifted his weight. It sent her sprawling to the ground with the hungry postman on top of her, Sophie gasped, took the iPad in both hands and swung her arms back.

Sophie's mum was lying on the floor wrestling for her life, flakes of dried blood from his feverishly masticating jaws were breaking off and landing on her face. As time slowed down a banshee wail materialised from behind her, a flash of pink shot past her face.

Sophie reached them as the postman lowered his head, the iPad caught him square in the face, with the run up and hefty swing, it batted him upwards. The flakes of dried blood were now joined by dislodged teeth.

Dead eyes rolled in the postman's sockets, trying to focus on something, his head had been knocked upwards into an unnatural angle. Sophie stood over her mother, she pulled her arms behind her and swung again.

The force knocked the zombie postman flush on the side of the head, he smacked into a small wooden telephone stand, there was an almighty crack as the front wooden leg splintered under the impact.

The postman fell to the floor and the table fell on top of him, the phone hit the floor and skidded towards the front door. "Mum, move out of the way!" Sophie shouted, her mum rolled away from the dazed attacker as Sophie raised her arms again.

SMACK.

Another blow landed on the base of the man's skull, followed by another sickening crack. Sophie looked at the iPad and saw that it was disintegrating, she lamented there was no App built for the pulverising of undead skulls.

She threw it at his head, the glass broke, spilling its guts of electronic components over the hallway floor. The postman lay still.

Sophie's mum looked across at the postman, with no nose his face rested completely flat against the ground, as if man and floor formed some kind of weird symbiant.

Sophie gasped, "Ha, that was close!"

Her mum looked up, "You're telling me!" she panted, "Help me up." As Sophie held out her hand there came a low moan from where the postman lay, fingernails scratched the laminated floor as fingers flexed back to undeath and he started to lift himself up.

Her mum screamed, the postman stuck out a clawed hand and caught hold of her blouse, reeling her in like a prize catch. His head turned horizontally, his mouth, now a patchwork of broken teeth, resumed their chewing air duties, anticipating their next meal. Sophie looked down, and grabbed the broken table leg, one end had a nasty sharp point on it.

She knelt down, grabbed hold of the postman's hair and pulled it upwards, as if she was opening a wheelie bin lid, as she did so she tilted it to one side. "Get off my mum you DICK!" and jammed the foot long shard of wood upwards through the man's exposed nasal cavity.

She felt the end of the makeshift spear hit bone, her hand was an inch or two from the postman's cold, dreary face, yet still a spark of un-life remained. She gripped the wood even harder and began to whisk.

The circular motion grew in size, and soon she was up to full speed, a slurry of brain and black blood slopped out of the growing hole, the grip on her mum's blouse abated and his body went slack.

Sophie's wild staring eyes were looking beyond the floor, still she stirred the wooden table leg, a hand gently landed on top of hers and she came to. "Thanks love," the comforting voice washed over her and Sophie finally saw what she had done.

She instantly released her hold on both the table leg and the head, they smacked into the floor, the leg still jutted out of the borehole whilst the head rested on it like a motorbike on its kickstand.

They had sat around the dining table in silence for the last ten minutes, Sophie's hands had just about stopped shaking whilst her mum was still sure she could feel someone groping for her. "I need a drink," Sophie's mum stood and walked over to an MDF drinks cabinet. She surveyed the contents and pulled out a bottle of single malt whiskey along with two thick cut crystal glasses.

"You have to be joking, that stuff tastes like fire," Sophie said, her mum ignored her and poured two large measures, sliding one over to her daughter.

"Your dad's fault, he got me onto this stuff, was more of a Babycham girl until I met him," she smiled, recalling some long forgotten night out.

The smile faded and she knocked back the whiskey in

one, before wiping the back of her hand against her mouth, "We have to get out of here Soph."

Sophie took a sip and recoiled, "But where can we go?" she spluttered.

Her mum poured another measure, "There's an army camp up the road, it's not too far, we can start there I reckon, should at least feel a bit safer from whatever the hell those things are," she knocked back the whiskey.

Sophie looked across and held her mum's hand, "Okay, but I am driving," she winked and pushed the glass back to her mother.

For the first time ever, Sophie and her mum were packed and ready to go in fifteen minutes, the postman's body had been dragged into the garden and the car laden with cases. Her mum slammed the boot shut, "Gimme a minute," Sophie disappeared back into the house, her mum smirked and got into the passenger seat.

Sophie reappeared moments later and opened the driver's door, pausing momentarily, she could see figures moving around the hills behind the cul de sac.

She climbed into the driver's seat, and started the ignition, "Let's get out of here whilst we still can."

CHAPTER V

A soft, gentle breeze drifted gently through the open door, lightly teasing Colin's short hanging hair. A hand still clutching the exposed meat of his chest flexed once, his head raised from its slumber, grey, pallid skin now wallpapered his body.

Eyelids rolled up like a curtain being raised at showtime, white spheres with a small black fleck in the centre stared forwards through the open door.

Basic motor function was returning, some primal synapses fired, it was all that remained of the complicated neural network which existed until it had been snuffed out an hour ago. All the thoughts, motives and desires associated with a human were now absent, replaced by a solitary yearning.

He gently sniffed the air, before looking across to a body lying face up on the floor a short distance away. He rolled onto one side, both arms acted like a jack and lifted him to his feet. Unsteadily, he shuffled across to the prone figure. Standing over her, it looked down, *MEAT?* He sniffed again, *NOT FRESH*, and instantly lost interest.

Colin turned to face the window, his frame stretched to its maximum capacity, but hunched where destroyed ribs and the weight of his body made him lean to one side.

The view looked barren, but he was compelled to go. He turned back to the point of his demise and meandered past a large red stain, now engrained into the carpet. He turned to the open front door and left.

Midday light fell onto skin which no longer required its nourishment. Eyes struggled to deal with the brightness, which caused him to instinctively raise a hand covered in dried blood to his face. Moving more steadily now, Colin made his way to the end of a dirt track, where it joined a main, but quiet road.

His head tilted to one side, as a faraway sound triggered a simple response inside of him, one became many, as the sound of moans rolled over the fields. Like a bat echo-locating a moth in the pitch black of night, he angled his body towards the sound and walked.

He trudged through lanes and fields which only up until a few hours ago were familiar and intimately known, now, they were just obstacles in his way. Where before a walk through the countryside meant enjoying the idyllic surroundings, it was now simply a slog.

Rhythmically raising and placing one foot in front of another, sometimes stumbling over slight dips and hidden bumps. The only thing that mattered was heading to the sound of the moans, growing louder with every shuffle, cresting a small hill, the small town of Foree honed into view.

It had been a settlement since medieval times, a fort had once stood on the hill overlooking the local area. With good sightlines of the local countryside it had provided a solid defence against rival feudal lords.

A small peasant settlement grew slowly over time, the rich soil and small tributaries provided ideal conditions to grow food and support a growing community. The moans that echoed around the vast valley indicated that this fertile land now provided a very different kind of food.

As Colin made his way down the hill, he heard a noise and turned his head. He could make out another figure a short distance away, his sight was the sense which appeared to have been affected the most by his rebirth to undeath.

He pivoted towards the silhouette and ambled over. This was mirrored by the other hill dweller, like dogs meeting in the park, they began to sniff each other as they got to within grabbing range, *MEAT?*

NOT MEAT, both reacted at the same time, partially recoiling with disappointment. They turned to face the sound of the moaning and made their way side by side to the growing din.

Where Colin was dressed in a once smart pair of trousers and shirt, his travelling companion was far more casually dressed. Previously a woman in her mid-twenties, it looked as though she had been disturbed in the night as she was wearing only a pair of heavily creased black pyjamas.

There were several open wounds visible, the most severe of which were on her neck and ankle. The latter caused her right foot to turn inwards, the ligaments all but severed and the appendage now nothing more than a macabre walking stick. Dried black scabs made her shoulder length wavy hair cling limply to her neck.

On the very edge of Foree was a new housing estate. Freshly built and named after a local Victorian entrepreneur, whose name barely resonated with even the most established families of the town.

Although it was going to be a fully closed in cul-de-sac, the back of the estate was currently open to the fields beyond. Its surrounding boundary walls had not been erected, it was from this direction the moaning could be heard the loudest, and where Colin, pyjama-woman and a number of other stragglers were being drawn to.

As Colin approached the estate, tiny fenced gardens gave way to a small part-grass, part-tarmac path. Having bumped into the fence and realising that it was solid, they formed a queue to walk down the path and into a parking circle which now resembled a zombie street party.

As they walked in between two houses, the moaning

reached its peak, a clutch of around fifteen zombies were already loitering, scattered around and looking in different directions.

Closed curtains twitched and half hidden faces looked out at the undead menagerie outside their abodes, of the sixteen houses in the estate, around half had signs of life inside. Colin and his newfound dead lady friend joined the congregation in the middle of the road, letting out guttural moans like his kin. All at once, a loud clang drew their attention to one house.

"I've gotta get out of here, let's take Bobbi and go now," a female voice shouted, a garage door slowly rose from the inside. All twenty of the undead turned as one like a school of piranha and shuffled towards the sounds of life, the moaning ceased and turned into gnashing of teeth.

The garage door was only about half a foot open, delicately painted fingernails of swirling marble clutched the bottom of the white metal garage door, trying to heave it open.

The door jerked upwards, but only by a fraction. By now the vanguard of the zombie task force was already on the drive, a second hand materialised by the first, equally adorned.

"I am trying to pull it up Dave, it's stuck, you could always help me you lazy bas..." the sentence was punctuated by an ear-deafening shriek. One of Colin's new pals had knelt down by the stuck door and after deciding that the left hand looked the tastiest, had clamped down with a mouth bereft of lips, teeth formed into a sick rictus grin.

The bite went in between the knuckles of the middle and ring finger, easily separating them from its owner. Dual squirts of blood shot out and hit the grinning zombie in its face like a broken fire hydrant, it masticated on its finger buffet.

By now, more of its brethren were by the garage door,

sensing food on the other side they fell to their stomachs and started to crawl in through the space at the bottom of the garage door.

"It fucking bit me Dave, hit it, HIT IT!" the female voice shouted, there followed a shuffling of jeans and a loud thud. A zombie milkman who was halfway through the opening, spasmed and became motionless.

It was a meaningless act of defiance, by now a score of zombies were in various states of entrance into the garage. Colin and his pyjama clothed chum formed the rear-guard, mouths chomping on imagined morsels.

Other residents, seeing that the undead gangs attention was on someone else, decided it was a case of now or never. Doors were unbolted and nervous glances checked on their uninvited guests.

Colin and around half of the gate crasher's who were waiting for the opportunity to enter the garage, turned and looked at the cattle appearing from their boltholes.

Colin and pyjama lady turned as one, homing in on a portly fellow a few doors down. He was in the act of waddling into his house, before re-appearing with armfuls of bags and clothes.

A family size SUV sat on the drive, and he fumbled in his pockets for the key. By now, those ghouls who were not in the process of getting through the garage door had selected their pick 'n' mix and were ambling towards their chosen fodder.

The SUV plink-plinked in recognition of the unlock button being pressed, a wave of relief crashed over his sweat laden face. He hurriedly opened the car boot and started throwing the collected items into the vehicle.

Colin and his feeding partner walked through freshly made flower beds, crushing dainty petals under their grimy feet. The chubby man wheezed, before heading back to his front door to collect more earthly possessions.

By the time he made it back to the front door, he was greeted not by Jehovah's Witnesses but by something a lot worse, two rabid visions of hell itself. Realising he wouldn't make it to his vehicle, he instantly dropped a bulging rucksack and a carrier bag of Jaffa Cakes and started to run. The soundtrack to his jaunt was that of screams, as they poured out of the garage opening, a mix of agony and pleas for mercy, interspersed with the cracking of breaking bones and the squelch of rent skin.

Henry York was not built for speed, a life of pie and beer had left atrophied limbs incapable of swift movement, he made it to the end of his garden, seemingly out of reach of his doorstep visitors.

Looking back, he smiled, *SO LONG SUCKERS*, in his haste he failed to see the lip where the pavement met the flower bed and was sent sprawling onto his front. He let out a muffled "Fuck," which was accented by the squeak of cheekbone on concrete.

Henry lay there for a moment before lifting himself slightly, in a temporary daze. He looked down at grazed hands, white lines with red tracks on a purple background were the least of his concerns. Before he could even think about attempting to lift himself off the pavement, he felt someone fall onto the back of his leg.

Colin was still a few paces behind, as his pyjama clad compadre lunged for the beached human. Her dirty body fell onto one leg, pinning the man to the ground. Filthy hands clawed away at the trousers, eventually tearing through the material which parted at the seam of the crotch. Finding a chink in the outer wrapping, she thrust her hand in and rooted around for something to sate her hunger.

Henry made a high-pitched squeal like a baby being tickled, which went up another octave, as a bloody hand slipped out of the hole in his trousers clutching pieces of meat and flesh. Colin knelt down by Henry's back, paying no heed to the sound of the squealing meal, now served up and waiting to be devoured.

Looking down he saw a band of white skin bulging out

the top of lunch's trousers, he grabbed a chunk with both hands and wrenched an opening.

This just increased the decibel level, pyjama zombie was multi-tasking by feasting on one handful of flesh, whilst the spare hand was pulling out further chunks of meat from the breach she had made. Colin was also reaching in and pulling out fistfuls of human flesh covered in a fatty rind.

Another of the undead cohort had now reached the still squealing Mr York, it knelt down by his head and placed jagged fingernails into Henry's eye socket. A blood soaked hand clutching a badly crushed eyeball was ripped out. The optic nerve was still attached and tried to send broken images back to the mainframe, the screaming intensified before ending abruptly.

A few occupants of Dacre Close had managed to drive away. Some though remained, unable to tear their attention away from the grisly feast outside, which they hoped they would not be invited to.

CHAPTER VI

Philip turned the ignition and the car slowly rumbled into life, Jim secured his seatbelt and looked down at his trousers, blood and pieces of brain matter still clung to them. For all of the rapid turn of events he had encountered since waking up just under an hour ago, he felt unperturbed. His mind was perfectly clear that he was going to survive, no matter what it took.

He looked across at Phil, who was focused on the act of reversing the car from the gory scene laid out in the small car park outside Warchucks.

"You must be loving this Phil," a smile started to spread across Philip's face.

"I'd be lying if I said I wasn't a little jealous of you getting the first zed kill between us Jimbo, had you pegged down as a rocking in the corner, shitting yourself, sucking your thumb kind of guy."

Philip slipped the gearstick out of reverse, and started to pull out of the industrial estate, in the rear view mirror the fire from Warchucks had taken hold of the rear of the building and thicker black smoke was freely pouring from the roof.

Philip looked down at the fuel gauge, "Hmm, think it might be wise to fill up now whilst we still can, no idea how long we'll have the chance to get petrol, before we either run out or the act becomes a game of zombie roulette."

Jim relaxed in the seat and looked out of his window, they were approaching a residential area, there were people pouring out of their houses, trying to fill cars with belongings.

"There's a petrol station just down the road from my flat, we'll stop off there and then get back to mine, okay?" Philip asked, concentrating on the road.

The last thing he wanted now was for the car to be damaged due to some momentary lapse in concentration.

He smirked, Jim was right, he was loving this.

"You remember the zombie mall in Reading?" Philip asked.

"Yeah man, that was a good day, actually that was a bloody good day, slightly different now though mate," Jim replied, recalling the three and a half hours they spent chasing people made up as zombies round a disused shopping centre.

"Yes and no bro, sure the guns fired plastic BBs and you couldn't shoot them in the head."

"Except for Shawabe huh?" Jim said, smiling.

Philip laughed, "Oh yeah! Man, that zombie dude took that shot right to the face, ruined the immersion if you ask me by storming off like a stroppy teenager."

"Dude, he got shot in the face near point blank with an air gun, he lost a tooth!"

"Mate, if you sign up to be a zombie, chasing paying customers round a derelict mall, you gotta accept that at some point, some airgun-toting redneck is going to shoot you in the face, all I'm saying," Philip replied, semi-annoyed, he took a left turn and cautiously made his way between rows of parked cars.

Jim let out a small laugh, "Was funny, especially when that zombie clown was chasing Gav round and round the ball-pit."

Philip edged past the last of the parked cars, and opened the engine up a little, "Mate, that was probably the best day of my life. Until now," he looked sideways at his brother with a cheeky grin.

"I FUCKING KNEW THIS WOULD HAPPEN," Philip yelled, pounding the steering wheel with the palm of his hand.

"It's like when we made the plan and they were all saying how stupid it sounded, and giving me those funny looks, well looky here pa, what's happening now, huh?"

"Seriously, you keep on about 'the plan', it's still not ringing any bells," Jim said, looking at people coming out of a newsagents with armfuls of stuff.

One man had litre bottles of water clamped between his arms and body, whilst straining with carrier bags of canned goods. He managed a few paces outside of the shop before one bag decided it could no longer carry its burden and shed cans of beans and alphabetti-spaghetti over the pavement.

Philip sighed, "Well, you should remember it, I do, besides, we'll go over it when we get back to mine," he looked at Jim "When we prepare." He said the last word dead-pan, not even laced with a hint of irony or humour.

Silence descended on the journey, interrupted occasionally when they passed houses or shops, they could make out people who were clearly no longer classified as human. Unable to focus on them for too long before they were out of sight, it was clear for now at least, the undead were in the minority.

In the main, the streets were busy with cars laden down with suitcases, pets and children looked out of closed windows with bemusement.

"I'll just put the radio on and see what they're saying about it," Jim reached his hand out to the 'Tuner' button in the central console.

Before it had even entered its airspace, Philip shouted "Don't you even fucking think about it Jimmy, not having that on in my car."

Jim stopped and looked at Phil, "You what? Something

the matter?"

Philip looked left and right briefly, then said matter of factly "Not having that propaganda shite on in my car, wait will we get back to mine and we can turn the telly on."

"Erm, you do know that they are probably just as full of shit as you and the radio are," an annoyed Jim said.

Philip turned quickly to his brother, smiling. "What was that mate? I haven't heard you swear for years, not since that time I grassed you up to mum and dad clouted you at the dinner table."

Jim went to reply, then closed his mouth, lost in thought momentarily, "He hit my head into my Sunday dinner."

"Ha, yeah I remember, had a bit of roast potato hit me in the head, was well funny."

"Everything's funny to you Phil, unless of course it happens to you, in which case it's the end of the world." Jim momentarily relived the hurt at the memory of his face meeting the plate.

It landed forcefully in the beef and gravy, causing a tsunami event which propelled the landmass of potatoes and vegetables into the rest of the family.

Jim knew he wouldn't be able to persuade his brother otherwise, so unlocked his phone and clicked on the BBC News app. The previous day's headlines of inflation rate drops, suicide bomb attacks, EU commissioners and former children's TV presenters being sent down for sexual assault were still showing.

The refresh symbol spooled round like a ghost driven hamster wheel, "Hmm, taking a while to load," Jim said out loud.

"Not surprising I guess, first thing that gets battered in these situations is the mobile service, everyone and their gran trying to phone people," Philip was carefully studying the road, "Not too long now bro," he added.

Jim waited, having to press the screen a few times to

stop it locking up, before the headlines rolled over. "Let's see, reports of murder and cannibalism, the government has called a COBRA meeting, says here that China has gone quiet with communications failing, a nuclear power station in Germany has gone critical, more reports of murder, oh, but some good news, they've cancelled Big Brother."

Philip had two reasons for choosing the Quantico petrol station above the three Shell petrol stations they had passed which were all brimming with vehicles and petrol-rage.

The first was the location, by the time they had filled up, they were literally a two minute drive from his flat.

The second was that it was the most expensive one in town, even with the world going to shit, people were still going to baulk at paying something close to the GDP of Malta per litre, thus making sure it would be quieter.

As they turned the corner into the road, there was a third reason to add to the list. Just past the petrol station was a bus diagonally straddling the entire road, forming a roadblock which completely prohibited traffic coming from the other direction

The road itself had terraced houses on either side. Some had a few quizzical onlookers peeking out from within, whilst others were a hive of activity as people retrieved items they deemed necessary for a sudden evacuation.

A Land Rover still rested against the rear end of the bus which bore signs of the impact, the emergency door was hanging off its hinges. The 4x4 driver was pacing uneasily by the rear of his vehicle, one hand clutched a phone to his ear, the other trying to staunch a head wound with a cream jumper, now two-tone with blood.

"That idiot must've booted it out of the petrol station and smacked into its ass, he should count himself lucky to still be alive," Philip said with disdain.

There appeared to be some movement on the bus, but

it was difficult to work out exactly how many people were there and what state they were in.

As they pulled up to the small four pump forecourt, they saw that two cars were already positioned on one side and in the process of refuelling. Philip pulled up on the other side, next to the shop and parked up, a Jaguar was on the opposite pump.

"Right, I'll get this done, you stay here Jimbo and see if you can find anything else out, have a look at how bad the roads are out of this dump." Philip unbuckled his seatbelt and exited the car, slamming the door on his way out, the car rocked from the impact. He quickly unscrewed the fuel cap and plunged the nozzle into it, squeezing the fuel into the cars innards.

He looked across to the Jag, and could make out a woman in the passenger seat, looking round nervously, she had dyed blonde hair, and even through the semi-tinted window, he could see that she had received numerous cosmetic enhancements.

"All bought and paid for," a voice boomed out, part obscured by the bulky fuel pump. Philip peered to his right and saw a well-dressed man, in the process of filling his car up.

He was about the same height as Philip, like his female companion he too bore signs of the plastic surgeons scalpel, short of carbon dating he could only guess his age to be in the forties.

He had slick, short black hair, swept to one side and held in place by a pair of aviator sunglasses, his clean shaven face seemed kindly enough. "The names Simon, Simon Ward, that's my little lady Lydia," the gentleman said, waving to the side mirror at the completely oblivious woman passenger.

"Philip, and that's my brother Jim," he motioned towards the interior of his car, before redirecting his attention to the spinning numbers on the pump.

"All gone a bit mad this morning eh Philip? We were

visiting mother over at Sleepy Willows when the owner said it was probably best we leave. They had a death in the night, but it seemed as though something was awry." Simon casually exchanged glances between the pump, Philip and the plastic doll which was his wife.

A small bell sounded, as the other forecourt inhabitant walked into the porta-cabin like building housing the twenty-four hour shop and cashier.

Snapping back to his car, Philip replied "Yeah, sounds like strange things are afoot at the Circle K, my brother encountered some zombies at his work too."

Simon stopped, tapped the petrol pump against his cars tank and replaced the petrol gun into its holster. "What was that? Zombies? Are you quite sure? Mrs Fitzsimmons didn't say anything about this at the home. You haven't been on the old sauce have you?" Simon peered closer at Philip and gestured with a 'drinky-drinky' motion.

Philip looked at Simon as if he had just discovered him on the bottom of his shoe, the pump clunked in his hand and he too tapped the spout against the metal rim before replacing it back into the main housing and replacing the fuel cap.

"Mate, what the fuck do you think? If they're dead, and then they're not, I'm pretty sure that means you've passed all the necessary tests to make you one of the undead."

"Prick," Philip muttered under his breath.

"My, my, you do have a potty mouth eh? And I'm pretty sure if there were zombies, vampires or whatever, that The Times would've mentioned it in dispatches," Simon rolled his sleeves up to reveal arms laden with steel wool like hair.

"Whatever, I'm paying up and getting out of here, believe whatever you want to Lord Farquhar, I've got more important things to do," Philip turned his back on Simon and headed inside the shop.

As he walked past, Jim got out, "Hang on, I'll come in with you, could do with a drink or something."

"Just don't scare the locals, looking like that," Philip gestured towards Jim's gore splattered trousers, and grinned.

They walked into the small petrol station shop and saw that aside from the bored looking cashier there was only one other person in there.

A short stocky man in his early thirties, wearing canvas shorts, a polo shirt, Jesus creepers and white socks pulled up as far as they could go, the elastic straining to maintain grip on the man's thick legs. The cashier was sat on a stool, with views over the forecourt, the blockade just outside of his garage dominion.

Two corridors of shelved goods formed a small processional leading to the counter. A small ziggurat of Pot Noodles peered out from forests of extortionately priced bags of tortilla chips and crisps. Handy fare for the wary traveller or local stoners too caned to walk the short distance into town to an actual supermarket.

Opposite the counter, at the far end of the building, two ancient drink fridges stood as sentinel guardians, keeping their partially cooled cans of liquid under guard from the rest of the shop. Metal ventilation grills just above the door appeared to growl at the intruders upon its space. Jim pulled on one of the handles, and after a moment of resistance, gained access to its carbonated treasure.

Philip scooped up two bars of Mint Aero and stood behind Mr Sandals, shaking his head at the man's choice of footwear. As he approached, the conversation between Sandals and the cashier hushed.

The bearded cashier bashed the till to input the price of a packet of Werthers Original and asked the customer "What pump please?" his voice dulled by the repetitious requests he made every day, sounding like a bored robot.

Before he could answer, a car horn sounded from the forecourt outside.

As one, the four people inside the shop all turned

instinctively to ascertain where the noise was coming from.

Aside from the three parked cars outside, and the crashed vehicles staring back, there was no other activity, or so it seemed. They all sensed movement from behind the Jag, and could just about make out a man standing by the driver's door, it wasn't Simon.

The horn sounded again, this time longer in length, more desperate. Jim edged closer to the long window which ran the length of the shop, trying to peer past the murk and grime of the filth-lined glass to make out what was happening.

He could see that Lydia was reaching across from the passenger seat pressing the horn, Simon was nowhere to be seen. He scanned the outline of the car, and then saw something lying on the floor, behind the car, it was an arm.

Philip dropped the Aero's and glanced at the man who was by the driver's door, there was something odd about how he walked, and he didn't appear to be holding himself normally.

He froze.

"Fuckity fuck balls," his words loud enough to make the bearded cashier stand up and walk over to the microphone between the till and the window.

Beyond the Jaguar, another two figures appeared, as if they had just been brought up from an escalator on the floor below, one was a teenage girl, wearing a plaid shirt, tight black jeans, black Doc Martens, black hair and thickly applied make up, the other was a bus driver.

The man who was by the driver's door stooped down and disappeared from view, the arm which was visible moments before was pulled from sight. The horn sounded again, this time it made longer, more desperate honks, like a gaggle of geese was milling around outside.

"Do something beardy!" Philip shouted, and the cashier kicked into life. A temporary burst of feedback emanated from the PA system outside. "Miss, I think you better get inside here, like, NOW," the speaker crackled, as more figures congregated outside.

The fridge door closed behind Jim, causing him to jump, he was the closest to the front door. Compelled by his experiences from earlier, he pulled it open and jogged to the fuel pump by Philip's car, his face contorted with revulsion.

As he reached the back of Philip's Corsa, he looked at the bus in the background. He could see that where the Land Rover had struck, the emergency door had now come completely off, leaving an exit wound in the side of the metal beast. From its innards spilled the previous passengers of the number 55 to Rooks Farm Estate.

By the Land Rover, he could make out a body lying at the back of the vehicle, by the clothing he worked out that it must've been the 4x4 driver. Crouched over him were three figures, each staring into what was left of his stomach cavity. Their blood stained hands reached past snapped ribs, pulled on strands of flesh, fished out an organ or yanked on severed and torn pieces of intestine, completely oblivious to anything else.

By now, Philip had walked outside to his brother, he was driven to see exactly what was going on, even though he had a pretty damn good idea.

Aside from the passengers chowing down on the very man who had caused the crash, the goth girl and bus driver were now joined by three other figures that had escaped their metal sarcophagus and were now scanning the area for food.

All of them appeared to have some kind of bite wound visible either on an arm, neck or in the case of the girl, the face. Dried blackened blood was visible from the wounds, torn open to the world. It was then that both of them heard a crack and a slurping sound from the other side of the Jaguar.

Jim was transfixed by the grisly tableau of the Land Rover driver being pulled apart with stubby, viscera covered fingers. Philip's attention however, centred on the noise behind the car.

He took a step to the side and could see the arm again, only this time it was lying unattached to a body. A pool of blood and tissue marked the spot where it had been pulled out of its socket, crouching down at this bloody junction was the man they had seen moments before.

Philip looked at Simons face, it was still, flecked in his own blood and with a look of utter surprise on it, his visage akin to Munch's The Scream. As he moved further round, he saw all of Simon's body.

Locked onto the bottom of Simon's right leg was another zombie, this one though had its entire bottom half of its body missing. It looked like a man, but it was impossible to tell.

It had long dank hair, covered in dirt and blood, a tribal tattoo grew out of a vest top, stopping at the elbow of the left arm. It was completely focused on tearing through what remained of Simon's calf, pulling strings of tendon and muscle out and then chewing on them.

It appeared to be utterly bored by the task, but was dedicated to this and this alone. He looked at the bottom of its body, and could see part of its backbone was visible, ivory white against the stark red of its meat.

The other zombie picked up Simon's arm, turned it upside down and poked blood stained fingers into the space the armpit used to be, trying to fish out some unseen tidbit. Another blast on the horn caused both brothers to come to, they looked at each other.

Then the zombies looked at them.

The one closest to Philip began to stand up, still clutching Simon's arm, chewing open mouthed on an unidentifiable piece of flesh. The half-zombie pulled its clawed hands from where the bottom half of Simon's leg used to be and started hauling itself under the car, towards the pair.

Those feasting on the Land Rover driver, who was now hollowed out like a pumpkin, also started to stand up and move towards the prospect of a new meal.

"Stop blowing the horn you stupid bitch, and get the fuck out!" Philip yelled at Lydia, he had pushed past Jim and was frantically pulling on the passenger door trying to get it open.

In the madness, Lydia had locked the doors and was shaking her head furiously, staring at Philip like he was some axe wielding maniac.

"GET THE FUCK OUT OF THERE!" Philip yelled, though he could barely hear himself over the horn.

Jim tugged on Philip's shirt, "Bro, we have to go, look," Jim pointed at the lumbering figures now homing in on their location. Jim felt something tug at his foot and looked down to see a hand trying to grab his leg.

"FUCK!" he shouted and jumped backwards, the hand failed to gain any grip and fell slack, though it instantly came back to life again as the zombie started to drag his way under the car.

"Back in the shop, now, if Barbie here doesn't want to get out, there's not much we can do," Philip put his arm around Jim and escorted him back inside, closing the door firmly.

The sandaled man and the cashier were both in the same spot as they were left in, unable to do anything except watch the tale of terror unfold before their eyes.

"Quick, you lot, get some shelves," Philip yelled, as he stood by the closed door handles, holding them together so the handle loops were aligned.

Canned goods and bags of toilet rolls were sent flying as the three men desperately tried to pull the metal shelves from the backs of the units.

Soon, each man had a shelf each and were stood by Phil. "Right, lets slot these in the handles and see if we can bend the ends, form some kind of brace or something," Philip commanded.

Philip slid one of the shelves through, it scraped the inside of the handles as it made a snug fit, "Looks like we might only need one." Philip then pulled back on the ends and formed a metal triangle, the door handles pulled taut by the bent shelf. He tested them by pushing on the door, they held firmly and he stood back, happy with his work.

In the time taken to reinforce the door, the zombies were crossing the forecourt, moving with purpose. "They move faster than I thought they would," Philip said to himself, but loud enough to be picked up by the others.

All four men looked out of the window at the zombie foot race now going on, the finish line was the small shop they were all stood in. A bloodied hand slapped against the bottom of one of the door windows, "Our old friend Paul is back then," Philip said, standing on tip toes and tried to peer down at the base of the doors.

"Paul?" Jim asked.

"Yes Paul. Paul, he's only three foot tall, he's even got a theme tune," Philip cleared his throat and began;

"On his way to town one day, to fetch some
moisturiser by Garnier,
Young Paul did happen to walk astray, and get struck
by a bus, oops, NO WAY!
His body lay so very still, all inside looked equally ill,
But then they rose and began to sway, and chomped on
those who could not get away,"

The three of them stood closed mouthed, arms folded, staring at Philip, now scooting round the petrol station amongst the spilt kitchen rolls and boxes of crushed cookies;

"He once stood as a colossus of a man, big and tough
with one hell of a tan,
But now he looks so grim and pasty, cut down to size
for being so hasty,
So heed this tale all those who hear, of dry and
wrinkled skin they fear,

Just because you look a bit rough, poor old Paul now don't look so tough."

Pointing to the bloody hand pounding against the bottom of the window;

"It's Paul, Paul, he's only three foot tall, if you want to see them, his legs are smashed against that wall. It's Paul, Paul…"

"You quite finished?" Jim asked, his brother stopped in mid-swing.

"Philistine bastards the lot of you."

Enjoying the sensory respite, Jim turned to the two other members of the petrol station, "Hiya, I'm Jim, and the insensitive X Factor wannabe here is my brother Phil, who are you guys?"

The balding cashier stroked his beard, his expression a mix of shock and irritation that the neatly stacked Fray Bentos pies were now bent and spread over the floor. He piped up "I'm Alan, been on since last night, someone mind telling me what's going on?"

"Well my bearded companion, it would appear as though the end of days is upon us, and that the dead……now walk the earth," Philip twisted his head as he completed his sentence to try and add an element of mystery to it.

"I'm Phil, pleased to meet you," said the stocky man, offering a sweaty hand to his new found comrades in arms.

"Fuck off are you, we're not having two Phil's here, I'm like the Original Philsta, you're some piss poor copy, you look more like a Duane," Philip said, menace in his eyes.

"But my name is…." Phil number two started to say.

"DUANE, as I just fucking said, wow, you really do border the line between idiot and complete twat," Philip squared up to him.

"Fine, Duane, I guess," he replied, backing down.

"Good, now we're all BFFs, let's take a moment and apprise the situation."

They looked out of the shop onto the forecourt, all of the zombies were now mere feet away from the window. Despite the car horn still tooting intermittently, all dead eyes were on the four human sardines encased within.

"Fuck, they do move faster than I thought, that's not good, always thought they'd be slow," Philip remarked,

"Perhaps fresher ones move faster?" Duane offered.

Philip bore holes into him with his glare, "Yes Duane, perhaps."

Pairs of blood soaked hands started patting the glass, leaving smears and prints on the already dirty windows. Vacant stares looked in, swaying from the impact of striking the barrier which was stopping them getting their food.

Their mouths wide open, a deep moan was coming out of every walking cadaver. A horn blast stopped in mid-toot, the four inhabitants of the Quantico petrol station craned to look at the Jaguar.

Through blood-rimed windows they could see that Lydia was peering out of the driver's side rear window, her face a mix of shock and excitement.

She turned quickly and Jim realised what was happening, "NO! DON'T OPEN THE DOOR!" but between the glass and the moaning from the undead trying to get in, there was no chance she would hear it.

As the door swung open, they could see that there was a figure by the rear passenger window. Philip was about to remark how it looked familiar when the realisation hit him, "Oh fuck, looks like Cilla has arranged a special reunion on today's Surprise, Surprise."

Now visible, Simon's corpse rose ungainly on one half eaten leg. Lydia's face went from elation to sheer hysteria in seconds. Even over the sounds of massed zombie moaning, they all heard a blood-curdling shriek as Simon lunged at her. His bloodied carcass fell on top of her and into the car.

A sudden geyser of arterial fluid jetted against the inside windows, and the shrieking ceased.

CHAPTER VII

They looked at each other despondently, the only sounds were of moans and hands rattling against the panes of glass. "We have to get out of here. Alan, there's got to be another way out of here, yeah?" Jim asked desperately.

Alan stroked his beard, his eyes darted back to the Jaguar, now internally decorated with dripping blood. "Err yeah, out back, though we still have to get past them," he gestured towards the braying crowd of zombies attempting to gain access to the shop.

"Okay, we can't get to the cars right now, so we are going to have to hope we can outrun them. Well, that and hoping that there are no more of them lying in wait outside the back door," Jim replied.

"I'll go get the keys, they're hanging up under the counter," Alan turned away from the ravenous pack of zombies and walked towards the counter.

"I'll go with him," Jim said and followed Alan.

"Woah, this is pretty mental huh?" said Duane, edging closer to Philip.

"Yep, you're not wrong there DUANE," he replied with disdain.

"This reminds me of that zombie film, 28 Days Later," Duane said enthusiastically.

Philip turned to look Duane straight in the eyes, "What the fuck did you just say Amish-boy?" he began to size him up.

"Erm, 28 Days Later? The zombie film..." Duane trailed off.

Philip grabbed hold of Duane's collar and bellowed "28 Days Later is NOT A GODDAMN FUCKING ZOMBIE FILM YOU COMPLETE AND TOTAL KNOB-JOCKEY!"

Even the zombies stopped moaning temporarily at the sound of Philip's raised voice. "Oh no," Jim said, recognising his brothers rant voice, "Go find the keys Alan, I better go save Duane, I mean Phil."

"Eh?"

"But there are zombies in it..."

"...they eat people..."

"...zombies..." Duane said, every few words segmented with big gulps.

"They're not zombies anus-head, they're fucking infected, zombies are DEAD, in 28 Days Later and 28 Weeks Later, they were very much A-FUCKING-LIVE, therefore they do not meet the necessary criteria of being zombies!" Philip spat out, his face now inches away from Duane's.

Duane wringed his sweaty hands, "But...the word zombie originates from Haiti and black magic. Y'know, stories of pissed off farmhands putting a spell on their masters and getting them to toil the earth. They were alive, so...."

Philip's eyes opened wider, "What the fuck did you just say rectal-fluid boy?"

"Phil!" Jim shouted.

"Yes," both Phil's replied looking over at Jim walking towards them, before locking eyes once more on each other.

"Put him down, we've got better things to do right now, like staying alive. Not arguing over the origins of the very things that would like nothing more than to gain entrance to this shack and devour our still warm bodies.

Let him go."

Phil glowered once more at Duane, made a motion to head-butt him which caused Duane to flinch, and then released him from his grip.

"Dick," Phil said angrily, barging past Duane with his shoulder.

Jim patted Duane apologetically on the back, "Don't worry about him, I've had the same argument with him before, he just takes this all very…..seriously."

"Guys, I got the keys, can we get out of here now please," Alan shouted from the back of the shop.

They all walked over to the counter, the atmosphere slowly cooling after the heated exchange. "So where you guys going when we get out of here?" Jim enquired.

Alan was concentrating on the collection of keys, before selecting one, "I'm going to get home, barricade the door and wait for all this to blow over."

Philip chuckled, "Nice one dude, how long do you figure that will be?" Alan seemed to ignore him, but he picked up some carrier bags from under the counter, and started moving around the ruined shop, picking up items of food.

"Where you going Phil?" Jim asked, surprised at hearing his actual name, it took a few seconds to realise he was the one being spoken to.

"Me? Oh, I'm going to head home to Newstead Haven, my families out there, want to get back and make sure they're okay."

"Well, the slow train to Dorkville beckons Duane, looks like Weird-Al has done his shopping," Philip pointed at the cashier returning with bags crammed full of supplies.

"I reckon we try and coax them down the far end of the shop whilst Alan remains crouched down by the back door, unlocks and opens it, then when the zombies are busy wondering what's going on, we all do one out the back," Jim laid out his plan like Hannibal from the A-Team, just without added carcinogenic props.

The other three nodded their approval, Alan made his way to the back door and placed his haul on the floor in preparation. The others made their way to the fridges by the far end of the shop, and started shouting and gesticulating at the congregation of flesh-eaters waiting for them the other side of a quarter inch of double glazing.

The three amigo's continued the zombie baiting, their antagonism riled up the undead, who started beating on the windows more furiously than before, causing spider web fractures to appear on its surface.

"Erm beard-man, you wanna hurry the fuck up unlocking that door, I'm getting a bad feeling about this!" Philip shouted.

Alan unlocked the door and gave it a push, "It's a bit stiff," he yelled.

Philip sniggered, "I bet it is you dirty bastard," his amusement was short-lived though when he noticed that the combined efforts of the zombies appeared to be working.

No sooner had Alan barged through the back door into the outside world, came an almighty crash of glass. The frame surrounding one of the windows gave way and swollen, bloody hands made their way in through the breach.

Hands clutched at thin air, snapping like hungry alligator jaws, but one found purchase on something, and pulled on a polo shirt. Duane-Phil was unceremoniously pulled towards the broken window pane by one hand, which quickly became three and four.

He struggled, but it was to no avail. "Help me guys!" he yelled desperately, Jim and Philip stood either side of him and grabbed an arm each, now forming the opposing team of a human sized tug of war.

At first the brothers gained some ground, and managed to heave him back into the shop, but more hands were appearing in the gaping hole where the window frame used to be.

Duane turned and looked at Philip, "I think you're going to…." he started to say, before another pair of undead hands grabbed his midriff and turned the tables in their favour.

Before they could muster another pull, the combined might of eight seemingly starved zombies told and Duane was pulled up to the yawning maw of the window frame.

Panicked eyes still fixed on Philip rolled and flickered, Jim and Philip looked down to see that Paul, Paul, he's only three foot tall, had managed to get a five finger death claw hold on Duane's stomach.

Like a fireman's Jaws of Life, the hand intensified its pressure until the skin broke. Another undead fist punched into his torso, rupturing the skin, the last fight went out of his body and his arms fell limp in Jim and Philip's hands, who released their grip.

Duane's body appeared to be glued to the side of the shop, held in place by vice like grips. Dead hands rifled through the assortment of human goodies on offer, settled on his intestines and hauled them out as if they were reeling in an anchor, urine and blood mixed by his feet as he gargled and fell silent.

The brothers stood back, "Hey guys, the doors open, let's get out of here!" Alan shouted, before he disappeared from sight.

"I'm sorry Phil," said Jim, who turned and jogged towards the rear exit.

Philip stood by the human feeding bag, he sighed, patted Duane on the shoulder and followed Jim to the back door. Behind them was a wet crunch as the spine snapped from the pressure and Duane's body was slowly pulled through the gap in the window, leaving a trail of skin and gore around the frame.

By the time they got to the back door, the only sighting of Alan was of someone running away from the bus of death, bags of shopping banging against his legs. "Ah well, it's not as if we were going to be pen-pals after this eh

Jimmy-Bob?" Philip was still flushed with exertion following the pulling contest with the undead.

They looked round the corner of the building and could see a host of zombies gorging on the cooling remains of Phil #2.

"They work quick huh? Not much left of the poor bastard already," Philip was making a note of the positions of the pavement dinner party.

"Gimme a mo," he said, and crouched down.

"You're not going to do what I think you're going to do are you Phil?"

Philip looked back up, winked and said "Only Usain Bolt can outrun me mate," as he leapt into action and sprinted towards his car.

The huddled masses around the front door of the shop were busy idly feasting on the succulent delights of fresh human flesh, some were still close to the passenger door of the Corsa. Philip paid them no heed, *I am getting my fucking car back, not losing it to these dead bastards.*

As he got closer to his car, he could see through blood sprayed windows that Mr Ward was still working his way through the first course of Lydia, served rare to bloody. Simon had turned his attention to her chest and as he pulled on her entrails with his teeth, her lifeless body rose and fell.

The Corsa driver's door was already unlocked and Philip quickly got in. He put the keys into the ignition and closed the door with a thud.

Disinterested eyes looked up from their forecourt side meal at Philip, those who had nothing more than a few toes to devour turned their attention to him and started to moan.

He turned the key, and the engine started, it seemed to falter slightly before coughing into life, "Thank fuck for that."

Philip slammed the gear into reverse, released the handbrake and stomped on the accelerator. He was by his brother in an instant, Jim pulled the door open and jumped in, slamming it behind him.

"Shall I take you back to mine m'lady?" Philip asked in his best Parker voice, Jim just looked at him. "Fine, sometimes dude you have no sense of humour," and pulled out of the forecourt of death, leaving the passengers of the 11:08 to Monroe Town Centre to their brunch.

CHAPTER VIII

Philip's ground floor flat was in a ramshackle three storey building which also contained a small independent art gallery. The entrance to the flats was an unassuming door to the side of the property, away from the floor to ceiling plate glass windows which ran along two walls of the gallery.

Philip pulled up to an abrupt halt a few feet from the door, singing "It's Paul, Paul, he's only three foot tall..."

"Have you taken some kind of blow to your head today mate, you're acting a little on the odd-side, even for you," Jim looked intently at his brothers animated form.

"Nope, just nice to be right. AGAIN," Philip turned off the engine and got out of the car. They entered the main door, before turning abruptly to another door at the beginning of a small hallway, which led to a set of steep narrow stairs ascending into the gloom.

Philip unlocked his flat door, left it ajar for Jim to follow, "Man, it's good to be home," he announced to the large living room.

Jim closed the door behind him and looked at the lounge it opened up into. It was the epitome of single-man, no item of furniture looked like it had been made within the last twenty years.

Aside from a large plasma TV, X-Box One and sound-bar, a two-seater sofa faced the collection of technology which lived on a cabinet which was clearly never made to hold such weight. Behind this was the outline of a window, made out through thin closed orange curtains.

His brother had disappeared into his bedroom, so Jim took the time to reacquaint himself with the flat. It had been a while since he had last been round, mainly meeting up in town for a few beers, or round Jim's in better times.

Against one wall stood two large bookcases, one was heaving with CDs, DVDs, video games and books. When Jim's gaze fell on the other, he laughed to himself, "It's grown since the last time I was here Phil," he shouted.

"Huh?" Philip walked back into the living room, clutching two identical rucksacks, one was dark blue, the other a light green, both looked new, robust and laden with hidden items.

He put them down on a coffee table covered in comics and letters, and joined Philip by the bookcase. "Ahhhh, yeah man, the collection has grown," he added, beaming with pride.

One shelf contained the Walking Dead hard-back compendiums, and other zombie graphic novels, two whole shelves were dedicated to other assorted zombie fiction. The remainder of the bookcase was brimful of zombie DVDs and Blu-Ray discs.

"Haven't gotten round to watching this one yet," Philip pointed to a Blu-Ray copy of Stalled, still incarcerated in its plastic wrapping, "Half-hoping I was gonna get time this weekend."

Interspersed on each shelf were various zombie figures from the celluloid and video game world, flyboy from the original Dawn of the Dead, 45 revolver idly hanging from a finger, stood paused in time in front of the George A. Romero section.

A couple of Pop! Vinyl zombies from the Walking Dead TV series squatted in front of the DVDs from Apocalypse of the Dead through The Battery and The Horde to Juan of the Dead.

In front of the remainder of the collection from Outpost, past The Revenant to the Zombie Diaries 1 and 2, other items like a Dead Rising Zombrex pen were also littered around in the shrine to popular culture zombies.

"Man, this must be the best day ever for you," Jim said, looking across to his brother, who was still enraptured by his pride and joy.

"First things first, can I borrow some clothes, jeans, a t-shirt or something, these trousers are beginning to honk," Jim said, indicating his stained attire.

"No worries man, there's some clean clothes in the airing cupboard in the bathroom, you clean yourself up and then we'll have a chinwag about what we do next," Philip pointed towards a half-open door.

Jim entered the bathroom and closed the door, sliding the bolt into a hole drilled into the doorframe. He pulled a pair of fading blue jeans, a black Crossfaith t-shirt and a black Genki hoodie with a cartoon Godzilla on the front from the pile of clothes in the airing cupboard and put them down on top of the closed toilet lid. He looked across at the mirror hanging over the green sink, a remnant of the 1970s.

Having not shaved since the day before, a thin layer of black fuzz was already spreading across the lower half of his face. He turned the cold tap on and splashed handfuls of water onto his face. Wet hands rested on the side of the sink as he looked at the reflection in the mirror.

He'd seen and done things already this morning that up until a few hours ago he thought impossible, yet he had taken it all in his stride. His mind cast back to the previous evening and a small wave of melancholy washed over him.

He looked back at himself again, *you love her.* He swallowed hard, *it's not too late, I can still make this work.* He threw more cold water in his face and turned the tap off.

You've been given a second chance by all of this, nothing to get in the way now, no crappy excuses. He snorted, "Except for the living dead of course," he said to himself, and smiled.

Mind resolved, he changed into the clothes he had retrieved.

Once dressed he glanced over to the bath, his brow furrowed with curiosity. "Phil?" he shouted, unlocking the door, "You having a bath this morning and forget to take the plug out?"

Philip walked in, and looked down at the bath, filled to just under the overflow, and then up at his brother. "You really are a n00b when it comes to this huh? How long do you think the water will keep running for Jimmy-boy? Forever? Think the electricity and gas is going to keep being supplied too?"

"First thing to do in a zombie apocalypse if you're at home, fill the bath and any other receptacles you have with water. It's the most basic of human needs, when it goes bad, you can still use it for cleaning etc." He turned around and walked back into the living room, "Come here, got something for you."

Jim walked back into the living room and to the coffee table where the two rucksacks sat. "Choose one," Philip said, "they're identical in content so doesn't matter which."

Jim picked up the dark blue one which was closest to him, sat down on the sofa, opened the top flap and peered inside. Two pairs of thick black socks were blockading the other items, he tipped the contents onto the empty cushion next to him.

The rucksack spilled its guts like a pisshead on a Saturday night out, a small pang of excitement like Christmas morning washed over him.

Philip piped up, "In no particular order, you will find socks, a water canteen, water purification tablets, wind and waterproof matches, an ordnance survey map, compass, torch, first aid kit, Swiss army knife, wind up radio and earphones, some protein bars, a can opener, waterproofs, fishing line, one half of a two way radio set and probably the most important item of the whole lot."

Philip sat on the sofa arm, next to Jim, "When shit goes

down and things, very much like your life right now, look like they're spinning down the toilet, when you wonder if you have the strength and energy to go on and survive."

Philip edged closer, "When the horrors of the apocalypse shred away the last vestiges of your sanity, you'll need......."

"Teabags?" Jim asked.

Philip sighed, "Knob." He stood up and walked over to an old battered wardrobe.

"Here, some other kit over here, a sleeping bag each and some army surplus boots I picked up dead cheap, you're still an 8 yeah?" Jim nodded, stood up and walked across to his brother.

"Dude, the next choice you get to make is one of paramount importance, it's time to play 8 out of 10 Bats......" Philip unlocked the wardrobe doors and opened them to reveal the bounty within.

Jim shook his head "You are one mental dude."

"What?" Philip protested, an outstretched arm showed him the array of accrued weaponry contained within.

"Whilst most people save up for a rainy day, you've been spending for a blood-soaked one eh?" Jim gazed at the assortment of crude implements.

"Mate, I believe in being prepared, I knew this day would come in one form or another. Hell, the zombie apocalypse was pretty low on my list of things that were likely to happen in my lifetime, but with all the social fractures nowadays, something like this was inevitable," Philip said with a great deal of conviction, Jim found himself unable to offer an opposing point of view.

"If it wasn't the walking dead, we could've been in a revolution with people finally realising that the government are a bunch of self-serving twats looking after their mates instead of the people who put them into power in the first place."

Philip continued his sermon, "Aliens, Kasha, dinosaurs, hell, fucking mutated giant fucking ANTS, anything, best to be prepared for one of these eventualities, when the only course of action left to anyone……is to survive."

Jim mockingly clapped his speech, "Very nice bro, thing is, as batshit crazy at this is, your forward planning has come in handy."

Philip smiled and slapped his brother on the arm, "Ha, knew it, so, you are a smasher or a slicer?" indicating to the two boxes sitting at the bottom of the wardrobe.

"Erm, no idea, what do you recommend oh mighty slayer of zombies?" Jim said sarcastically.

Ignoring his brothers tone Philip replied "Well, depends on what you feel more comfortable with, let's consider the facts, as documented, it does seem that in order to finish them you have to destroy the brain, your little run in at work showed that."

Jim nodded, "True, we've seen a fair few have pretty horrific injuries, and although it slowed them down, they still came back."

Philip nodded furiously, pulling out the notebook from earlier, flicking through pages. "For sure, Paul for instance, I mean WHAT THE FUCK, your dick has more meat on than him, and he still came for us, still didn't lack any strength either as poor Duane's guts will testify to."

Jim shot him a look, "Okay, okay, that was a little harsh, but you get my meaning, that bird from your work was Fifty Shades of Fucked Up, but she still came back."

Philip scribbled notes on a particular page. "So, you need to mash the brain up, popular opinion says that it's the hypothalamus, right in the middle of the ole grey matter is the thing that drives them to do what they do," he continued, furiously writing in his notebook.

Jim looked into one box, it was full of blunt weapons, hammers, crowbars, even a rolling pin. The other contained bladed weapons, a brand new machete was on top, beneath that he could make out a few axes of differing sizes.

"Help yourself Jimmy, take whatever you want, I've got

mine already," Philip pulled out a drawer at the bottom of the wardrobe unit, a towel laid over the form of two items.

Philip knelt down and pulled the towel off, revealing a cricket bat and a knife with a handle, "What's that thing Beefy?" Jim asked.

Philip pulled out both weapons, resting the cricket bat against the wall. "This my friend, is a trench spike, genuine World War One," he picked the weapon up, and slid it onto his hand.

"Double edged blade, steel pommel and knuckleduster hand-guard if they get in close," he turned it around in the air, demonstrating each feature as if he was some salesman in the art of maiming.

"Where's the chainsaw Phil?" Jim asked, laughing,

Philip's face was like stone, "Are you fucking joking? If you want every deadhead in a half mile radius to descend on your very location, be my fucking guest Ash."

"Jesus, okay mate, just asking, I've obviously not put as much thought into this as you," Jim said.

Philip relaxed, "That's okay Jimbo, you'll pick this shit up," completely missing his brothers jibe.

Jim rustled through the box of blunt items, "What's this Phil?" pulling out a strange hammer.

"Ahh, good choice, that my friend is a tiling hammer," he took the object from Jim's hand, "Look, it's got pointed, tapered ends so should go in and out quickly, not field tested in any guide I've read, but seems sturdy enough."

"Erm, guides?"

Philip sighed, "Yes idiot, guides, the world today is awash with literature on pretty much everything, and hell, the Internet has even more. For example, the items in your bug out bag are a mix from the seminal Max Brooks Zombie Survival guide, the Official Zombie Handbook, UK Edition, of course, and the Zombie Survival Manual."

Jim looked at his brother bemusedly, "Mate, you have gone to a *lot* of effort with all this."

"Thanks," Philip replied, and handed back the tiling hammer to Jim. "Tell you what, was going to save it for myself, but as I've got me trench spike, you can have Wilma."

Jim looked blankly at Philip, "Who the hell is Wilma?"

"Not who Jimmy.....more like what...." he reached to the back of the drawer and pulled out a small bundle wrapped in a white towel with Japanese characters on it.

With all the delicacy of removing a soiled nappy from an infant, he carefully unwrapped the tenugui, revealing a bladed weapon some two foot in length, encased in a black scabbard.

"This my friend, is a wakizashi, made from tempered steel, this shit can cut through almost anything, here feel the weight." Philip handed the weapon to Jim, who held it by the handle, and slowly withdrew it from its scabbard.

"Nice."

"So, we've got the foreplay out of the way," Philip licked his lips seductively. "Let's get stuck into the main course, the plan, which you've managed to completely fucking forget about."

Philip sat on the sofa, carefully re-packing Jim's rucksack with the spilled items. "Remember a few years back, my birthday when you me, Jon and Mike went into town? *Way* too many beers, knob jokes and flatulence, the discussion fell onto what we would do in a zombie apocalypse."

Jim sheathed the wakizashi and sat next to Philip on the sofa, "I can barely remember that night Phil, if you recall I spent the last part of the night speaking to god down the porcelain telephone."

"You've forgotten all of that night?"

"Yeah, think so."

"So you don't remember me sticking my finger up your arse?" Philip looked at Jim straight in the eyes.

Silence.

Philip fell about laughing, "Man, you are too easy. Well,

okay Leonard Shelby, let me enlighten you, without the use of tattoo's......obviously."

Philip continued the packing, "My plan is simple, we need to get to a remote location, away from any heavily settled areas. Ideally with access to fresh water, wildlife and where the terrain is not easily traversed when your fibula is sticking through your skin."

Having finished packing, he pulled the drawstrings tight, clipped the locks together and passed it to Jim.

"Wales. That's where we need to go, I've had a look, and think we should aim for Rhayader." He pulled a map from his bag, and unfolded it, scanning the page until he pointed at a spot.

"There, the town itself has a population of two thousand odd, which isn't ideal, but from there we should be able to work our way down the River Elan, find an isolated spot and hold up. There are reservoirs nearby too, so fresh water, hopefully snag some wildlife, grow our own food, y'know, try to survive this thing."

"I think I'm remembering stuff from that night now," Jim said slowly.

"Good, like what?"

"You have cold fingers," Jim smiled.

"Knob. So what do you make of the plan?" Philip folded the map up carefully and placed it back into his bag.

"Sounds good to me, just two things, first we should stop by mum and dad on the way there, make sure they're alright."

Phil nodded in agreement, "Definitely dude, it's on the way, I've tried calling but not getting an answer, phone networks probably up the swanney, what's number two?" whilst sniggering.

Jim smiled, "Second is to get Sophie, or at least try, she said last night she was going to her mum's, so it's not too far from our folks, is that okay?"

Philip looked back, straight faced, before smirking, "Course it is you bummer, she's gonna tell you to do one, but understand why you have to try."

Jim nodded, "Thanks mate, well I'm good to go, except there's one thing I need to do before we leave this town."

Philip picked up his notebook and stuffed it into his rucksack. They gathered up the remaining food from his cupboards, which consisted mainly of pasta, individual hotel portions of Nutella and tomato ketchup. Loading the car up took no time at all, Jim sat in the passenger seat awash with nervous energy.

"Hang on bro, gimme a mo," Philip shouted.

He walked to his front door and slammed it shut, pulled out a brush and a can of matt black paint, he daubed in capital letters;

DEAD INSIDE, DO NOT ENTER

"That should keep fuckers away from my stuff," he hauled a bulging duffel bag onto his shoulder and headed outside.

CHAPTER IX

Henry York had turned into a visceral fondue party, around a dozen zombies were now picking clean every bone and ligament they could. Colin worked his way through a rib, having gorged on several pieces of rump, back and a kidney.

Dotted around the estate were other groups of the undead, some feasted on other less fortunate inhabitants who ran the gauntlet of escape and failed, whilst some bore the mark of being freshly reanimated.

Colin dropped the rib onto the ground and stood up, he took a few paces forward before being overcome with a strange sensation. He bent over and threw up chunks of undigested Mr York. From other puddles of offal, it was clear that he wasn't the only one.

His stomach partially emptied, the yearning to feed again compelled him to lurch towards the end of the road, where Dacre Close ended and more houses began.

As he lumbered forwards his dining buddy Ms Pyjamas appeared at his side. Her broken foot had turned almost completely around after tackling Henry York, making her gait even more ungainly.

Fresh moaning could be heard from multiple areas of the sprawling suburbia laid out in front of them. With a motley crew forming up around them, they shuffled towards the nearest hubbub.

They say that in any group, you're only as fast as your slowest member, if you're in an undead travelling party, this would mean that you wouldn't travel very quickly at all. For zombies though, this rule does not apply, each of them was focused on one thing, getting to the closest moan, ideally before the best bits were already snagged.

The town was charged with desperate energy, people were trying to get themselves and the people and things they cared about the most out of town and to some perceived sanctuary.

Some had no idea where they were going, merely following neighbours, the sheep gene kicking in. Others had barricaded themselves in their homes, curtains drawn shut, the warbling of radios and televisions carried out through half opened windows.

Occasionally the odd zombie lingered outside these abodes, drawn to the noise within, hammering on doors and windows with rigor mortised hands.

Colin and his undead posse ignored these, instead they were being pulled to the loudest moan in Foree, the place where the pickings were ripe.

Most people in Foree worked in the larger towns and cities nearby. In the main, traffic flow into and out of the town was pretty light aside from rush hour. Where, from nowhere, the main road through the town became as clogged as an artery of a champion pie eater.

With just under half of the town now intent on leaving, at the same time, the traffic report had gone from a crawl to a standstill.

This made for the longest stationary human sushi conveyor belt in the area, three miles of honking vehicles were attracting quite the undead crowd. Even in the midst of unbridled terror and absolute bewilderment, some people were still evidently dicks.

Like a swarm of ants, the undead coterie trudged onwards, their numbers swelled with every street they marched through and every corner they turned.

Some of their number would be attracted to pockets of life, trying to winkle out shell-shocked survivors from makeshift encampments.

Five well-dressed, but very dead men surrounded one unfortunate soul who had sealed himself within an old fashioned red telephone box. Their moaning was incessant, hands pounded on the metal and glass coffin as if trying to wake him from a bad dream. The occupant had sunk to his knees and was praying to whichever god would listen.

The sound of angry horns grew nearer, now drowning out the moans being carried in the air. The zombie cabal turned a corner past a Greggs, doors wide open, a loud slurping sound from a zombie draining marrow from a baker's spine echoed from within, whilst another worked their way through an arm now barely more than bone and scraps of skin.

The massed metal snake of vehicles began here, the tip of its tail formed of two old Ford RVs.

"C'mon you bastards, move goddamn you, MOVE!" shouted Bruce, smashing his palm onto the horn again.

The sound that came out did not match the size of the vehicle at all, this seemed to inflame Bruce's rage even more.

His wife Sandra sat next to him, her mind in another world. She was knitting a pair of turquoise trousers for her grand-daughters doll, the sound of Meatloaf's 'Bat Out of Hell' oozed from the small speakers mounted in the doors.

"That's not going to help dear, we are just going to have to be patient, seems everyone is leaving town today," she said, not even looking up from her craft.

This antagonised her husband further whose expletive laden response was muted over the horn being smacked again whilst Marvin Lee Aday extolled the virtues of being gone when the morning comes.

As Sandra finished a stitch, she pulled it closer to look, "There, this'll look just f…" she was interrupted by a pair of hands grabbing her head through a half-open window, shock-ridden eyes looked first at her husband and then towards her assailant.

Another hand grabbed her ear and started to twist, Sandra let out a small whimper which escalated into a gentle sobbing.

Colin continued to twist the ear whilst Ms Pyjamas clutched the woman's head, holding it in a firm and untender embrace. One hand lay over her mouth, the other wrapped around the other side of her head, fingers splayed over the eye socket.

Colin twisted further until a popping sound pierced the quiet of the cab, Bruce had turned to look at what was happening but was paralysed by fear, his jaw slack with terror.

The sobbing became a glass shattering scream as the ear detached from Sandra as if she was a Mrs Potato Head toy.

Ms Pyjamas seemed to gain more grip too as she fell slack in her hands, her slender fingers biting further between her eye socket and nose and inside her cheek. In one move, she yanked both of her hands, and Sandra's face opened up like an umbrella, the scream lost its resonance.

Ms Pyjamas released the eyeball and it swung like a conker on a string, gently bouncing off both sides of Sandra's chin. She kept hold of her cheek however and now pulled with both hands, the skin stretched and then tore like expensive wrapping paper, the white flesh pulled away to reveal the gift inside as a mass of tissue, muscle and teeth.

The tear now reached the gaping hole where Sandra's ear used to be, and Ms Pyjamas gave one last tug and pulled off a sheet of face.

She sniffed it, put it in her mouth and chewed it, before losing interest, it fell to the floor where one of her kin picked it up and repeated the process.

Ms Pyjamas reached forward and slid grey fingers into the flap of skin which was now the only border between Sandra's neck and what was left of the side of her face.

Her fingers dug deep and she pulled, plucking the carotid artery with the caress of a drunken bass playing giant. It plinked in a shower of red syrup, giving Ms Pyjamas the appearance of a fierce Celtic warrior.

Sandra's spirit cashed out as her life force was pumped through the gouge in her neck, Ms Pyjamas delved further into her throat and pulled out chunks of meat.

Bruce came to, and opened his door, before turning and jumping out of the RVs cab. He was met by a female paramedic, who stared at him with spheres of nothingness. He stepped back instinctively, repulsed by her appearance. Her head was charred and puckered, her lips had been completely immolated and rows of white tombstone teeth chattered in her blackened gums at the prospect of dinner.

Her eyelids had been completely burned off, singed, fused muscle held her eyes looking forwards from her head. She staggered toward him with outstretched fingers like daggers, reaching out to him like metal rakes.

He backed up again but only into the open car door, which refused to yield. Bruce held his hands in front of him, pleading, as the paramedic stumbled forwards and stabbed through his arms, pulling him to her soot covered uniform.

She sank her teeth into his throat, he gargled on his own blood and relented, sinking to the floor as other zombies crowded around him, eager to eat.

"Where did Mr Driver go?" asked Timmy, his face scrunched up, making his freckles merge into one giant ginger blob on his nose and cheeks.

Sunita swung her legs under her chair, looking around at the rest of her year four classmates, "I don't know, I think he said he was going to see what was happening and why everyone had stopped."

Rows of curious eyes peered from the mini-bus windows at rows of stationary vehicles all around them. "I don't think we'll be getting home soon," Britney opened her bag up and rummaged around for a Fruit-Shoot bottle, her eyes lit up before proceeding to drain it in one.

The mini-bus was firmly ensconced in the traffic jam which led back to a few hundred feet from the school entrance, on the outskirts of Foree.

"I wish Mr Driver would get back soon, I want to get back to mummy....and Minecraft," said Reece, before huffing and flicking through his pile of football stickers.

"Look! They must be having a race, lots of people are running to the end of that street," Timmy prodded a sweaty finger against the glass. Through smeared windows, scores of people were running from the road behind the minibus, turning around occasionally to check on something in the distance.

A woman in her early thirties ran by the mini-bus, glanced inside and stopped, sweat beaded on her forehead along with a thin river of blood. "That lady looks silly," said Sunita, who followed it up by blowing a raspberry at her.

The woman stopped and peered inside, looking frantically over to the driver's seat, "Where's the driver?" she shouted, pointing to the empty seat. Only to be met by more blown raspberries and Timmy exhaling on the glass and drawing a smiley face in the condensation.

By now, the nine children on the bus had all moved to the same side, and were pulling various faces at the woman outside. Her head jerked to her right, as if pulled by an invisible string, she glanced back at the children and mouthed "sorry," before turning and joining the small stampede. The flow of human traffic had gone from the fast moving and fit to the old and lame.

"Timmy, look, isn't that your daddy over there?" Reece pointed to a hunched man walking with a bunch of other figures behind the stationary mini-bus.

The children moved to the back of the bus and looked through grimy windows. "Are they playing the game too? They must be the ones who have to catch the other people," said Britney. The chasers were now only a car length away from the children.

"DADDY!" shouted Timmy and he started banging on the rear windows with small sweaty hands, the other children quickly joined in, nine high pitched voices all shouting "Daddy," through the rear window.

"Look, he's heard you, your daddy and his friends are coming here, perhaps one of them can drive the bus and get us back home?" Sunita asked.

"Let's open the door and let him in, my daddy is the best driver *ever*, he drived me and mummy to the circus and there were *lions* there, and men with chairs and a whip trying to stop them from biting them," Timmy said as he pressed down on the rear door handle.

The door refused at first, but as the other children joined in, it popped and released its hold, swinging open. "Daddy! Why are you chasing those people?" Timmy asked, looking sideways at a face that looked familiar yet different.

"Have you been eating jam on toast as you have lots of jam on you?" Reece asked, pointing at the mans face smeared with red goo.

Scores of black-dotted white eyes settled on the small children sitting in the back of the mini-bus looking blankly back at them. One by one they emitted a moan, before stumbling towards them.

"Daddy, if you can drive this bus then we can catch the

people you're chasing," Timmy said excitedly. He was met by more moaning, a hand shorn of its skin reached up to Timmy's face, skeletal fingers clutched his cheek and started to pull.

The knitter formerly known as Sandra rose from death, one half of her face and neck was completely exposed to the world like a half-made, but wonderfully accurate, anatomical model. Her jaws ground together as she plopped through the open window and onto the road.

Pushing herself up on broken wrists, she stood and wobbled slightly. Her feet slowly getting used to movement again as she caught up with her attackers, her eye still rocking from side to side.

Colin and his ragtag band of followers made their way through avenues of abandoned cars, small screams could be heard a short way in the distance, temporarily drowning out the cacophony of moans which had been guiding them to this point.

Small bands of zombies stood by cars, hitting windows with balled, cold fists, people inside catatonic with fear looked beyond them at visions known only to them.

The screams died down and the zombies continued their inexorable march down the vehicle lined road.

CHAPTER X

Philip flashed nervous glances up and down the street, the only sound was the engine idling. He gripped the wheel tightly in one hand, the other surgically attached to the top of the gearstick.

His peripheral vision caught movement and he quickly looked to his left to see Jim walking through an open door, he stopped momentarily and inhaled deeply before he closed the front door and got into the car.

"Well?" Philip asked, relaxing slightly.

"Yeah, it's done," Jim looked down at a tiling hammer and hand covered in thick congealed blood and brain matter.

Philip patted his brother on the shoulder, "You did the right thing I guess, just got to ask…"

Jim wiped away a tear from his eye, "Yeah, what's that?"

Philip pulled the notebook from the door tray, "How was the ole tiling hammer?"

"Eh?"

"The hammer, on a scale of one to ten, how efficient was it? Was it easy to use? Did you need more than one go? Is it damaged at all?" Philip had his pen poised above the paper.

"Erm, I've just caved my elderly zombie neighbours head in, I didn't realise you wanted a full blown product review," Jim pulled out a cloth from the glove compartment and wiped clean the hammer head.

"What are you doing anyway? Saw you with that bloody book when you turned up at my work, what is it?"

Philip sighed, "Fine, I'll tell you on the way out of Shitsville."

Most of the residential roads were now empty, whereas most days you could barely make it down Jim's road for all the parked cars, today you could happily swing a dead zebra round in the middle of the street and not hit a single thing.

"So…" Jim began.

"Okay Nosey Noserson, fine, I'm making my own Zombie Survival Guide, the main difference being mine will be actually grounded in real fucking life, not some assumed vision of the apocalypse based on film, TV or plain ole superstition," Philip tossed the notebook across to Jim.

Jim turned the book over and opened it up randomly choosing the 'Weapons to fuck shit up," section, as he read the entries, he let out a small laugh. "What's up Chuckle's?" Philip asked angrily.

"Nothing, just liked your description of Fire Extinguisher."

"Thanks," Philip puffed out his chest with brotherly pride.

"You didn't even swear either, are you sure you wrote this?" Jim laughed.

"Fuck you bro, fuck you," Philip replied and stuck two fingers up at him, though he couldn't keep a straight face for long.

"Okay Max Brooks, so in your humble apocalyptic opinion what is going on?" Jim asked.

"Well, let's look at the facts, this all happened after Sputnik went bang-bang last night, the whole red sky thing must have been something inside that probe. Something it pulled out of the guts of that meteor, which then reacted with the earth's atmosphere. We're looking at a Class Three-"

"Class Three, what the hell is…" Jim butted in.

"-dude, shut the fuck up, it's rude to interrupt. A Class Three is one step away from Mr and Mrs Skinjob ruling the whole goddamn planet, it's bad, like you trying to pull on that Greek holiday bad," Philip finished.

"Man, you so funny, I seem to recall getting off with that one girl," Jim said sheepishly.

"Two things, one, I am fucking hilarious, two, that was not a bird Jimmy-boy, only men have an Adams apple," Philip grinned inanely at his brother.

"So, alien shit in the sky means it's global, most outbreak scenarios form on the basis of one isolated incident somewhere, which then spreads, if you can find it in time, you can contain it. That's why zombie survivalists suggest you look out for odd news reports, family murders with odd characteristics, areas being sealed off etcetera."

Philip changed gear, keeping the car within the thirty mph speed limit, weaving his way through back streets.

"Thing is, that didn't happen now, it looks like *everyone* got hit at the same time. I'd guess that everyone on this planet at the time that thing went KABOOM is probably infected. So, apart from the amount of bacteria and likely infection you'll get if one of these zeds bite you, that won't transmit a virus to you. Cos you, me and every other happy go fucking lucky member of society is already a ticking zombie time-bomb."

Jim leaned back in the seat and flicked back to the index of Philip's notebook. "Makes sense I guess, Mrs Lundy was still dressed the same as yesterday, so she must've died in the night, no other way that some mysterious thing got her, as when I went indoors, the place was sealed up pretty tight."

"Exactly, when you die now, you come back as Zack. At least popular culture was right, that in order to finish them, the trusty destroy the brain seems to work. I'd probably stick my neck out and say that providing the brain is intact on death, and that no zombie is using it as an aperitif, you'll reanimate. One thing though, how long did it take whats-her-face to come back?" Philip enquired.

Jim thought back to his run-in earlier, "Not long actually, must've been minutes, she came back quicker than the driver."

"Okay, and the people on the bus of death appeared to come back at different times too, so it doesn't seem there is a set time on when you come back, which doesn't really help," Philip pondered.

Philip stopped at traffic lights, the roads were still practically empty. "Cool, so we have an inkling of what the hell is going on, as it's going on everywhere. I think the chance of it just blowing over are unlikely, so we crack on with the plan. Head to ma and pa's, see Sophie, get to Rhayader and just try and find somewhere we can all hole up and see this through. In the meantime, I want to try and make something which will be of use. This shit is real now, if it's passed on to unborn babies and that, we should try and record what we find out, for our sake and theirs."

Jim, flicked through the pages back to the 'Weapons to fuck shit up," section, pulled the lid off the biro attached to the notebook binder and scribbled down his thoughts.

"Cheers bro, I'll put you down as a part-contributor," Philip nudged his brother.

"One question Phil, the roads out of this place must be rammed, guessing the last thing we want to do is get stuck in traffic."

"Already ahead of you my friend," Philip replied.

The small hatchback pulled up in front of a grass verge, bordered by hip length grass gently waving in the breeze.

They had turned down an unmarked road shortly after driving through a small uncompleted commercial estate, 'Monroe's Future Tomorrow - Today' read the sign. Given all that had happened in the last day, the future of Monroe and indeed everywhere mirrored the half built, and utterly abandoned buildings.

Shadows seemed to move beyond paneless window frames and piles of breeze blocks. Jim ignored them and looked instead as to where they were going, which seemed to be nowhere.

"Erm, Phil, have you brought me here to have your way with me and kill me?" Jim looked around anxiously.

Philip slowly turned his head, and slid a hand onto Jim's knee, he said in a gruff voice "Take off your trousers boy, papa needs a new bitch."

He smiled and slapped him playfully on the face, "You'll see," he winked and revved the engine gently.

His Corsa was eleven years old, it had scraped through the last MOT with lashings of gaffer tape and a heavily stoned mechanic. Philip had gotten a half ounce of White Widow from 'man in pub' in the knowledge that 'man in garage' would pass his car providing it wasn't a complete death trap.

The 1.2 engine had lost more than a few horses over the years but what it lacked in speed it made up for in sheer bloody mindedness, in that regard it echoed its owner.

Philip took the handbrake off, and started to head towards the end of the road. "Erm dude, this isn't Grand Theft Auto, no road, look," Jim pointed ahead.

Philip ignored him and changed gears, not to gain speed, just a bit of traction. The car mounted the grass verge, the skirt could be heard scraping against the ground, Jim looked up at the roof, his hands clasped behind his head which he was shaking sideways in disbelief.

Corey the Corsa stuck its nose into the tall grass, like a cat sticking its head through a venetian blind trying to catch a fly.

The back wheels gripped the grass ramp and slowly hauled the entire vehicle onto the verge, which was now snuffling around in the undergrowth. To Jim it looked like they were in an organic car wash, grass like reeds brushed past the window horizontally, a clump of nettles moved past his eye line, gutted they couldn't sting him.

Suddenly the view in front cleared, the final row of grass bent to the whim of the steadily moving car. A few feet in front lay another unfinished tarmac road, running into the horizon.

"What? Where are we? What's this road?" Jim looked around with amazement.

Philip laughed, "The look on your face, this side is owned by a different company than the one we just went through. They've been fighting for months about which dumb fuck was to scythe through the last twenty five feet of countryside they had yet to desecrate. This comes out on a little road in a few miles, we may have some traffic at some point, but we won't be caught up with the other pricks who are all trying to get out the same way."

Philip navigated the car carefully off the grass embankment and onto the tarmac, feeling the cars relief at being back on proper road again, he started to accelerate.

Philip looked sideways at his brother, whilst sliding on a pair of mirrored sunglasses to dim the late afternoon sun.

"Dude, in these times, you need a little faith."

CHAPTER XI

"Where we heading to next Rev?" asked Billy, tipping the box of .308 rounds into his hand, and standing them up in rows on the pine dining table, forming them up like a bullet version of the Terracotta Army.

"We'll head into Foree shortly, we've cleared out all the outlying farms and villages from here to here," rough, worn hands indicated a swathe of countryside on a map stretched out on the table.

He removed the mottled white robe and rested it on the back of a chair, he dug deep and emptied the contents of his jacket pocket onto the table, knocking over some of the carefully placed bullets.

He took a cigarette from a crushed card box, lit it and took small but quick drags. "We've done our bit, just have to wait for the other chapters to get back to us now," he picked up and threw a radio to Billy, who caught it against his chest.

"Find out where the others are, I want to be ready to head out soon, we have plenty more to do. Are Dan and Justin back yet from their little sojourn?" the Reverend peered down at Billy, who was thoroughly dominated by the foreboding presence that loomed over him.

"Yes Reverend, Lewis said they got back about half an hour ago, with, some, erm..." Billy trailed off into silence.

"What is it Billy?" the Reverend blew smoke out, staring straight into his eyes.

"I don't like those two sick fucks, they just put me on edge is all," Billy looked down at the remaining rounds in his hand. The Reverend took another series of brief drags from the cigarette, the ash bent over like a broken stone bridge.

"Now now, they're chosen too, like us, just they're a little more…enthusiastic in their endeavours. Their methods may be unorthodox, but in the end days, we have use for men of such talents."

As he finished, he flashed a snarled grin, "Be careful they don't hear you call them that either, or you might very well find yourself ending up as one of their 'volunteers'."

Billy recoiled further, "Yes Reverend."

The tall man put a paternal hand on his shoulder, "You are one of the chosen Billy, find the strength in that, and the cause we have all been selected for. We do this all for Her."

Billy looked up and smiled, "Thank you Reverend," the Reverend patted him on the shoulder, finished the cigarette and cast the ash and filter to the floor, before crushing it underfoot.

"Where are they?" he asked quickly.

"Over in the barn," Billy replied, idly toying with the radio handset.

"Good, now get on that thing and find out where the others are," the Reverend turned and walked out the front door into the cool afternoon air.

Closing the door, he turned towards the barn, which lay at the end of a wide gravel track. In front of it was parked a white box lorry, the bottom three feet of which had a grey-brown skirt of dirt and dust, some wit had written 'CLEAN ME' on the driver door.

It had been parked facing down the track, so the rear was facing a large set of heavy, double wooden doors. The trucks roll door was open, half-light coming in through the plastic roof leaking onto a stained wooden floor.

The Reverend pulled one of the barn doors open and walked inside, dust and grass particles disturbed by the entrance hung in the air, made visible by rows of light shining through gaps in the wooden walls.

A well-built man placed a large wooden box on the floor, before looking up at the visitor, "Evening Reverend, I trust you have been busy this afternoon?" he pulled up his trousers as he spoke.

"Good evening Dan, the day has provided many more for Her flock, it won't be long now before Phase Two commences, which is why I'm here, have you…" the Reverend started to ask.

"Yes, we have," said another voice, deeper in the bowels of the spacious barn, hunched over a table was a man with greying hair, working on some object unseen.

He turned to the two men, and removed a pair of thin framed glasses. He rubbed his eyes, "We have managed to get fifteen…volunteers, for our little project, did have sixteen, but the Taser must've disagreed with him."

The Reverend gave an imperceptible nod to Dan, who returned the gesture and continued his work. "Fifteen is a sign of providence Brother, I trust you left the sixteenth in their Ascended state," the Reverend walked over to the man at the table.

"I did, I also gave him a little assistance, wasn't fair on him to come back and be trapped in that block of flats with no food," a flash of malevolence ran over his face, delighting in the memory.

"Well done Brother, now, how are your plans coming on? I have yet to be convinced that this little scheme of yours has merit, there are others amongst us who feel that this is a needless distraction from what we should be doing," the Reverend looked over a collection of metallic objects and wires on the table.

The man stopped work instantly, swivelled slowly on a tall stool, and looked at the Reverend. "We are few

Reverend, and we have so very much to do," he paused, smiling at some unshared memory.

"If we can find one of the locations, then my work can bring......Rapture to so many, and with little exposure to any of the chosen. Let's remember that so far, the military has not had a part to play, that *will* change, and we need to use the correct tool for the job."

The Reverend cast an inquisitive eye over the eager man, before looking beyond him to the assortment of parts lying on the table behind him.

"So Justin, have you perfected the charge?" he moved and stood by the seated man, rummaging through the detritus.

Justin swivelled back to his work, "Yes, of a fashion, although a little unconventional, it will do the job, with minimum collateral damage."

"And how are the 'volunteers', are they ready?" the Reverend asked softly.

Justin stood up, "Oh yes, we have sedated them all, ready for transportation. We just need to get them prepared and looking their best, Dan is unpacking their suits now," he walked to a shaded part of the barn.

The Reverend put down a small empty plastic box on the table and followed Justin deeper into the straw laden building.

He could make out shapes lying in the distance, as he got closer the shapes materialised into human form. Each was bound and gagged, lying on their backs and completely silent. He stood over the nearest one, a man in his early twenties he guessed, dressed in a vest top and jeans, pieces of straw entangled in his ginger hair.

"How long are they out for?" he asked, studying the unconscious bodies lying in perfect lines like dominos. They were a complete mix of race, gender and age.

Justin stood over a middle aged woman with a purple rinse, lost in thought.

Mother? You're not my mother, I did not spawn from you, you would share her distaste for my actions. But you do look so very much like her, the way the light catches your…

The Reverend coughed, Justin looked across "A few hours, we can put them under for longer, but it gets riskier if we do," he said distractedly.

"I will get the location for you, get them ready, if this works we might wish to replicate this elsewhere, do you have the necessary equipment?" the Reverend asked, thinking how peaceful the captives looked.

Justin knelt down by the woman, straightening out a silver necklace around her neck. "I have enough for two more batches like this," he indicated towards the line of pacified prisoners.

"If you want more after that, I will need some more supplies, but given the situation that should not pose a problem."

"Let's see how you get on with this lot first, I need convincing, I trust you and Brother Dan will be on site to supervise this?" the Reverend asked.

Dan walked over to the two men, sweat glistening on his brow, "The only way to do this is for us to be on site Reverend, we came to you with this plan and we will see it through," he wiped a thick arm across his forehead, the grey t-shirt darkened with perspiration.

"I believe in the pair of you, you helped us prepare for this eventuality, tidy up here and be in the house in ten minutes, I have something to say before we continue," the Reverend said, the two men nodded in agreement.

A paint specked lectern stood in front of three rows of chairs, a banner behind read 'CHILDREN OF ISHTAR'.

People milled about, conversation bubbled around the room, settling immediately as the tall robed man strode through a door, clutching a wooden staff and a thick leather bound book.

The congregation each found a seat and stood

watching the bedecked figure walk to the lectern and rest the book on it, he raised a firm hand and indicated his flock to be seated.

He pulled his hood back, and gazed out at the group in front of him. "Today, we have helped many to Ascend, and fulfil the wish of Ishtar. It is Her desire that the gates of the netherworld are flung open, the doorposts smashed and the doors left flattened," he paused, taking in the adulation of the audience.

"It is Her wish that the dead rise up to feed on the living and then for the dead to outnumber them. We have all been chosen by Her, as it was foreseen, it has come to pass, the end of days is upon us, only we have prepared, ONLY WE WILL PREVAIL!," he shouted, casting a steely gaze amongst the enthralled gathering.

"We offer a simple choice, willingly embrace Rapture and Ascend with Her in their hearts, or we will force them, such is our charge. This is just the beginning, to Ascend is to be spared from the purge that will follow, where the evil and the wicked will flourish. To Ascend is to be taken unto her bosom and fight the unfaithful," he raised the staff aloft.

"Only then will the world be cleansed and we THE CHOSEN, can take back what belongs to Her," he scanned the room.

"Others will call us deluded, misguided and even insane, but who is really deluded? Those who make laws to swell their own pockets and those of their accomplices?" a murmuring washed over the crowd.

"Who is misguided now? Those who sit in their stone tombs, worshipping false idols every Sunday morning?" the cry rose louder.

"WHO IS INSANE NOW? THOSE WHO TOIL EVERY DAY MERELY TO EXIST AND SETTLE DEBTS FOR THINGS THAT THEY DO NOT NEED?"

People rose to their feet, fists pumping in the air, the

Reverend raised both hands aloft, the staff forming one half of a silhouetted pitched roof.

"Through Her writings and guidance, we have prepared for this day. It is now time to spread Her word. Brother Billy has spoken to the other chapters, they have completed their part as we have fulfilled ours," the group settled back into their seats.

"Most of you are to rendezvous with our fellow brothers at the mill on Tidsley Plain. Brothers Billy, Frank, Dan, Justin and I will remain here to complete our work, this town needs to be cleansed," nods of approval bobbed around the room.

"The wheels of government still turn, the armed forces are starting to organise, we have a statement to make to show our dedication to Her," he looked over the congregation.

"Go, continue expanding Her army, for the time of judgement approaches. Those told to remain, please come with me," he bowed, and then headed towards the dining room, leaving his accoutrements resting on the lectern.

As he entered the dining room, he pulled the robe over his head and slung it over the back of a wooden dining chair, the other four men followed him to the table where the map still lay.

"Brothers, they have started to set up a 'safe-zone' nearby, from the reports on the radio, numbers at the moment are only a few dozen, with limited military support," a rod like finger pointed to an area on the map, a sprawling complex.

Justin unfolded his glasses, put them on and peered at the indicated spot, "Ah, RAF Upper Heyford, mothballed in '94, did you know that they shot some scenes of World War Z there? Quite ironic really."

Billy piped up, "The radio reports say there are some contractors on site now, repairing some of the buildings, to make them habitable, for a time at least. Most of the military has been deployed to the larger cities, apparently the Territorial Army are taking on these safe-zones."

Justin pored over the map, looking at the surrounding topography and access roads, tracing his fingers over possible points of access.

"Here, the main gate will be here, leads right up to these main buildings which are the most obvious choices for conversion to temporary accommodation," his hands a blur of activity, indicating areas on the creased map.

"Will it be a problem?" the Reverend asked, looking pensive.

Dan looked up from the map, "Not at all, if anything, it makes the task easier, with them setting up, we should be able to get in with minimum fuss, and even if we're challenged, it'll be no problem dealing with the weekend wankers."

The Reverend looked pleased, "Good work Brothers, get it done, when you are finished, radio in and we can let you know where to join us."

He looked round at each man, "By now, most of this town will be quarry or among the Ascended," he walked over to a gun cabinet, and pulled out a double barrelled shotgun. He checked down the sights and returned to the map.

"The others? They will soon be one or the other. We shall start here-" pointing to a small shopping mall.

"-and work our way round other areas where survivors will be grouping en masse," he slid two cartridges into the breech, "Our work now begins in earnest," and snapped the weapon closed.

CHAPTER XII

"If you want to see them, his legs are smashed against that wall…" Philip sang, although it had been slow going at times, the country lanes were pretty deserted. It was only the odd occasion they had to reverse and pull over for some larger vehicles, but in the main, they had made good progress.

Jim looked forlornly out of his window, the late afternoon sun was waning and starting to retreat back into the heavens. "Don't worry dude, we'll find them," Philip punched Jim on the arm, "Eh me ole roister doister, don't be disheartened, we should be there in an hour or so, kinda having to go round the houses a bit, but should mean we stay off the main roads, so it's all gravy."

Jim looked ahead, endless narrow corridors of hedgerow, tarmac and sky, before he looked back, "Yeah, I know, just mad to think that this time yesterday I was looking forward to a nice meal out, now I'm trying to not be a meal myself."

"There you go, that's the spirit you fucking miserable bastard," Philip said, and re-focused on driving.

As they turned the corner, the hedgerows eased off, leading up to a crossroads a few hundred metres in the distance, where two figures stood watch. "Slow down Phil, they may need help," Jim said cautiously.

"Yeah right, or they might want some horseradish sauce and bread to mop up your gizzard," Philip replied sarcastically.

"What the fuck is a gizzard anyway? Sounds a bit stringy, must remember to Google it if and when society manages to haul itself back from the abyss of annihilation." Philip peered at the figures growing larger on the horizon, they had seen the car and were looking in their direction.

"I don't think they're zombies," Jim said keenly.

Philip leant forward "Oh fuck."

"Wait they're soldiers!" Jim exclaimed excitedly.

"Yeah, I know, fuck, fuck, FUCK," he replied, starting to slow down and evaluate his options.

"Erm, I think this is a good thing mate, I mean, they're soldiers, you know protect and serve."

Philip looked at him and stopped the car abruptly. "First, American cops use Protect and Serve, y'know, the same American cops that kicked seven bells of shit out of Rodney King and killed Elvis," Philip started to look around.

"Second, name one fucking zombie film where the military or any one in a law abiding capacity was not a complete and total knob-jockey," he added.

Jim pointed forwards, "Erm, I think you could be right," Philip looked ahead and could see the two soldiers running towards them, their rifles pulled to their shoulders.

"STOP RIGHT THERE!" they commanded.

"For fucks sake, I just want a break, and not to be used as motivation for a round of soggy biscuit," Philip started to put the gear into reverse.

A shot rang out, the sound of displaced air wooshed past Philip's face.

"Oh balls, army fuck-nuts are going to kill us and wear our heads as helmets."

"Phil, shut up."

"They're going to skin us alive and then wear our skin

and cavort around the countryside twixt bedecked in moonlight."

"Phil, shut up!"

"And then they're going to make love to each other whilst wearing our skins and we'll still be alive, but flayed and looking at ourselves fucking against a mighty oak."

"PHILIP, SHUT THE FUCK UP!"

Calm descended, "Thank you," Jim raised his hands, looked at Phil and shrugged.

"Always knew you were a fucking camembert guzzling surrender goblin, they'll never take me alive!" Philip shouted, and looked forward, only to see the two soldiers standing in front of the car, guns raised and aimed squarely at them.

"I hope my one is the giver," he said, defeated.

The soldier on the driver's side started moving around towards the door, his SA-80 still trained on Philip.

Philip turned slowly, raised his hand and extended his middle finger, the soldier stopped stock still.

"You're not one of those nutters then?" the soldier asked, his voice trembling with nerves.

Philip looked across at Jim, "Great, we've bagged a couple of geniuses," and pressed the button lowering his window.

"Oooohhhhh, we're going to eat your brains!" he shouted, the soldier tensed before his mate shouted over.

"Ben he's having you on, relax mate."

Ben relaxed slightly, lowering his weapon, "Oh, good, sorry for shooting at you, my bad," he said sheepishly.

"That was you was it? Nice one dumbass, I only packed five spare pairs of pants, didn't envisage having to use one this early into our little trip," Philip replied, "Do you mind?" he gestured towards the door,

"No, no, of course," Ben murmured, and moved back from the door.

The brothers got out of the car, "I'm Jim and this is my brother Philip, we've just left Monroe, heading up to our folks in the sticks, where are you lads from?"

Both soldiers shouldered their weapons, and started to remove their helmets, "I'm Jay, this is Ben, we're in 4 Rifles, out of Bulford, not too far from Monroe. Been out in town there, few nice pubs from what I can remember."

Philip closed the door and walked over to Ben, "So what are you boys doing out here? Figured the military would've been kicking ass and taking names in the cities, not traffic patrols in the middle of nowhere," he looked at them suspiciously.

Ben shot a look to his mate, "Well, we kinda had a bit of an accident, had to head back to base to relay orders, when Benny boy here zigged instead of zagged, turned our ride over, trying to get back there now," Jay said, giving Ben a look to remind him he hadn't forgotten about the crash.

"Why don't you just radio in?" Jim asked.

"Would do, but everything's gone tits up, all we get now is static. We had just set up in the outskirts and were told to get back and tell the techie's to sort it out."

Philip laughed, "Do you two actually have the faintest clue what is going on right now?"

The two soldiers locked eyes again and looked back, "Not really, just told that there were massed civilian disturbances and to offer assistance to the locals, get them packed and ready to evac to some safe zones which they're setting up, why, what do you two know?" Jay asked, his eyes narrowing.

Jim turned to his brother and opened his hands, beckoning for him to relay the day's events.

"You two aren't necrophiliacs are you? Cos if you are, your little hobby just got a little more edgy. Zombies my friend, all over the shop, we have seen shit today that would make your dick drop off."

Philip then began to, colourfully, impart the sights, sounds and smells they had encountered since the morning, the two soldiers listened intently, a mix of disbelief and fear emanated from them.

"So there you have it, we got out of Dodge, and are now heading up to our parents place, hoping to get there before it gets dark. Kip overnight, find his ex, watch him get dumped again, which you two are totally invited to by the way. Before we then head over to the land of the leeks," Philip said, his mouth dry from speaking for so long without pause, "What are you two going to do?"

Ben rubbed his face with his hands, trembling slightly, "Well, we need to get back to base, but if what you're saying is true, I'm wondering if we should. My missus is six months pregnant, have to get back to her, make sure she's okay."

Jay nodded, "Yeah man, I could do with getting back to my mom and pops too, if I can protect anyone, it would be them."

Jim turned to Philip and gave him a look, "Fine," Philip said, rolling his eyes.

Jim turned to the two soldiers, "Why don't you two come with us? Even if it's just for a bit, get to our mum and dad's tonight, rest up, you can then head off tomorrow to get back to your families, what do ya reckon?"

The two soldiers nodded and picked up their gear, "Cheers guys, sounds like a plan," Jay said, a smile returning to his face.

Philip walked to the back of the car and lifted the boot, "Chuck your gear in here and let's get a move on."

Jay and Ben walked round the car, as Ben walked round, he heard a rustle in the bushes, the narrow country lane constricted around him, "Erm guys, did you hear something?"

The four men stopped, and scanned their surroundings, senses heightened, they were met with silence, "No worries, probably just the wind," Ben said and started walking again.

An arm shot out of the foliage and grabbed Ben's

shoulder. Like a mechanical grabber in an arcade machine, it hauled its prey towards the wall of leaves and branches. "Help!" he yelped and the others rushed to his aid, his body was yanked into the thick undergrowth.

Ben screamed, Philip bent into the car, and pulled out the cricket bat, Jay instinctively raised his gun.

"Don't you fucking dare shoot that thing, it was probably your shooting that got their attention," Philip shouted, and pulled the bat to his shoulder.

Jim unsheathed the wakizashi and ran to Ben, who was still screaming, "It's got me, it's got me," over and over again.

Jim looked into the bush, but could not make anything out, "Jay, pull him out," he shouted. Jay ran round, grabbed hold of Ben's other arm and pulled as hard as he could, the two brothers stood guard either side of him.

Jay heaved and as he did so, Ben was wrenched out of the thick growth, a trail of blood glistened on the green leaves.

He brought with him his assailant, who had broken teeth embedded in his lower arm, the zombie was dressed in cricket whites, mottled with grass stains and blood, his face a map of scratches from being hauled through thorny branches.

"I've got him," Jim shouted and thrust the wakizashi forward toward the undead cricketers head. Jay was still pulling his mate free, and instead of the keen blade plummeting into its head, it stabbed into the base of its neck, instantly severing the spinal column.

Jay continued to pull and with the main resisting point now broken, the head separated from the neck in a sickening sound of torn skin and snapped veins.

What they could see of zombie Botham's body was held slack in nature's embrace, unfortunately the head still clung onto Bens arm like a bulldog clip.

Ben looked down at his arm, and the zombie looked back, his screams grew louder. "Hold still!" Philip changed his stance and executed the perfect pull shot.

A loud SLAP signalled willow against cranium, and the zombies head was ripped from its desperate bite. The skull was smacked back into the English countryside, Philip raised a hand to his eyes, "That's a six if ever I saw one," his pride at his shot selection was short lived, by the sound of Ben screaming still further.

Jay let his comrade in arms go and looked at his mate's limb, Ben looked down and clamped a free hand on the gaping wound. A steady stream of warm blood seeped from the bite, "Oh fuck, oh fuck, oh fuck," he said over and over again.

Jim and Philip looked at each other, turning over their respective weapons, already pondering the scores out of ten for the Survival Guide.

"Ben, chill, I'll grab the first aid kit out of my gear, hang on mate, we'll get you sorted in no time," Jay pulled open his rucksack, frantically searching for bandages.

"Man, there is no way I'm coming back as one of them," Ben muttered, his hand reaching down by his side.

"No goddamn way."

His hand unbuttoned a fastener on his belt, "If you find her by any miracle, tell her I love her, and I thought of her now-" his hand rested on the grip of his Glock, "-at the end," which he pulled out of its holster and placed under his chin.

"BEN, NO!" Jim shouted, a crack resonated around the country lane, a puff of red mist erupted from the top of Ben's head followed by fragments of bone and brain.

Like a Thunderbird who had just had his puppet strings cut, he collapsed into a heap on the floor, life extinguished.

The three men stood over him, "Rest in peace bro," Jay said, the two brothers looked down with a mixture of shock and exasperation.

"You stupid bastard," Philip growled, kicking out at the camouflaged body.

Jay looked across, heckles raised, "What did you just say?"

"I called him a stupid bastard, cos that's what he was. A STUPID FUCKING BASTARD! Providing that bite wasn't infected we probably could've stemmed the bleeding and SAVED HIS WORTHLESS ASS," Philip squared up to the soldier.

The two men were in each other's faces, "He would've come back as one of them," Jay snarled back.

Philip drew closer, "No he fucking wouldn't, did you not listen to one fucking word I just said? We are *all* infected, every single one of us, you, me, Jim, this dead stupid bastard here. Hell, every single person you have met, fucked or had a drink with is," he retorted.

Jay looked down at Bens lifeless body, then at his hands, "You serious?"

Philip stood glaring at him, Jim moved to their sides, "Afraid so Jay, everyone, if you die, you come back as a zombie, all you gotta do is not die," he rested a hand on their shoulders.

Jay backed down, and raised his hands in acceptance, "Okay, cool, I didn't know.....we didn't know."

Philip flexed his shoulders and started to relax, "That's cool, now let's get his stuff and get the hell out of here before more of *them* turn up," a blood smeared cricket bat pointed at the ragged neck of the entangled zombie.

Jay nodded and started to gather items off his chum, he prised open stiff fingers from the pistol grip and put the safety on.

"Let's go guys," he climbed into the back of Philip's

car. The brothers got in, and continued their journey.

Whilst Philip drove, Jim wrote into the notebook, detailing the events they had encountered, and adding new entries into the Weapons section. He also made notes on 'Travel', paying particular attention to staying away from hedgerows.

All the while, Jay sat in the back, looking out of the window at the countryside moving past in an endless collage of green.

The light from the sun was starting to fade, the fiery orb idly disappearing beyond the horizon. "Here we go," Philip reported, "We're here," pointing to a house a short way in the distance, a waist high wall corralling it in the midst of fields and hills.

As they pulled into the dirt track, Jim looked up towards the side of the house where a car was parked, "That's their car, looks like they must be at home."

Jay appeared from behind them, looking at the house, pointed towards the front of the building, "Something's wrong with this picture, why is the front door open?"

Philip slowed the car down, his heart rate started to rise, the front door was yawning open, a large hole was visible one side. "Oh no, I hope mum and dad are okay," Jim said, raising a hand to his mouth, as Philip parked the car just behind a Volvo.

CHAPTER XIII

Philip jumped out of the car and dragged the duffel bag from the seat behind him, he opened it and set it down on the floor. Jay extricated himself from the back seat and stretched, before pulling Bens pistol out from his belt and taking the safety off.

"No," Jim said forcefully, "no guns, it's going to be dark soon, we don't want to attract any roamers nearby."

Jay nodded, and jammed the gun back into his belt, "Okay, but I don't have anything else."

"I do, help yourself," Philip pulled a crowbar from the duffel bag, Jay peered inside and saw that it was full to the brim with various hand weapons.

"Fuck, you have come prepared," Jay felt the weight of a lump hammer, swinging it in the air and making large figures of eight.

Jim unsheathed his wakizashi and walked to his fellow road trippers, "Ready?"

Philip nodded, "I've got a bad feeling about this," he muttered, before standing up and walking tentatively towards the open front door.

As they got closer they could see where the door handle and lock should be was now a gaping hole. From the looks of it, the door frame had also taken a pounding.

"Look," Jay pointed to a spent cartridge on the floor,

the two brothers looked at each other and gulped, preparing themselves for the worst.

Jay barred their entrance, "Look guys, I don't mean to be funny, but perhaps it's best you don't come in yet, let me check it out, you two stay here. I'll give you a shout when I'm done."

"Thanks Jay," Jim put a hand on Philip's shoulder.

"Yeah, thanks mate, that would be good, take this," Philip added, holding out a torch.

Jim and Philip stood guard by the front door, their minds racing with endless possibilities. Jay turned the torch on and gently pushed the door open with his foot.

The hallway was laden with chunks of door and splintered wood. Just inside the doorway, the torch found another spent shotgun shell.

He took a few steps inside, the door closed slightly behind him, as if it was consuming Jay into its inky black depths. The thin beam of light moved from the shotgun shell, along the hallway to another doorframe, which was also partially splintered, small pieces of buckshot glistened from within their embedded holes.

Scrolling down the frame, he could see a large dark stain at its base. Further splatters were sprayed down the walls from an impact, he walked to the doorway and looked inside the room.

"Oh no," Jay said softly, the light rolled over a body lying perfectly still on the floor. Another dark stain had spread out under its head, like a large circular cushion, a broken wine glass lay off to one side.

He walked to the body and looked down, he could see a perfect circle puckered on the woman's forehead. Her face looked peaceful and relaxed, eyes closed, Jay could almost mistake her for being asleep.

Jay looked at the window and could see a hole in one of the panes, spider web cracks spread from the impact, his head dropped, *how the hell am I going to tell them?*

He walked over to the sofa and pulled off a tartan

blanket, unfolding it, he laid it carefully over the prone lady.

"What do you think has happened?" Jim asked nervously.

Philip stared ahead, "I don't know, I'm not sure I want to know."

"We should've got here sooner," Jim said, struggling to keep his bubbling emotions in check.

Philip turned to his brother. "Dude, we got here as quickly as we could, it hasn't exactly been plain sailing today what with the impending end of the world, stoving co-workers brains in and surviving zombie sieges in petrol stations."

Philip put a conciliatory arm around him, "You never know, they might not even have been here," he added.

"What about their car?" Jim asked, Philip fell silent, and hugged him tighter. Their introspection was broken by a sullen looking Jay walking from the house.

The brothers looked at him expectantly, but his body language confirmed their fears. "What did you find?" Jim asked, he could feel his stomach tightening, Jay stopped and looked at the pair.

"Guys, I'm really sorry, your mum, she's….." he started to say.

"No man, don't you fucking say it," Philip's hands balled into fists, the grip on the crowbar tightened.

Jim looked away, his bottom lip trembled, "Err, what, err………what happened?" he asked, fighting back tears.

Jay looked at Jim, "Someone shot her, they were outside the house, looks like a rifle round, she was hit in the head, there's no way she would have known about it, and she wouldn't have suffered," he said timidly.

Philip started to walk towards the house, incandescent with rage, "Bastards, who the fuck did this? We gotta find them," he growled.

"Did you find our dad?" Jim asked quietly.

Jay looked over to him, "No, I checked the house, no

sign of him, but I think he might've been killed too. There's.......there's signs that someone else was shot, but there's no body."

Jay put a hand on Jim's arm, "I'm really sorry guys."

Philip's eyes narrowed, "FUCK! FUCK!" his screams echoed around the countryside, Jim moved towards him, trying to calm him down.

"How do you know eh? How do you know? It could be anyone lying in there, you've never met my mum have you. Or have you? Have you been boning my mum?" Philip demanded.

Jay raised his hands, "Phil, I'm sorry, I don't want it to be true, but it is, there were pictures in there, it's her, it's definitely her, I'm really sorry."

Philip dropped to his knees, his eyes tightly closed, willing it to not be true, Jim sank to him, eyes puffing up and turning red, they grabbed each other, lost in their sorrow.

Philip released Jim slightly and looked up at Jay, "Where's dad? If he's not there we should go and find him, he could be injured, he might need our help!"

Jay looked away, holding back his own emotions, "….Phil, I would love that to be true, but I just don't think that's possible, there was a *lot* of blood in there, whoever the other person was, there is very little chance they would still be alive."

"Bollocks, you don't know though, do you? You're just guessing, Jim, we can do this, we came all this way for them, we can't just abandon dad can we? Let's find him, say it," Philip stared frantically at his brother.

Jim gripped him tightly, "Phil, we have to look at this logically…."

"ROBOT, I fucking knew it, you always hated him…"

Jim slapped Philip squarely across the face, his head rocked to one side, he looked back at his brother, lip trembling.

"How dare you Phil, you don't have a monopoly on

grief you know, you're not the only one suffering. What, you think just because I'm not signing up for your crusade of walking aimlessly round a zombie infested countryside, probably looking for another zombie, that I don't care? You selfish bastard."

The words hung heavily in the air, Jay looked down at his feet, unsure of what to do or say.

Philip looked into Jim's anger-laden eyes, and sagged, "I'm....I'm sorry bro, just I....I shouldn't have said that, I'm sorry, just.......I was so sure we'd find them, you know?"

Jim's features relaxed back into grief, he nodded weakly, "So did I Phil, so did I."

Philip opened his arms again, "Sorry," he said, they hugged again, lost in their joined suffering. After a few minutes, they clambered to their feet, Jay offering them a hand.

Philip stood in front of the damaged front door, "We gotta bury her, can't leave her like this," he said, his voice wavering with barely repressed anguish.

"It's the least we can do for her," Jim stood in solidarity by his brother's side.

They went to the carport and got two shovels from the collection of garden equipment, with the moonlight casting a solemn, gentle glow, they dug a hole in the back garden.

Every push into the soil both hardened their resolve and raised their heartache. By the time it was done, their hands were blistered and sore.

Whilst they dug the grave, Jay had gone back into the house, found some clean sheets and wrapped Francine's body, encasing it in white cotton.

The mood was sombre as the brothers entered the house through the back door and walked down the hallway. Both examined the damaged doorway and stain before entering the living room.

Memories of Christmas mornings and birthdays flooded back, of arguments and celebrations, family gatherings and afternoons of watching TV.

Jay was waiting for them, kneeling down by what looked like a pile of washing, sheets wound around a featureless body. With no forewarning, realisation kicked in and both of them started to weep.

They embraced, holding on to each other with a tight grip, as if by squeezing harder they could undo what had happened.

Jay stood, head bowed, a priest in army fatigues, he waited patiently for them.

As they slowly lowered her body into the shallow grave, tears fell off their faces onto the makeshift shroud. The moonlight gave the body an eerie glow, as if it was illuminated from within.

"Do you want to say something?" Jay asked solemnly.

Jim stood forward, "Mum, you gave us everything we needed, and were always there for us. You made us the men we are today, I always thought we would be able to look after you and dad as you got older, but…." he drifted off.

Philip stood by his side and put an arm around him, acting as a shock absorber for Jim's heart rending sobbing.

"I love you mum, thank you for everything you've done for us," Philip released his brother and picked up a shovel, gently shaking the displaced soil on top of their mothers wrapped body.

Jay stepped forwards, "Don't, I got this, you guys get indoors, rustle up something to eat and drink, I'll be there in a bit."

He took the shovel from Philip and let them walk back into the house, taking a deep breath, he laid Francine Joan Taylor to rest.

The kitchen held an air of sterility, like the house was holding its breath, desperate to forget the events of the day. Jim and Philip had gone through the cupboards and were cooking up some pasta and meatballs. "Least the gas is still working huh?" Jim idly stirred the vegetables and sauce in a pan.

Philip looked across, "Who the hell would do this? I mean, it's not as if mum and dad are Bonnie and Clyde."

"Were..." he corrected himself, and fought to hold back more tears.

Jim shook his head, "No idea Phil, guess that people just react differently to all this, some go inside their shell, whilst others.....well, do this."

Jay walked into the kitchen, sweat beading off him through exertion, he gave a nod to each of them, and sat down at the dining table. "What do you guys wanna do?" he looked at each of them in turn.

Philip sat down opposite, "Stick to the plan I guess, his ex is just down the road from here, we'll have summat to eat and drink, then head off there," he looked to his sibling, "Jim, is that okay with you?"

Jim nodded, "Yeah, sounds good, thanks Phil," lost in the continued act of stirring the sauce. They ate in silence, with no electricity, they had dinner by candlelight.

As they packed up the car with what they could find in the house, Philip stood in the hallway, transfixed by the shattered door frame and the large stain on the floor. "Guys, come here a minute, got something I want to show you," Jay said, breaking the silence.

As they got to the car, Jay stood there holding his assault rifle, "Figured it made sense to show you how this works, in case, y'know, something happens to me." He passed his rifle to Jim, pulled Ben's from the boot and gave it to Philip.

"Don't need to fire it, I'll just show you how to load it, take the safety off and aim using the scope," he ran them through each process in turn. Finally, he pulled out the Glock, and demonstrated the same.

"Thanks Jay, you're alright you know," Philip opened the duffel bag, "Help yourself to whatever you want from there, just..." he started to say, "...if you could help us with our little guide that would be cool."

Jay laughed, "No worries, now can we get the hell out of here?"

Philip looked across to Jim puzzled, "Everything alright Jay?"

Jay picked up a meat cleaver and run his finger along the edge. "Everything's fine, just I've seen enough films to know that I don't want to be the token black guy, standing outside some deserted farmhouse in the middle of nowhere with two white guys," shooting both of them a big, beaming smile.

Jim laughed, "Ha, you're alright, they don't build the Wicker Man until July," a ripple of laughter rang round the group. Pulling away from the house, both Jim and Philip gave one last look over their shoulders to the place they once called home, before turning onto the main road and heading towards Foree.

As they pulled onto the main road, it was clear that whilst the roads into the town were pretty clear, the roads leading out were clogged like a toilet bowl stuffed with disposable nappies.

They drove past a mile and a half of abandoned vehicles, some had doors open, others had windows smashed and lined by blood. Interred within some were the ones who had turned, but were now unable to escape their metal coffin, moaning and squirming, still held tight by their seatbelts.

"This is pretty FUBAR," Jay's eyes locked onto a school minibus, small bones and strings of meaty pulp lay strewn around the flung open emergency doors at the rear. He put his hand to his mouth, and suppressed an urge to vomit.

They could hear moans being carried on the still night air, they seemed to be coming from the centre of the town, it was apparent their numbers were plentiful.

"Here we go," Philip said wistfully, and turned into a small cul-de-sac, a string of intestines rested on a sign;

CLASS THREE

DACRE CLOSE

What lay within was a microcosm of what was happening up and down the country, and further abroad. Wherever humanity laid its cap, it was being mercilessly stalked by the dead.

"Dear god," Jim looked around at the carnage, small puddles of pink goo were scattered on the tarmac. Body parts of every kind were strewn haphazardly, as if a giant macabre Piñata had burst above the small estate. "I hope she got out alright," he added, though his mind was already thinking back to the last house visit they had made.

They pulled into the drive, and got out, "Fuck me," Philip exclaimed, on the front garden of the house next door were the skeletal remains of someone.

It was impossible to make out the gender of the victim, as it had been picked clean. Torn clothes hung off the shell of the person, "This one must've tasted good, they've not left anything."

Jim walked up the pathway, his attention was pulled to something lying in the garden, his heart started throbbing through his ears, *please, no.*

He walked over to the figure and noticed it was dressed as a postman, a large crater made up most of its face, a table leg stuck out of the hole.

"Looks like Pinocchio won't be telling Gepetto any more lies," Philip said as he walked past Jim to the front door.

"I'll stay here and make sure we don't get any guests," Jay pulled out his SA-80, and scanned the houses, flashes of movement were visible, but there was no one else on the streets.

Jim tried the door handle, it opened without resistance, turning the torch on, it leapt onto a pool of pink and red matter lying under a small broken table.

Philip raised the crowbar, and surveyed the scene, "This must've been where Mr Postman met his end, bodes well that he's outside and not lying there," he pointed out, Jim nodded, a flush of relief washed over him.

They walked into the living room, trying to avoid the head debris littering the floor, but the odd crack underfoot reminded them of what they were standing on.

The house was quiet, nothing stirred from within. Philip spotted the kitchen at the back of the house and headed off, determined to see if anything could be of use.

Jim cast his torch over the living room, before resting its bright gaze on the dining table, there was something on it. He walked over and resting against a smashed iPad was a half-sealed envelope, he rested the wakizashi on the table and shined the light on the envelope.

Jim

He turned it over and broke the seal, gently retrieving the folded paper within;

Jim,

I hope, somehow, that you find this. Seems like the world has gone to crap huh?

Me and mum are safe, despite the best efforts of the postman, we're getting out of here as we need to get somewhere safer.

I understand if you don't want to, but if you want to find us, we are heading towards the army base outside town, they say that they are going to be setting up safe areas nearby, so it makes sense to get to one.

Hope to see you, love

Sophie

X

Jim smiled and hugged the letter *still got a chance*, "Phil, you ready to go?" he shouted.

Philip appeared from the kitchen, carrying a Sainsbury's Bag For Life filled with food, "Oh yes, they had some more orange digestives too, they are all mine Broski 3000."

He saw Jim holding the letter, "Another Dear Jim letter dude? Man I'm sorry," Jim tucked the letter into the envelope and shoved it into his back pocket.

"Au contraire mon frère, her and her mum are heading to that army base outside of town, reckon it'll be safer there than here."

Philip frowned and looked back. "I don't mean to burst your bubble el duderino, but an army base in the apocalypse is about as safe as a teenage girl at a Top of the Pops recording in the seventies."

Jim picked up the scabbard, "But they're full of soldiers, armed to the teeth, sounds pretty ideal to me."

Philip walked over to the hallway, "Of course, what could go wrong, two ladies in a base full of men overdosed on testosterone and semen. Yes, they are tooled up, pray tell dear brother, how loud do you think fifteen assault rifles on full auto are? Enough to wake the dead perhaps?"

Jim hurried over to Philip, "Balls, let's get a move on," the pair of them rushed outside.

"Jay, there's an army barracks nearby, you know of it?"

Jay stopped looking around the neighbourhood, "Yeah, just Logistics though, they'll have some combat troops there, but nothing major," he said, before climbing into the back of the Corsa.

"That's something I guess," Jim said, breathing a sigh of relief.

Philip laughed, "Yeah, something indeed. Instead of heavily armed troops, they can fight off the undead with paper clips and staplers eh?"

Jim glared at his brother, Philip shrugged nonchalantly, "What? Perhaps a nice thick ring binder?"

Jim's eyes flashed with anger.

"Fine, yes, yes, let's go," Philip clambered into the car. Jim cast a final glance round the devastation, glad that Sophie had escaped, but equally concerned for what lay ahead.

CHAPTER XIV

Wendy's clients had always remarked on how soft yet firm her hands were, the thirty something chiropractor spent hours a day cracking peoples bodies back into shape. Now those same hands were one of many pulling at the chain link fence, a wave of moans and guttural snarls rumbled from the horde, chiming with the rattle of the wavering barrier.

Another burst of automatic fire raked the undead masses, 5.56 rounds tore through the first few ranks, tracer rounds pierced the inky blackness of night like subsonic fireflies. Bodies stuttered as the rounds caused them to jig under the impact, the odd zombie dropped as bullets pierced skulls, desiccating the soft tissue within.

"We've been here for hours now mum, things don't seem to be getting better, all I've heard in the last hour is that," Sophie raised a hand, as the staccato sound of the Light Machine Guns thudded from positions above them.

A lull briefly made their ears ring, before the LMGs opened up again, sending another volley of stinging lead into the braying undead crowds.

Her mum had covered her ears, "What love?" she shouted.

Sophie shook her head, *we've got to get out of here.*

Since arriving they had been interviewed by a stern

looking General with a bushy moustache before being ushered into the mess hall, where another twenty odd civilians were also housed.

All had escaped Foree, like Sophie and her mother, all had struggled to get out, the roads clogged with stationary vehicles and the undead swarming round them like ants surrounding a piece of fallen fruit.

If she hadn't driven on the wrong side of the road, Sophie doubted whether they would be here now, the tales of her fellow mess-dwellers bore tales of desperation and utter horror.

One woman was near hysterical, repeating the same mantra over and over again "…the children, get the children…"

All attempts to calm her were met with the same phrase over and over again, steadily increasing in volume until the offer of help was rescinded.

Each group kept to themselves, clustered around bolted down tables, sipping lukewarm tea and wrapped in army blankets.

A solitary guard stood by the mess doors, he looked more nervous than anyone else. Sophie walked over to him, "What's going on, do you know?" he looked back at her, lines of sweat ran from under his helmet forming vertical transparent canals to his chin.

"I-I-I have no idea ma'am," he stuttered, looking utterly bewildered, he clutched the rifle to his chest like it was the last thing on earth.

"Well, we have to do something, it sounds like World War Three out there, is this place even safe?" she asked, this time more firmly.

He disengaged eye contact and stared into middle space, "Yes, we should be fine. They will just be thinning the numbers," he said, though with less conviction than before.

Sophie sighed, she was going to get nothing out of him, she walked back to her mother and sat down again. "Not so sure we should've come here now."

Her mum looked back, "Where exactly should we have gone? My sister lives miles away, and from all accounts this is happening everywhere, where would we go?"

Sophie looked down, thinking of everything that had transpired and everything they had seen.

Her train of thought was interrupted by the mess doors being slammed open, the moustachioed General stomped in, flanked by two dishevelled soldiers. Both of them were stoic, their uniforms ripped and stained, they carried rifles which ended in bayonets, coated in black goo.

The General climbed onto the closest table, his chaperones halted and cast glances around the room. "May I have your attention please ladies and gentlemen," the hall was hushed, even the sound of gunfire and wailing seemed to dissipate.

"As you can all hear, we are under attack, the…..people that have been attacking everyone have effectively surrounded this base, and seem intent on getting in," his words hung in the air, families pulled each other even closer.

"I have orders to relocate you all to a safe zone which we are in the process of setting up, it's a short drive away, but is better equipped to deal with a larger number of people," his cobalt blue eyes danced around his audience.

"We will shortly prepare you for this journey, prior to you going we will have to…..purge the attackers from the main gate in order to effect your safe egress. This will be noisy and we would ask that if any of you are…sensitive to this, that you let Private Thompson here know so he can obtain ear defenders for you," the words carried out to each corner of the hall with ease.

"We will be getting you out of here very shortly, so please gather any belongings you have and be ready to leave," he went to step down when Sophie shouted out "What's going on out there? Are we going to be safe anywhere?"

The General paused, half in motion, before pulling up to full height and searching out the person who had spoken, he fixed her with his gaze.

"Young lady, there is not much I can tell you. We have a handful of soldiers trying to keep back a couple of hundred of these…attackers, ammunition and other ordnance is in short supply," he boomed.

"And as for the second part of your question, I say yes. There will be safe zones under military control that will provide you all with the protection you need," he hesitated, "It's just unfortunate that this is not the place. I envisage we will be overrun within the hour," the entire room inhaled sharply.

He raised a hand up, "That is why we need you ready to go. The men and women here will do everything to ensure your safety, that is what we do, regardless of what happens to us, *you* are our priority."

He nodded to the two guards beneath him, who turned and made their way back to the door, "Get your stuff ready to go, you will be collected shortly."

He spun round and jumped off the table, as he reached the doorway, he leant into Private Thompson who was guarding the door and whispered something to him. The private snapped to attention, bolstered by the General's words.

They exchanged salutes before the General and his guards disappeared into the night beyond the door. Private Thompson shouldered his rifle and started to walk amongst the people, asking them if they required assistance.

Sophie turned to her mum, "Great, on the move again, let's get our stuff together."

Her mum smiled and patted her on the cheek, "Already have done, what little we have, everything else is in the car, and I doubt we'll be able to get back to that."

Sophie smiled back at her mum, "Guess the last thing I need now are my hair straighteners," she winked at her mum.

Five minutes later, the doors opened again, one of the General's bodyguards marched into the room, full of purpose. "Okay, it's time," he said authoritatively, "When you leave the building, the truck is backed up a little way down the path, keep together, follow us and whatever you do, do not wander off."

The soldier turned around and headed back out the door, people looked around at each other, before trudging off behind him. Private Thompson stood at the doorway, beckoning people to go through. Sophie and her mother joined the queue towards the back, and followed the others through the doorway and into the still night air.

It seemed like they had gone through a portal between the barren void of the mess hall and the outside world awash with sensations. Light flickered on the horizon from tracer rounds and what appeared to be fires, the sound of gunfire and moaning was all pervading, acrid clouds of smoke made them cough. A little way in the distance they could see two red lights, like an angry robot squatting on the ground.

Two soldiers were helping people to clamber into the back of the transport truck, they sat on hard metal benches facing each other, the claustrophobic cloak of night and fear lay over them.

Sophie and her mum were hauled into the belly of the truck, with visibility reduced, they had to grope around for a place to sit. As they found a space, Sophie looked out of the back of the truck and could see a throng of people shaking the perimeter fence.

She looked closer and could see the tell-tale signs of reanimation, heads cocked at ungainly angles, missing limbs, appendages twisted in unnatural angles, all clamouring to gain entry to the undead cafeteria within.

The back of the truck slammed shut, quickly followed by a slapping above the rear wheel arch, the engine revved, stowed in its bowels, it sounded like a malevolent growling animal.

Private Thompson stood behind the truck and shouted over the engine "Get ready, there's going to be some loud bangs and then you lot will be getting out of here pretty sharpish, hold tight-" he swallowed hard "-and good luck," giving them a thumbs up.

He pulled his rifle to his shoulder and headed towards a ladder resting against the mess wall, leading to the sloped roof.

The air in the back of the truck was laden with sweat and bulging terrified eyes, from close by they heard WHUMP-WHUMP-WHUMP.

The truck gunned its engine once more, this time slowly gaining traction on the ground. Ahead, amongst the intermittent gunfire and groans came three large explosions, which shook the truck, the engine deepened and the speed increased.

There was a clatter from the front, as if something had just hit a shower door, reverberations ran down the length of the vehicle, Sophie leant forward and looked out of the truck.

She could see scorched earth, and the gateway lying broken, one gate now formed a metal welcome mat, whilst the other was bent back on itself, crushing a number of the undead, flesh and bone protruded from the mesh, like a twisted sandwich maker.

Like the tide, their brethren were surging towards the breach, shots rang out and some fell. She could make out a thin line of soldiers standing in the distance, muzzles flashing, before the truck turned and the camp fell out of sight, she leant back and squeezed her mother's hand.

The journey was made in silence, occasionally someone coughed or cried gently, but no-one spoke, each of them locked in their own thoughts. The truck settled down into a steady pace, and rhythmically rose in time with the bumps in the road.

After what seemed like forever, the truck turned up a

road lined by fences, instantly familiar to the truck passengers, the same sort of fences they had seen ripped apart earlier that evening.

The truck pulled to a halt, air brakes hissing like a lazy snake, after a short delay, with muffled voices coming from the front, the truck moved again. As they passed they saw one soldier standing by a small wooden shack, another held the gate open like a nightclub bouncer.

Once the truck was clear, the two guards heaved the gate closed and resumed watch.

The truck stopped and reversed to a concrete loading dock, dim lights shone in the bay, casting a gentle glow on open wooden crates and boxes. Another hiss of air-brakes was followed by silence as the engine was switched off, the crunch of boots on gravel before the back of the truck disengaged and fell away.

"C'mon folks, let's get you all inside, there's plenty of beds for everyone, think the chef has even got some grub on the go," said a soldier and started to help people disembark.

Sophie and her mum were helped off the truck and pointed in the direction of an open doorway, dazed survivors were milling around inside a large abandoned aircraft hangar.

Zed-beds were lined up in rows with identical blankets and pillows stacked on top of them, the smell of cooking meat hit them, they walked inside, eager for some respite.

CHAPTER XV

"So many people to help Ascend, and oh so little time," the Reverend loaded two more shells into his shotgun.

A short distance away lay a couple still holding hands, gaping holes in their back riddled with shot and blood. He snapped the shotgun back together and continued to walk down the pavement, passing coffee shops and a discount book shop.

"Reverend, I think we're nearly done here aren't we?" Frank asked, cradling an eighties Self Loading Rifle in his arms, he retrieved a rollie from behind his ear and lit it.

The Reverend looked over to him, "I think so, the only place left to check is Sainsbury's, got to be some folk in there who are in need of some of our guidance."

"Hey Rev!" Billy appeared from behind them, holding his Remington rifle in one hand.

"What is it brother?" he asked sternly, staring down at the man.

Billy fought to catch his breath. "The zombi….I mean Ascended, they're getting closer boss, not going to be too much longer before they're on us," he said, panting.

The Reverend looked past Billy down a long line of card and charity shops, a small fire set in the smashed front window of Top Shop cast a flickering light over a number of deformed humanoids, lurching towards them.

"No matter, let's finish up here, brothers Dan and Justin should be at the site now, by the time they are done we will be onto the next objective, ahead of Ishtar's children," he gestured to the approaching figures.

They all turned and jogged down the pavement, the glass fronted supermarket was ahead of them, emergency lighting visible at the back of the store, shapes moved around inside.

They ducked in through a hole in the facade, boots crunched on broken glass, Billy's smudged robe got caught on a bent piece of metal, he took a moment to disentangle himself.

Frank and the Reverend peered into the gloom. It was clear they were late to the looting party. Near empty shelves spread as far as the eye could see, here and there laid the odd clutch of item deemed unwanted by the desperate masses.

Billy caught up to his accomplices, straightening out his garments, "Sorry Reve..." a raised craggy hand silenced him immediately.

The Reverend gesticulated towards the back of the store, they held their breath and listened intently, they could make out the sound of a scuffle and laughing.

The three men turned and walked in front of the row of checkouts, the tills had been smashed and pulled apart, people believing that the money within would be of some use in these anarchic times.

The Reverend stopped and pointed down a row which according to the overhead signs previously stored 'Cereal, Long-life Milk and Breakfast Bars'. At the far-end stood a circle of figures gathered around something lying on the floor.

The Reverend pointed to Billy and then to the back of a checkout, Billy nodded and padded over to his assigned position.

He looked at Frank and tipped his head towards the group at the end of the aisle. Frank nodded, gripped onto his SLR a fraction tighter and started to creep down the aisle.

The Reverend followed behind him a few paces and pulled the shotgun into his shoulder, eyes trained on the growing gloom.

All the aisles were split in half by a long passageway wide enough for two trollies to easily pass. Frank reached the end of the first half of the aisle and checked either side of him, he turned to the Reverend and nodded. He then edged across to the other side, the figures in the distance were between two fresh food counters, he counted five, all were dressed in hoodies, clutching makeshift weapons.

The figure on the floor was bearing the brunt of their ire, hands raised in supplication were only met with sickening kicks or a beating from some implement.

Strip lights cast a lazy glow over the figures, the murk kept their faces hidden, stolen away within their pulled up hoods. Frank aimed the gun forward and moved to one side of the aisle, he closed an eye and aimed down the iron sight, the targets bobbing up and down in his vision with every laboured, silent step.

The Reverend reached the halfway point and took cover by some collapsed shelves, he stole a glance at the back of the shop, but from this distance he could not see anything else.

Frank crept slowly, now only around fifteen feet from the group, he neared the end of the aisle. He strained to make out some detail of the men, who were still laughing and goading the person on the floor, he reached the end of the aisle and moved his finger to the trigger.

"Oi mate."

The voice was right by his ear, he instinctively turned, and looked into a V for Vendetta mask buried in a black hoodie, the grinning plastic face regarded him sideways on.

The Reverend had started to inch down the aisle when he saw Frank's head turn quickly to his side. A baseball bat swung into view and Frank dropped to the floor, the clatter of his SLR hitting the floor got the attention of the food counter-gang, who looked across at the intruder.

Frank's head swam, he looked up and saw the mask glaring back, a bat rested on his shoulder. As his eyesight returned, another mask loomed into view and then another, each person bearing various makeshift weapons. He raised a hand, which was greeted by a kick to the side of his head, which then violently met the bottom of a metal shelf, splitting his cheek.

"Bring him over here, Benny boy here needs a friend right now," said a muffled voice off to one side.

Frank struggled to come to his senses, the two blows still rung through his head which made him feel drunk and groggy. He felt hands grab him under his arms, and he was hauled along the gritty floor, his feet dragging behind him.

"And bring his gun you Muppet," came the same voice again, he heard someone pick up something metallic behind him.

He struggled to open his eyes, when he did so, his vision was wobbly and indistinct, like watching old TV shows on the internet. He could make out the figure which up until recently was the object of their attention. That baton had now been passed to Frank, the person still writhed gently on the floor, every time they tried to clutch at one of the gang, they were kicked and punched.

The gang opened up into a semi-circle, forming a small gladiatorial pit between them and the sides of the meat and fish counters.

A stinking, fetid puddle of defrosted ice slush joined the two counters like a rancid fish smelling river. The arms holding him dropped Frank onto the ground, his hands splashed into the brine, kneeling on all fours he looked across at his floor buddy.

Dressed in his Sainsbury's uniform, his floor companion painfully started to sit up. Frank could make out dark contusions on his arms and neck, probably from the kick-in the thugs had meted out to him.

"Hey Benny, don't you want to say hello to your new playmate? He's come all the way from…what the fuck, are you in the KKK or something mate?" said the voice, obviously the ringleader.

Frank looked up, all of his captors were wearing the same mask, their only distinguishing features were the colour of their clothes and their weapon of choice.

The group laughed loudly, the painted grins echoing the noise which seemed to engulf him, he looked across to Benny, "Don't worry pal, it'll be alright."

Benny quivered, his hair was matted with black viscous liquid and water, his head jerked and turned around. Frank froze, "No, god no," Benny stared at him with cue ball eyes, his battered face seemed to perk up, and jaws kicked into life like a thresher.

"That's quite enough fella's," the voice caused the mob to turn as one. They were greeted by a tall man dressed in what used to be a white robe stood at the end of the cereal aisle, a double barreled shotgun levelled at the closest member.

They all froze, locked in time as if the Reverend had pressed pause in need of a toilet break. The leader alone stood tall and looked over at him, "Fuck off granddad, one of you, six of us, even if you shoot that thing, we'll still have enough left to fuck you up."

The Reverend looked over them one at a time and then down to Frank and Benny, he coughed.

"Oh shit," said one of the gang and brought a shovel down onto Benny's back, who was in the process of crawling across the fishy floor towards Frank. Benny hit the floor hard, then tried to right himself like a turtle on its back.

"Plus granddad, we have your man here, now how about your drop your boom stick, and I don't get creative with this," he raised a fire-axe slowly into the air, the dull light glinting off the edge.

The Reverend tightened his grip on his shotgun, "I

strongly suggest you boys leave…..now. Or you will incur my wrath."

The leader tilted his head back and laughed, causing the pack of hyenas to join in. "You are one funny old bastard, 'incur your wrath' who the fuck do you think you are? Samuel L Jackson? From where I'm stood you look more like Casper the paedo ghost," the mask removed all trace of emotion.

"Now, drop it," the leader grunted again, this time with more menace.

"No," the Reverend replied with the force of conviction. Frank looked across to Benny who was still trying to pick himself up, he clamped his hand to the side of his head, trying to stifle the growing headache.

The leader looked back, defiant, "Fuck this," and swung the axe at Frank's head.

In the space of a few seconds, Frank's headache subsided and then raged anew, he heard tiny pops from the side of his head. The axe bit through his fingers with ease, cocktail sausage like fingertips jumped up from the axes blade.

The axe head landed with a THUNK into the side of his skull and became stuck. The boss tugged on it, and in turn pulled Frank's head back with it.

Frank felt funny, his headache had definitely got worse, his hand felt lighter, he put it in front of his face. He looked closer but could only make out four little bloody stumps, each squirting a tiny jet of liquid into the air.

"Huh, that's weird," he said and tried to turn his head sideways, it wouldn't move.

Suddenly he felt like someone was pulling him sideways, "Stop it, I've got a pretty bad headache, I'll deal with it tomorrow," his words started to slur.

The Reverend's shotgun fell slack in his grip, looking at Brother Frank who was attempting to make sense of what was happening. The boss put a boot to the side of Frank's head and jerked the axe clear.

With a squeak of metal on bone, the axe head came free, and Frank lurched to one side. "Just one scoop for me mother," he said, his deformed hand waving in front of him, trying to catch the liquid being pulsed into the air.

The leader looked down at the two men, Benny was hungrily tucking into the fingers gently marinating in a fishy jus.

"Don't claw me. With your spoon," Frank spluttered and collapsed face first into the puddle, blood trickled from a three inch gash in the side of his head just above his ear. A flap of skin had started to peel away from his skull where the axe had been retrieved, curling up at the edge.

"Okay, okay," said the Reverend reluctantly, "But you will pay for that," he put his arm out to the side holding the shotgun, before raising it slightly.

Billy could only see three of the group by the counters, the Reverend was obscuring sight of the others, but he knew what the sign would be. As soon as he saw the Reverend raise the shotgun, he pulled the trigger.

Shovel man was next to the ringleader, standing impassively over proceedings, his head jerked suddenly, joined by the sound of a loud clap from the front of the store.

The shovel clattered to the floor, quickly followed by its bearer who landed on Benny, pinning him to the ground. The force of the landing made him spit out Frank's index finger, he growled in annoyance as he had just chewed the nail off and gotten to the good bit.

The Reverend pulled the shotgun into his stomach, the man with the baseball bat had picked up Frank's SLR, and was in the process of studying its workings when the shotgun blast hit him in the kneecap. He howled like a rhesus monkey and collapsed, the rifle once again clattered to the floor.

The Reverend swung the barrel over to the next man, a slightly chubby member of the merry band, whose

Superdry hoodie hugged him like Clingfilm.

He let out a muffled whimper before 400 pieces of discharged shot met him square in his guts. The claw hammer he was carrying dropped to the floor as he slumped against the wall. Fat fingers desperately tried to push torn pieces of intestine and stomach back into the smoking cavity.

Billy had reloaded, when he looked down the scope again, he could see that Frank was lying on the floor, along with another man. He could make out two more masked men, both paralysed by shock, he aimed at one holding a large wrench and fired again.

The Reverend switched his attention to the two remaining members. As he bore down on them, one crumpled, a small splatter of blood shot out from the eyehole of the mask. It was followed by the back of his hood being tugged back and viscera shooting out of a hole from the rear of his head.

The leader steeled himself and pulled back the axe, "Come on then you bastard," he yelled.

The Reverend passed the shotgun into his left hand, slid his right hand into the robe behind his head and pulled out a Jennings .22 pistol which had been taped in-between his shoulder blades.

The leader froze and raised his hands, "Okay mate, you got me, you got me."

"I have," the Reverend replied dead-pan, lowered the pistol and shot him in the hip, the leader instantly dropped the axe and sank to the floor, clutching the wound. The Reverend walked over to him, the gun pointed to his head.

"Do it you bastard, fucking DO IT," squirming on the floor in agony, his jeans saturated with blood.

"Looks like I nicked an artery there my son, how long do you think I have left?" the Reverend asked.

The boss pressed both hands firmly onto the wound, "What do you mean? I'm the one bleeding out here."

The Reverend crouched down, "I know, I meant, how

long do you think I have to inflict untold pain and misery on you, before you bleed out," his eyes stabbed into the leaders, holding him in his thrall.

The man writhed some more, he looked up at the sounds of footsteps to see another white robed man standing behind the other. "Billy, go check on Brother Frank, and then how our fellow shoppers are doing."

The Reverend laid the spent shotgun behind him on the floor, pulled back his hood and tugged the scarf down from his mouth and nose.

The small pistol was still trained on the fallen man, the Reverend reached across and pulled the mask, stretching it until the elastic gave in and snapped. "Ow, bastard," said the leader.

His face revealed, the Reverend could see that the colour was draining out, like a sucked M&M, patches of hair dotted his spotty face. "There, I can see you properly now," he was greeted with a "Fuck you," and spit in his face.

Billy crouched down by Frank, he felt for a pulse and detected the briefest sign of life. He looked down at him and tried to stick the flap of skin back to his head. Like a broken bit of Velcro, it held for a moment, before unfurling again, "Is it my turn to walk Sparky?" Frank asked.

Billy rubbed his tired face, Frank started to convulse, his mouth dispensing a thick white froth, a gurgling sound and then silence.

Billy stood up and walked to Frank's assailant, he was whimpering and clutching what was left of his knee, the gunshot had stripped away the skin, meat and sinew, leaving only bone and scraps of flesh, he kicked the bat away and picked up the SLR, placing it on top of the counter.

He looked over the counter to see that another member of the gang was sitting on the floor, this one was mumbling to himself, clutching his innards which looked like maggots bursting out of a dead mole. Billy knew the other two were dead, he had put bullets through both of their heads.

"Reverend, Fra…Brother Frank is gone, two of them are wounded, pretty badly and two more are dead."

The Reverend thought for a moment, "There were six of them, look for the other one, this lot are going nowhere……for now," he grinned at the leader.

Billy started to hunt around the counter, Benny waved a lazy arm at him, still trapped beneath the dead body, before Billy disappeared through an open door into the warehouse beyond.

The Reverend stood up, and looked across at the counter, he smiled and walked over to the gang member, playing 'Keep The Guts In The Body' game.

The gang-leader sank back, he couldn't feel his legs anymore, and the world looked as though it was a negative of an old photo.

The robed man reappeared in his vision, slapping him in the face. "Now, now, don't pass out just yet, I've got something for you," he said, holding a long fillet knife in front of his face.

The leader was now hex code #FFFFFF, ghostly white, veins were visible under his near-translucent flesh, he was shivering slightly, the grip on his wound weakening.

The Reverend pulled the knife back, and then stopped, "No, you don't deserve to Ascend, you're one of the people that are here to test us. You form the very reason that will cause Ishtar to raise her army to purge true evil from this world. Hey, don't pass out now."

The Reverend grabbed the man's hand, turning it palm down, in his grip, he parted the fingers, two to each side like a Vulcan greeting.

He looked at the man, who looked back with grey fading eyes, "I SAID DON'T PASS OUT!"

The blade slid in slowly, width-ways through the webbing between the middle and ring fingers into the hand, the man let out an agonised feral howl. The Reverend slowly pushed the blade further, it met bone and resisted slightly, forcing him to apply more pressure.

There was a crack and splintered pieces of bone broke through the surface of the skin. The man now was wide-eyed, emitting sounds akin to a trapped animal, the Reverend paid him no heed and pushed the blade further.

He stopped with the knife half embedded into the hand, "Nothing to say?" he asked, greeted only by a blood curdling scream.

The Reverend grabbed the knife handle and cranked it violently ninety degrees, the leaders back arched in excruciating pain before he slumped back, unconscious.

The blades edge visible through the skin, the Reverend levered it upwards, slicing the top of the hand open.

He got no reaction except a spray of blood, Billy appeared in his periphery, "Nothing Reverend, he's gone."

The Reverend was transfixed on his patient, "No matter, get fatman's hammer and drag him to the checkouts."

The Reverend stood up, threw the knife into a sink and placed the shotgun on the chest of the passed out man. He picked up a handful of metal skewers from behind the counter and hauled the bleeding man to the checkout.

By the time he got there, Billy had already headed back to get the other wounded man, whilst he waited, he reloaded the shotgun and rested it in the bagging area.

He could hear screaming behind him as Billy dragged the last man down the aisle, his ragged, devastated leg left a red trail down the tiled floor. The three injured men lay in a row on the floor, "What do we do now Reverend, the Ascended outside will be on us soon enough."

The Reverend brought his scarf up over his mouth and nose and pulled up his hood, "We leave them a gift, an offering of peace," and started to drag the nearest man outside.

CHAPTER XVI

MID-WEEK SPECIAL
YOUR CHOICE OF MEAT
AND A PINT £7.99

Colin stood staring at the sign, somewhere in the recesses of his decaying brain an electric signal pulsed, a flash of lightning encoded with meaning and feeling. The receptor though had been disconnected, the plug pulled, the flash reached the meeting point and fizzled into nothingness. Ms Pyjamas stumbled past him, nudging Colin gently and joined in the other undead banging on the thick wooden door.

The zombie horde had swelled in number from the traffic jam which had eventually sealed the fate of so many inhabitants. Those who hadn't reanimated were laying either in puddles of expelled meat or scattered in pieces over the road, torn asunder by the frenzy.

The Salisbury Arms was the last vestige of hospitality on the road out of Foree, steadfastly refusing to be bought out by a local scheme proposing to build a sizeable shopping mall.

Its refusal meant the plans were scaled back, becoming more of a large shopping arcade than the glass and concrete retail beast that was promised, the pub remained unspoilt by progress.

In most towns up and down the length and breadth of the United Kingdom there is always one pub that people fear to tread. Unsupported storied of glassing's and people exiting head first via windows, helped create a myth that no amount of paintjobs and potted plants would change.

The locals had turned up early, intent on two things, protecting the place that meant more to them than their own homes, and secondly drinking the bar dry in case it was indeed their last day on the planet, on both counts they were doing an admirable job.

They had barricaded the main door with fruit machines and tables, then jerry-rigged a generator to the jukebox, drowning out the moans from the undead with everything from Bryan Adams 'Summer of 69' through to Rammstein's 'Sonne'.

They hadn't had a knees up quite like it since Pete 'The Bastard' McGiven had his assault charge withdrawn, on the basis that the key witness had become a semi-permanent resident of Coma-land.

As far as they were concerned, if it was indeed the end of the world, they were going to go out doing at least one of the things they loved doing, getting pissed.

It was somewhere during a full blown rendition of 'Bohemian Rhapsody', including an ear shattering screeching air guitar solo, that the undead, running out of grub in the metal picnic hampers at a standstill in the road, turned their attention to the bastion of booze.

Stiff, cold, dead hands had been hammering on the exterior now for around ninety minutes. The only thing they had achieved was having Breed 77s cover version of 'Zombie' dedicated to them around the twenty minute mark.

"What do you want next?" yelled Mark, although propped against the jukebox, his legs swayed like a drunk Elvis, his pint swirled like a whirlpool spraying the sticky carpet with beer.

Disturbed from his vodka-induced slumber, Martin lifted his head from the bar and shouted "Give us a bit of Tom will ya."

Mark scrolled through the concertina of CD covers, before running a finger down the glass in an attempt to aid his eyesight, the entire process was nearly enough to tip him over.

He mashed E3 – 12 into the keypad and watched with amusement as a CD was retrieved from its harness and reeled into position, the opening refrain of 'Delilah' burst into life.

Mark pushed himself upright and tottered over to the bar, men and women were linked in arms, screaming the words, or at least the ones they could remember.

He finished the dregs of his pint and clunked it on the bar, "Give me another will ya Mel, I've got to go for a piss," and set off on his next adventure. The disinterested barmaid picked up his glass and started to pour his fifteenth pint of Doombar.

Ms Pyjamas was banging on a patch of wall as well as any decent rhythm section member, the lack of progress seemed to not bother her or any of her other hundred-odd deceased companions. Colin looked at the building, his simple mind trying to find his own patch to bang on, he sidled down an alleyway, his progress barred by a tall wooden gate.

Maybe because it was a little bit out of the way, none of his zombie pals had ventured this far. *MEAT*, he raised his hands and hit the gate, it moved.

A lot.

He tilted his head sideways and let out a quizzical moan, before walking through the gateway.

Bloody thing, the foam spurted out of the spout, the physical representation of a wet, raspy fart. She sighed, *last thing I need with this bunch of pissheads,* she yanked the handle up, and made her way towards the hallway.

Colin ambled down the alleyway, kicking empty plastic crates as he walked. A small number of the group hearing his moan were now in pursuit, eager to access the buffet inside.

His way barred by piles of metal beer barrels he turned to face a solid wooden door, he balled his hands into tight fists and started to bang.

Mel opened the interior door, unhooked the keg from the line and dragged it behind her, wiping her hands on her black jeans.

KNOCK-BANG-BANG-BANG

She cocked her ear to the side door and sighed, noticing that the chain was swinging from one end.

Fucking pissheads, why can't they just stay indoors?

"Fuck sake Mark, you don't have to go outside to smoke you know!" she shouted furiously.

BANG-BANG-BANG-KNOCK-KNOCK-BANG

"Okay! Okay! Gimme a minute, the latch just shut behind you is all," Mel pulled down the knob on the door, which popped slightly out of the frame like a stuffed belly being unhindered from a belt after Christmas dinner.

She pulled on the handle and was met by a grey face with a hangdog expression, its mouth opened and let out a happy moan.

MEAT, Colin raised his arms and lunged at the woman in front of him. Supper was a lot smaller than him, but looked like she was more than just skin and bone. His jaw hung slack, it seemed an eternity since he had fed last.

Mel screamed, and held a hand to her mouth, as if venting her terror had manifested it in zombie form. Behind the man's shoulder appeared more of his kind, Xerox copies of humans, baying for human flesh.

Colin clamped his hands around her shoulders, forcing her back against the wall, her head struck it with a dull thud and she seemed to droop slightly, partially stunned.

Her face fell upwards, eyes flickering with contrasting messages, trying to focus on the ceiling.

He leant forwards and sunk his teeth into her throat, he felt a puff of air blow over his face as her windpipe was severed. Blood discharged from the tear, coating everything red in a foot wide radius, she sank to the floor, gasping and gargling on her own fluid.

Martin bellowed a nonsensical chorus, something about Jemimah being unable to take any more, still entwined with his fellow revellers. "I love that song me," he slurred, and made his way over to the jukebox.

"I need something with a bit of life," bloodshot eyes tried desperately to focus on the tiny words.

In the interlude, the drunken revelry abated, people having forceful discussions on how much they loved each other, and how they should just shut up and listen mate, *listen*. Martin punched the keypad, and watched the CD dance over into the player, he looked at the bar, and saw that they had some gate crashers.

"Oi love, did you forget to get dressed this morning or summat?" shouted Pete 'The Bastard'.

Ms Pyjamas ignored the comment, and staggered into the pub, joined by a flood of her friends. The jukebox belched The Offspring's 'Pretty Fly For A White Guy' into life, vibrating the boozer.

Every living member of the pub looked over to Martin, and gave him a disapproving shake of the head. Martin shrugged and picked up a bar stool, smashing it against the wall. He bent down and picked up a broken stool leg with a spindle jutting from it, the tip had splintered into a nasty sharp point.

Others reached for pool cues, horse brasses, ashtrays and beer bottles, smashing them to form jagged glass hand posies. The zombies kept on coming, forming a thin grey line barring exit from the pub.

The living screamed war cries and profanity laden

taunts, and charged the undead, who in turn shambled towards the living, arms outstretched, teeth gnawing the air. They met in a melting pot of unbridled violence, the battle for the Salisbury Arms began.

In fairness, it was more of a fracas, when one side in a conflict had drunk enough alcohol to sedate a blue whale, grace and tactics were never going to feature highly.

What it did give them, fearlessness, an inflated sense of skill and an increased pain threshold gave them the edge in the initial exchange. Broken glass lanced into dead faces, gouging and rending putrefying flesh, ashtrays caved in skulls and horse brasses smashed clavicles.

The living looked up from the initial exchange and cheered, until the first of the fallen simply rose anew, damaged but still heavily intent on eating them alive.

Ms Pyjamas looked into the startled eyes of a middle aged man with a wispy beard and a headband made from a tie he retrieved from the lost and found earlier in the day.

Old Rambo shouted a nonsensical challenge "I'LL-FUCK-YOU-UP-YOU-MOTHERFUCKING-DEAD-BASTARD-RAT-WANKER," and clocked Ms Pyjamas round the side of the head with his personalised pool cue.

It smashed upon contact and he was left holding something which now amounted to nothing more than a large splintered pencil, he looked down at it and jabbed it into Ms Pyjama's chest.

She looked down and then back up at the old man, before closing her right hand around the man's throat, crushing the life from him.

Ms Pyjamas reeled him in like a winch, eager to feast on some mature steak. She cranked open her jaw and inched closer to his shoulder, as she was about to make contact, Big Marge shoulder-charged her head on, reluctant to let her prize go, the three fell to the floor in a heap.

"BUNDLE," shouted Martin, and leapt at the zombie with a diving elbow drop, the undead skull smacked against the floor, his moment of wrestling glory was short-lived. Still sitting on the floor, he looked down, and saw that the zombie had recovered, Ms Pyjamas bared her teeth and sank them into Martin's bicep.

Martin tried to stand up, but his showboating had given the zombies the time they needed, and three of their kind loomed down on him. He screamed, but was quickly muffled as he was counter-bundled in return.

The dead were gaining the upper hand, what they lacked in speed they made up in resilience. Pete 'The Bastard' had ripped off a zombies arm and was in the process of administering the appendage to the same zombies head, but it was still fighting him with an inner fire and perseverance.

Old Mary's weapon of choice was a large cut crystal ashtray, its pointy sides and her unnatural strength were demolishing zombie heads with wilful abandon. She smacked another to the floor with a double handed backhander.

"Take this you wee bastard!" she yelled and raised the ashtray in the air, as she did, two zombies appeared from behind her and sank craggy teeth into her wrists. The ashtray fell to the floor smashing the prone zombie's skull, monochrome hands still clutching the heavy glass object.

The zombies ranks were being swelled by the seemingly endless queue from outside, for every deadhead vanquished, six more took their place. The Salisbury Arms was littered with broken bodies, packs of feeding zombies and an ever dwindling number of the breathing.

The survivors were being forced back to the windows at the front of the pub, with the front door barricaded, any chance of escape seemed forlorn. Yet another was pulled into the rabid throng, leaving two with their hearts still beating unaided in their chests.

Pete 'The Bastard' looked across at Neville, who was permanently sporting a Miami Dolphins baseball cap, even though he had never left the county.

They nodded, and let loose a deafening cry "FOR THE SALISBURY!"

Untold pairs of dead eyes regarded them with disdain, reaching for the last survivors. The pair shook their heads and turned to smash in the small windows. At first they resisted, but with an almighty effort, a pane capitulated and smashed, leaving a jagged portal to the outside world.

Neville pointed over to the bar, "PETE, LOOK OUT!," 'The Bastard' looked across to the bar.

"Sucker," Neville said slyly as he leapt through the hole, his heroin fuelled waif of a body flew through like a piece of cotton threaded through a croquet hoop.

'The Bastard' looked back at the breach, "Oh you little tinker, I am going to-" he looked into the bar and saw that row upon row of pairs of pearly white eyes were staring at him, working out the choicest cuts. "-CHEESE IT!" he shouted and pounced through the broken window.

Unfortunately, he was not as girth-restricted as Neville and he was jammed halfway in and halfway out. He could feel cold lollipop fingers crawling up his leg, pinching his skin.

He looked around, breathing in the cool night air and saw several undead stragglers who were now almost upon him. "Oh fuck," he uttered as he was double teamed by the zombies inside and out. Gradually pulled apart, his innards slopped down onto the pavement and the bar sofas.

Mark slowly opened the door of the Gents, trying to make sense of what until now had been the sounds of screaming and dull thuds.

The CD whirred back into its housing, and the only sounds were that of chewing and slurping. Mark edged the door open enough for him to squeeze through, he spied the open back door and ran.

Colin had his fill of barmaid Mel and tried to grab the fleeing dessert, but missed by a mile, he let out a disappointed moan and ambled after him.

In the afterglow of the massacre, a number of loud BOOMS were heard from a large building opposite. What was left of the barmaid twitched, turned her head to the sound and started to haul herself to her undead feet.

He could hear the man looking for him, he tried to suppress his panting which in his head sounded as loud as a steam train in a tunnel. He had managed to clamber the racking and was lying down on top of it, clutching a broken length of pipe to his midriff.

Who the hell was that dude with the shotgun?

The memory chilled him to his very core, he seemed cold, calculated and calm. When the shooting started, survival instinct kicked in and he flung himself to the floor, crawling on his belly and into the deserted grey warehouse.

He knew there was more than one of them. Sean had been taken out before the psycho shot Dave, there was no way he could've done that without help. He held his breath again as he heard boots scuffing on the dusty floor beneath him.

The footsteps grew quieter and he relaxed again, *got to get out of here, get back to the flat, they don't know where I live, I can do this.* He waited and closed his eyes, thinking of last week when they had all gone out, he could taste the acidic cider.

A scream from the shop made his eyes open with a start, *SHIT, OH SHIT,* he rolled over to the edge of the racking and looked back where he had fled from.

He could make out someone leaving the warehouse, *it's now or never,* he tucked the pipe into the large pocket on his hoodie and started to climb down.

His feet tingled as they hit the floor, sensation returning, mixed with adrenaline, he pulled the mask off and laid it on a shelf.

He breathed in deeply, and let the stored air release, checking that no one was around he started to tiptoe towards the loading bay, *on easy street now*. The loading bay was empty, he looked around again, no streetlights were on but it seemed clear enough.

He turned and walked towards the brick wall surrounding the large area where delivery trucks used to come and go, the large gates closed and padlocked.

The wall was a few feet taller than him, but he heaved himself up with relative ease. Casting one last look at the supermarket, he turned and climbed down. His feet swung in the air, not quite making it to the ground, his hoodie was gathered up around him from his descent, it was at that moment he felt something cold against his skin.

He plopped to the floor and immediately felt claustrophobic, he spun around and looked straight into the egg white eyes of Ms Pyjamas, who sniffed him, before snarling. Ray gulped and reached into his pocket for the pipe, another moan came from the side, and then another, his hand gripped tighter.

Ms Pyjamas and her foodie pals surged forwards, pinning him against the wall, Ray yelped like a scorned dog as dead hands held him in place. Feeling something clammy against his side he looked down to see a small claw of a hand pinching his skin.

The dead girl looked up at him and grinned, he returned the smile before grimacing with pain as the child's hand tore through his skin, inquisitive fingers dug into the bottom of his lung and started to pull.

Ray emitted a sound like a slowly deflating balloon, he tried to struggle but resistance was futile, the pack of zombies held him to the wall and started to unwrap supper.

Colin was a little way from the feeding frenzy, *NO MEAT*, and turned away, a sudden loud bang got his attention and he joined a new procession heading towards the sound.

He shuffled as fast as his leaden legs would allow, still leaning over broken ribs, he overtook some of his more crippled brethren. He rounded the corner and was nearly taken out by a running man, he snatched at him and then another, but failed to connect with either swipe, he heard moans from ahead and continued moving forwards.

He rounded another corner and could make out more of his kin in the distance, shuffling towards the front of the shop. He sniffed the air and smelt spilled blood, a nearby moan confirmed it and he ambled forwards.

His lean helped with his momentum, and he took the lead from the rest of the pack, ahead, something tweaked into view, *MEAT*. He started to slow, and looked down.

In front of Sainsbury's was a narrow grass verge that ran the length of the front windows, designed to break up the monotony of concrete. The strip of green served no real purpose, until now. Colin's ears pricked up, he could hear humans mewling nearby, the stench of sweet blood grew heavier as he got nearer.

The gang-leader came to, dragged back to reality by excruciating pain, he tried to move, but every movement resulted in further shots of agony. He gritted his teeth and looked to his right. His mind took a few seconds to translate what he was seeing into actuality, his hand was staked to the ground by a long thin metal skewer, he screamed.

As he did so, another howl of pain sounded nearby, and another, each aware of their impending doom. Colin knelt down by a human who appeared to have been prepared especially for the banquet, he shoved his hands into the warm exposed intestinal tract and pulled out readily prepared chunks, the meal started to cry.

He could hear others tucking into the other courses, the snap, crackle and pop of leg bones being pulled out and picked clean played over agonised pleas for help and mercy, all of which went unanswered.

Elsewhere, others drank deeply from a fountain of blood, before wrenching finger bones apart, down to the wrist and chewing on them like chicken drumsticks.

Others joined in, the screams of pain quickly subsided, replaced by the sound of chewing gristle, and the slurping of marrow. Others pressed probing fingers into eye sockets and ear drums, seeking inner sustenance when the more accessible cuts of meat had gone.

In the space of twenty three minutes, nothing remained except bones, strings of ligaments and twelve metal skewers sticking out of the grass.

Ms Pyjamas, fresh from her fill of Ray re-joined the horde, after emptying decaying stomachs of chewed meat, they rose and moved off in search of fresh supplies. It seemed all of Foree was now echoing to the sound of moans and screams.

CHAPTER XVII

"I'm not happy about this, just so you know," Philip said grumpily.

"Duly noted bro, but we could do with some idea what the hell is going on everywhere," Jim scanned through static filled radio stations, a voice appeared out of the ether.

"…must destroy the brain, that's the only thing that seems to actually stop them. All the reports I've seen say as much, zombies have been seen with no arms, no legs, but still they attack!"

Another voice interjected "You keep saying that word…zombies, surely that can't be right!"

The sound of scuffles in the background "Well what else are they? This phenomenon started last night. When someone dies, they come back to life again, imbued with one desire and one desire only, to eat the living. They ignore their own kind, no evidence of them attacking animals and consuming them," replied the stern voice.

"Told you," Philip said, in his 'told you so' voice.

"*Shush,*" replied the two passengers.

"Okay Doctor, so what should people do, everyone is hearing so many contradictory things, stay in your homes, go to the safe zones, what should they do?" asked the DJ.

More scuffling is heard in the background "Leave him

alone!" shouted the interviewer.

"It's quite simple, I would suggest you stay at home, if you can, barricade any means of entrance on the ground floor of your residence. Gather any food, water and supplies and take them upstairs, if you don't have an upstairs, make sure your barricades are built to last."

"Dude, are you noting all this down? It's in the other guides, but we could do with making a note of all this, and who this bloke is," Philip asked aloud, Jim scrabbled around for the notebook and started to scribble down what he could remember.

"Get upstairs and if you can, destroy the stairs leading from the ground floor, if they do get in it will be make it harder for them to get to you. Do not turn your radio or TV sets on too loud, they appear to be extra sensitive to noise, less so to sight. But still, turn your lights off and use candles or portable lamps where you can."

Jim continued to scrawl in the notebook, the interviewer piped up again, "Okay, so let's say they manage to do all that, how long is this going to last?"

Silence.

"That is impossible to say, most projections were based on localised outbreaks, which then spread. This is not the case here, we have been hit once, and everywhere. Unless by any miracle we can get on top of this situation in the next twenty four to forty eight hours, I think we will be facing a species extinction event. If not all, then a large majority of humanity will be one of....them," the scientist replied, gasps of shock could be heard in the background and then booing.

"What do you want me to say? I am giving you my opinion, for every one of us that dies, they come back as one of them, unless the brain is destroyed, then this goes on and on. If one of them dies, it makes no difference. Look at Manchester, we are receiving reports that eighty five percent of the population there is now dead," the words sank in through the speakers.

"Okay, so what can we do Doctor? There has to be something? God knows there has to be something!"

"God?"

"Sir, you believe that our only salvation lies in some higher made up being? This is science, and science does not lie, does not discriminate based on gender, skin colour or social class, this infection is in *all* of us. We are all going to die at some point, and when we do, those closest to us will have to make sure that we stay that way. My advice is simple," he added.

"Go on...." the DJ said.

"If you are with your loved ones, cherish the moments you have with them, if you can, fight them, destroy them, but do not become sentimental. If you see someone you love has become one of those things, do not hesitate. Destroy it, because *it* will not hesitate to kill you."

He coughed, people could be heard sobbing and heckling in the background, the DJ called out for silence. "Doctor, what can we hope to achieve against these......these things?"

Silence.

"Hope is a most human invention, it exalts us to great heights but can also make us perceive things which do not exist. My only advice is survive."

"That was Doctor France speaking to us from our London studio, in other news, the German government has confirmed that a team of specialists has contained the meltdown at Brokdorf, though it is feared that..."

Philip cranked the volume switch to low and said "Look peeps, we're here, I think..."

The car rolled up to a scene from Apocalypse Now, small fires burned in front of them. Jagged pieces of metal stuck out of the ground as if they were a new variety of flora, one half of a large metal gate lay on the floor, broken bits of chain link fence jutted out in all directions.

"Holy shit Batman, what the fuck has gone on here?" Philip asked, mainly to himself, but still aloud.

Both Jim and Jay were leaning forward, taking in the scale of the devastation, even at night, the area looked like a complete death-trap, and they hadn't even spotted a member of the undead yet.

"Look at that," Jim said, pointing to the other half of the gate, it had been slammed into the perimeter fence with such force that it had crushed a number of the zombies together, nodules of arm, leg and body part bulged through the holes. Even despite the destruction, broken jaws still churned at the sight of food, dead eyes locked onto them.

Jay pointed to a number of small charred craters from which spewed flame, "Looks like they mortared the gate, not sure why though, they must've known that whatever was outside, was going to get in," he said, dumbstruck by what he saw.

Philip turned the ignition off and held the top of the steering wheel with both hands, "You really want to do this bro?"

Jim turned, "I have to Phil, if she's in there, I have to find her, I have to know."

Philip nodded, "We best get tooled up then, no telling how many deadheads are going to be in there, we need to be ready," he pulled the duffel bag from the rear passenger seat and headed round to the boot.

Jim and Jay followed him, still surveying the scene, Philip was a hive of activity, the trench spike tucked into his belt. He was rummaging around in the bag, "What are you doing Phil?" asked Jay, his eyebrows arched.

Philip looked up, grasping a sledge hammer and a large kitchen knife "Improvising," Jay and Jim looked at each other and sighed.

Jim slipped the scabbard into his belt, and picked up the tiling hammer, Jay slung an SA-80 over his shoulder, one hand gripped a meat cleaver, the other a lump hammer. "Who wants the other rifle?" he asked.

Philip turned to Jay quickly, "Me, me! Pick me Jay!

PICK ME! I'm good for it, I've been working out real good, I'm ready."

Jay sighed, "There you go, the safety is off, make sure you point that thing away from us *please*," pointing to the rifle lying under a pile of weapons.

"GET THE FUCK IN!"

Jay turned to Jim, "He gets that, so you get the 9 milli glocks, take one, and get the clip out of the other," he pointed to the pistols.

Jim picked up the gun, "Okay, so on a scale of zero to hero, I feel pretty damn manly right now."

Philip slung the rifle over his shoulder and pulled something out of the boot, "What the hell is that Phil?" Jim asked.

Philip held aloft some-*thing*, "This my friend, is the devil of ingenuity, fat end for smashing skulls, and then a handy spear-pike thing for stabby-stabby," he said, sounding pleased.

Jim and Jay looked at each other and sighed, "This is going to be a long night," Jay said.

Philip closed the boot, "Right, listen to me, no-one fires a gun unless you absolutely positively have to, we have an unknown number of Zack inside the perimeter, stick to melee weapons, if the shit gets too much, we meet back here, the doors are unlocked, get in and honk the horn *three* times."

"No worries," said Jay and Jim, nodding their heads.

"Three shall the number be. No more. No less," Philip said, beginning to smile.

"No worries," replied the other two.

"Thou shalt not count to four, nor either count to two-"

"We got it," Jim replied.

"-unless you then proceed to three," Philip continued.

"Okay Phil, we got it!" Jim said.

"Five is right out," Philip chuckled to himself.

"Your brother is a bit of a dick," said Jay, Jim nodded

in agreement.

They headed towards what was left of the gateway, and tentatively walked over it to gain entrance to the army base, they were met by the creaking of metal and a wall of low end moans.

"Balls," Jim whispered, they all held their weapons a little tighter and cautiously stepped inside.

The sun had long since disappeared, the moonlight casting only a pale glow. Tall floodlights stabbed through the smoke and gloom with halogen daggers, creating patches of light.

Ahead of them, around thirty to forty feet away was a large building, the doors to which were swinging gently, like a saloon bar in the Wild West. Jay signalled the two brothers to head to it.

As they got closer, the sound of moans seemed to spread around them like a duvet, it was impossible to ascertain exactly which direction they came from. Scattered around like confetti were body parts. Some were identifiable, others were clumps of bone and tissue.

Philip saw a head laying on its side, half of its face had been burned, looking like Two-Face, eyes turned in their housing and locked onto him, long teeth sticking from blackened gums chattered, eager to tuck in.

He walked over to it, turned his hammer-knife combo upside down and plunged the blade through where the ear should've been, the eyes rolled inwards and the chattering stopped.

Philip placed a boot on the head and yanked out the blade, "Sweet, works like a treat," he scrunched the gaffer tape which held the blade in place.

They were halfway to the open doors, when a figure staggered to the doorway, silhouetted from behind by yellow light. "Hello?" Jim asked, gently rocking the hammer in his hand.

The silhouette raised a hand and fell forward, clutching their chest. They jogged over to it, ready to strike, they could see that it was a man, dressed in army fatigues. He raised a hand, "Stop," he croaked, lifting his head to reveal a face heavy with sweat and blood, but still a well maintained moustache.

Jay ran over to the man, "It's alright sir, I've got you," he cradled the man gently and sat him down.

The General looked Jay up and down, "Ha, a deserter eh? I should have you SHOT!" Jay tightened his grip.

The General laughed, "I have always wanted to say that, at ease Private, I'm General Hemlock, commander of this base…or was."

"Sir, what the hell happened here? The gates they…" Jay started to ask.

The General gripped him tighter and let out a small growl. "Fuck, not sure how long I've got," he fought back the waves of pain.

"Let's get him inside," said Jim, offering a shoulder to General Hemlock, they carried him into the mess and rested him against the bar.

Jim walked over towards them, "Can we get you anything General?"

Hemlock looked up "Now you mention it, they do have a rather nice single malt here," pointing behind him. Philip rested his hammer-pike against the open door and disappeared behind the bar, looking for the whiskey.

Jay sat by the wounded General, noticing that he was clutching his side, "Sir, may I?" he pointed to the affected area, the General looked at him and nodded weakly.

Jay peeled back the Generals hand and noticed a jagged piece of metal sticking out from in-between his ribs. Jay gasped and looked at the old man, who shook his head, "It's too late, I can feel it son."

"Sir, what in the name of all that is holy and pure happened here?" Jay asked, his mind swimming with what he had seen outside.

Philip returned with half a pint of Glenlivet. General Hemlock let out a pained laugh, "That's a proper measure, *finally,*" he took the glass from him and took a large gulp "That's the stuff, good find son," he cradled the glass to his chest.

"Sir?" Jay asked again.

The General nodded, "We had a number of civilians with us, those….things had us surrounded, only a skeleton crew here, everyone else had been sent to the cities, we were all that remained," he grimaced again, a small runnel of blood trickled from the corner of his mouth.

"We had word they had set up a safe zone at an abandoned RAF base, Upper Heyford, we packed them on a truck and sent them out. Only way we could clear the gate was to light those bastards up," the General took another mouthful of whiskey.

"Upper Heyford? How far away is that?" Jim asked, his mind racing with questions, "Did you see a woman and her mum, about ye high?" he added, sticking his hand out in the air.

"Sir, where is everyone else and where are the zombies?" Jay asked, trying to stem the bleeding.

The General held up a hand, "Settle down chaps, one at a time, first, Upper Heyford is about forty odd miles away, in Oxfordshire, and yes there was a woman ye high with her mother, but there were a number of civvies like that," he finished off the whiskey, holding the glass to his mouth, letting every drop disappear down his gullet.

"As for the others son, no idea, after the blast, they got in, so much blood, I crawled away and passed out, when I came to, gone…..no idea where, or why they didn't find me," he clutched his side tighter.

"Son-" he said, the dribble of blood had turned into a gush.

"Yes sir?" Jay asked, reaching around his back for the cleaver.

"-you know what you have to do, keep these two safe…be a good chap…." he let out a rattle and fell still. Jay lay the General down and looked at the two brothers, who nodded back at him and looked away.

Jay raised his arm, "Yes sir," and heaved the lump hammer into General Hemlock's skull, his body shook with the impact. A loud crack echoed through the mess hall.

Jay gave another almighty blow, which careened through the skull and mashed up the pink squishy mass within. General Hemlock shuddered as if someone had walked over his grave and then fell still.

"Sir, may you rest in peace," Jay hung his head over the General, offering a silent prayer.

HONK

The three men spun and looked at the doorway.

HONK-HONK

They looked back at each other, thinking the same thing.

HONK-HONK

"Well, someone didn't get the fucking memo, either that or one of you two built a time machine at some point in the future, and came back to this exact moment just to really piss me off." Philip pulled the rifle from his shoulder and tensed, Jay stood up, still clutching the bloody hammer, whilst Jim gripped his weapon a little tighter.

They edged towards the doorway, eyes set to scan, trying to pick out any indication of movement.

HONK-HONK-HONK

"Okay, seriously," Philip jogged over to where the mess hall ended and night began, "Oh fuckballs." Jay and Jim caught up.

"So where the hell have this lot been hiding?" Jim asked. Between the mess hall and the bombed gateway stood around two dozen zombies.

"Hi guys!" shouted a man's voice standing by Philip's car. "I thought I better warn you about this lot, before, y'know, they erm….ate you," he added, he was dressed in army khaki and was holding a rifle with a bayonet affixed to the end.

Philip looked down at the ground, "Okay, so this is it, years of preparation-"

"In your head," Jim piped up.

Philip looked across and scowled at his brother "-have come down to this. Ladies, let's dance," he slung the rifle back over his shoulder and picked up the sledgehammer-spear. Holding it aloft he walked in front of Jay and Jim, eyeing the undead horde.

"Jim, Jay, strange army man who better not be fucking with my car, fight and you may die and then be reanimated. Run and you will live, at least awhile, though your pantaloons will be stained brown-" Philip shouted.

"Is he always like this?" Jay asked, unable to take his eyes from Philip.

Jim nodded, "He's always had a penchant for the over-dramatic."

"-dying in your bed from knob-rot many years from now, would you be willing to trade all the days from this day to that, for one chance, JUST ONE CHANCE-"

"Get on with it bro," Jim said under his breath.

"-to come back here as young men and tell these zombie fuckwits that they may nibble on our testicles but they will never take......OUR FREEDOM!" Philip spun the homemade weapon above his head and charged towards the nearest zombie, Jim and Jay looked at each other and followed suit.

"Sir, I challenge you to single combat!" shouted Philip, a man dressed in what used to be a very expensive grey suit stared back with a slack jaw and intense eyes.

Philip raised the hammer and brought it down square on top of the zombies head. The blow juddered up his forearms into his shoulders as it compressed the zombies head into its neck, the night air chimed with the crack of bones.

"Ha! You look like R2D2!" he bellowed hysterically, and he brought down the hammer again, the skull cracked open and sank into the top of the zombie's chest. Two eyes peered ahead from where the bottom of its throat should be, black congealed blood oozed from the flesh caldera and the zombie collapsed to the floor.

Jay had pulled the cleaver out and was engaged in a form of brutal ballet, each pirouette and cabriole ended in one weapon or both being smashed into the dead. Broken bodies lay in his wake, his form seemed effortless.

Jim was a little more formulaic, dashing in and bringing the tiling hammer down into the top of the skull with a dull thud. It lacked Jay's panache, but was as effective.

Philip heaved the hammer again, panting heavily, "Fuck me this things on the weighty side," he lanced a prone zombie nurse through the head, the weapon serving as a crude gravestone.

He left it there and walked towards a male zombie clad in a gimp suit, "Man, I bet you dropped the ammal nitrate soaked orange just after reanimation, danger wank gone wrong?" The leather clad man waddled towards him, his bulbous form bursting out of the skimpy outfit, his moans were muffled.

Arms outstretched, he reached for Philip's head, he dodged to the side and kicked the back of the dead gimps knee, causing it to fall flat on his face, the body wobbled like day old jelly.

Philip knelt on its back, pulled out the trench spike from his belt and rammed it into the back of its skull, his flailing extinguished.

"Phil watch out!" Jim yelled, Philip turned to see an old woman in a blood caked cardigan looming out of the gloom at him.

"Shit!" her sagging tights acted like a bolas, tripping her up, her withered body fell on him.

He struggled to get leverage under the mass of layers she had on, the stench of lavender, special brew and piss engrained into her very being. Her craggy face lunged at his, she opened her mouth to reveal bloody gums, her false teeth long since lost.

She gummed him, trying to get some kind of purchase on him "Urgh, that is gross, get off me you revolting toe-tag hag!" He brought his fist, still curled around the trench spike handle, round onto the side of her head.

The handle was essentially a knuckle-duster, and her emaciated form folded to one side, Philip rolled over on top of her, tilted her head forward and thrust the blade through the base of her skull and into her cerebral cortex. It sunk in up to the hilt, he twisted it both ways before wrenching it out.

"Phil, your new girlfriend just wanted a little kiss," Jim shouted, evading the clutches of another zombie and tapping the tiling hammer through its skull.

Philip let out a sarcastic laugh, "Yeah, yeah, still better looking than yours," he said, pointing to a large dead lady lumbering towards Jim, bingo wings bouncing with every lolloping stride.

Balls.

She struck him like a bowling ball hitting a pin, sending him to the ground, the hammer flew out of his hand and disappeared into the gloom. She eyed him up like a giant cake, Jim half-expected her to lick her lips, she fell to her knees, straddling him.

"She's a bit keen!" shouted Philip, now on his feet and engaging a one armed mechanic, "On your first date too!"

Jim tried to squirm out of the grip of her legs, which held him firmly in place, he reached down and started to pull Wilma out of her scabbard.

Podgy fingers reached for him, Wilma became free, as

she moved in closer, he thrust the blade into her head, it cut through bone as if it was melted cheese, she fell loose. With a degree of effort, he heaved her to one side and stood up.

Jim looked around and saw that the undead numbers had been thinned considerably, "Guys, let's get out of here!" Philip and Jay looked around and gave a thumbs up, they all ran towards the gaping gateway.

"Good going!" shouted the solider enthusiastically, his uniform was heavily stained with dried blood. The three clattered over the fallen gate, "Who the fuck are you Mister Honk-a-tron?" Philip shouted, pointing the gore soaked trench spike at him.

The soldier took a step back, "Me? Erm, I'm Tom. Tom Thompson."

Philip started laughing "Man, your parents must've hated you eh Tom-boy!" The four men stood around the car, sizing each other up.

"I don't mean to be a party-pooper, but shall we save the introductions for the road," said Private Thompson, pointing behind them.

They all turned around to see the dregs from the fight lurching towards them, with more indistinct figures appearing out of the murk in the distance. Philip nodded "C'mon, get in you lot, we best head off to this RAF base. Get the girl, kill the baddies, y'know, save the entire fucking planet."

CHAPTER XVIII

The box lorry rumbled up the dimpled strip of tarmac towards a large metal gate garnished with coils of rusting barbed wire. The headlights sliced through the mid-evening haze, rolling over two white faces standing either side of the closed gate doors.

They looked at each other, one cast his SA-80 over his shoulder and retrieved a clipboard from a small wooden shack, the other cradled his rifle in his hands, finger hovering over the trigger guard.

The air brakes hissed and jerked the lorry to a standstill, the soldier with the clipboard walked up to the driver's door, looked up and through the window. His colleague bookended him, standing guard by the passenger side.

"Good evening gents, where you guys from and what you bringing in?" the clipboard wielding soldier asked, a furrowed brow visible under his helmet. The chin strap pulled on too tight, squeezing his face into a perfect circle.

Justin wound the window down and rested an elbow on the sill, "Evening officer, we've come up from stores at Brize Norton, told to get here as soon as possible." Dan rolled down his window and smiled at the armed guard who stood emotionless in front of him.

His mate scanned down the clipboard, "Brize Norton? Not got anything down here from you lot, who sent you?"

he looked back up at Justin, slowly lowering the clipboard, his free hand reaching back to his weapon.

Dan laughed, "Hell sent us," Justin leant back into his seat and in one fluid movement Dan stretched out his arms, both ended in two silenced Beretta's.

The silencer of one pistol swung to within an inch of the soldiers face by his door, the other in line with the empty window frame of the driver's door.

The passenger side soldier tried to bring his assault rifle to bear, whilst his comrade in arms fumbled for his. Four whip like cracks rang out in quick succession, two rounds were discharged at near point-blank range, puffs of red mist blew out from two holes in the soldiers forehead, the signal to his body ceased and he collapsed like a badly made house of cards.

The other raised a hand to shield himself, both rounds ripped through the clipboard and slammed into his jaw. The impact forced a sliver of jawbone through the back of his neck, a vapour trail of blood tracing the path of the shot. He clamped a hand over his shattered face, eyes ridden with surprise and pain, Justin slammed the driver's door open which sent the soldier flying to the floor.

He leapt from the cab and landed on the stricken man's chest, "Look at me soldier man," he said in a low, sinister tone. He reached round his back and slowly pulled out a long thin stiletto blade.

The soldier looked into eyes filled with insanity, his reflection visible in maddened pupils. Justin brought the blade slowly across the trooper's eye line, revelling in the man's terror.

He held it there for a few seconds and placed it to the man's temple, giving a tooth filled grin before slowly sliding it steadily through the skin and into the frontal lobe.

The soldier gently convulsed as his body was overcome by incoming damage reports, before he flat lined. Justin stared into the man's lifeless eyes, willing a reaction, disappointed, he yanked the blade out in a single pull, a jet of pressurised fluid shot out from the exit wound.

He looked at the blood flecked face, examining the exposed bone and tissue, before wiping the knife on the soldiers sleeve and climbing back into the lorry.

Dan hurriedly dragged the bodies into the shack, retrieved their weapons, and hurled them over his shoulder. He unbolted the gate mechanism, and kicked the doors open, beckoning Justin within. The lorry belched forwards, Dan hauled himself into the passenger seat as it passed, a short way in the distance lay a large concrete building, bathed in stark white light from towering floodlights.

Like a weary train passenger, Rob's head fell forward, snapping him into the waking world, he forced tired eyes open, but was met only with darkness.

What the hell is going on, where am I?

He racked his brain trying to dredge the last memory he had stored. Broken thoughts came back, fear, terror, someone was after him, he remembered running from a well-built man who had chased him from the newsagents.

He remembered dropping the crowbar he had been carrying, why he had it eluded him, but he knew he needed it.

Who was he?

Recall hit him. Turning the corner into the alley which led to his house he ran into another man, thinner, but toned, as if he had been expecting him the entire time.

Shit.

He remembered the man's eyes, wild with anticipation, a hand holding something jabbed out towards him, a sudden jolt followed by darkness.

Now even more darkness.

Rob tried to shake his head clear, it felt heavy and tight, like something had him in its gentle clutches. He raised a hand to his face, that too felt heavy, like weights were attached to his fingertips. He heard a gentle clunk as something at the end of his hand hit something attached to his face.

What the fuck is going on?

He started to panic, trying to touch his face again, he couldn't feel anything at the end of his fingers, but something was definitely there, clinking against something in front of his face. His breathing became heavy, his breath returned quickly back to his face, warm, damp and stale.

He heard more mumblings from around him, "Hello?" his voice wavered, "Who's there? This isn't funny you know, what have you done to me?" his words greeted by more sighs and gasps.

His eyes were acclimatising to the dimness, though his view still appeared to be through some Vaseline smeared Edith Piaf gauze. He put both his hands on the ground and tried to force himself to stand, he could hear the muffled sound of metal grinding against wood.

Beneath him, he could sense movement, gentle undulations which told him that he was in the back of a vehicle. Looking around, human shapes slowly materialised out of the gloom, their heads a uniform size, their bodies bulky and ill-fitting.

"Who's there?" cried out a woman's voice, still the sounds were dulled by the force field on his head.

Dan turned to Justin, replacing the spent cartridges in each pistol magazine, "What the hell was that Reverend bloke on about back at the farm?" Justin stared ahead, lost in the horizon overlaid by images of torn tissue and dripping blood.

He looked at Dan, "No idea, I swear these Doomsday cults get more hypocritical and pretentious every few years," he wrenched on the gearstick, keeping it at a steady rate.

"He'll get his, let's have us some fun first, kinda intrigued as to how this'll work now," he sneered, drawing closer to the building, "There," he pointed towards a closed unloading bay.

The van turned in an arc, before reversing up to the raised platform leading to the back of the building. Justin killed the engine and picked up a bag tucked under the seat.

"You do realise that this is completely bat-shit crazy Juh, even for us? I thought those ripper killings we done were fucked up, but this cranks it up to eleven," Dan looked at his friend, both smiled.

"Yep, this is most definitely one of our more avant-garde creations, but when some wanker gives you lemons-" Justin pulled out an Uzi from the bag and cocked it, "-kill 'em and shove them up their dead ass."

Rob felt the vehicle stop and then move backwards before a shudder through his backside told him that the engine had been turned off. He heard two doors thud and then two sets of footsteps crunch their way around him. More voices could be heard, metal clanging against metal, panic spread through the murk.

The roll-door squealed as it was pulled upwards, Rob turned his head to see that it was night time outside, two figures could be seen stood by the door opening.

"Hello? Can you help us?" he asked the figures, he was greeted first by silence then a gentle cackling.

The heavier set figure leaned against the opening, whilst the thinner man jumped into the back of the vehicle, he heard a click and a beam of light hit him in the face.

"Well hello there campers, this is your captain speaking, we have now arrived at your final destination, please ensure all trays are stowed and you have all your belongings," said a forbidding voice.

As the light shone around him, Rob turned to take in his surroundings, he was struck dumb by what he saw.

His view was like peering through smeared windows,

but he could make out there were at least a dozen or so people with him in the back of a seven and a half ton lorry.

Every single person he saw was wearing what looked like a riot helmet with a transparent visor pulled down, the sensation of hearing underwater was now apparent. He peered closer and saw that everyone was also encased in black body armour, the kind he had seen SWAT teams wear on way too many American shows.

Fear constricted him, his heart beat faster, thudding through the top of his head like a hammer in a bell tower. He pulled his hands up to his face and looked at them, it took him a few seconds to realise what he was seeing.

Each hand was covered in thick neoprene gloves, and on top of each finger protruded a six inch blade, honed to a razor sharp edge.

Why the fuck have I been turned into Freddie Krueger?

"Hey, you!" a voice snapped him out of his thoughts, he looked at the face, and his heart sank. "Remember me ginge?" Justin asked, giving Rob a huge smile.

"It's you, the man from the alley, what have you done to us?" Rob demanded.

Justin laughed, "I've made a few improvements, to help with a little science project me and my associate rustled up," he cast an eye over the armoured bodies propped up in the lorries hold.

"I'll fucking gut you," Rob snarled and went to stand up.

Justin darted over to him placing the Uzi barrel under his chin. "I think not pretty boy, shut up and stay still," Rob remained motionless, "Thank you," Justin stepped back to the roll door.

"Do you know the problem with zombies? I mean, the real problem?" Justin asked rhetorically, "They kill, sure they do, in pretty horrific ways, rending skin from bone, pulling out gall bladders like we pull out money from a cash machine," he waved the Uzi round like an orchestra conductor.

"Problem is, they kill, then they eat, kill, eat, kill eat, all that wasted time. My friend and I decided to cut out the eating bit, and help zombies to kill a little quicker, hence why you now all look like Edward Scissorhands cosplayers."

Realisation dawned on Rob, "No, please, you don't have to do this," he begged, Justin placed a finger to his lips.

"Shhhh, settle down now Ron Weasley, you'll ruin the big reveal," Justin hissed.

"I've taken your concerns on board, and really, they are….close to my heart. Well, all of yours," he added, placing a bag onto the floor and rifling through it slowly.

Rob sat there, *close to my heart*, he looked down, the armour jutted out from his chest due to him being sat down. He looked closer and could see that taped to his chest was a small plastic box.

A red light blinked into existence, joined by a solitary beep, he looked up, gasps of fear spread through the armoured cohort.

"I added the beep-" Justin said, grinning like a loon.

"-I had to actually physically add that to each device-" he added, stifling laughter.

"-IT'S JUST FOR SHOW!"

Rob looked at the maniac who was holding a small rectangular box in his hand. The other figure clambered into the back of the lorry, *it's him, the man I was running away from.*

"Hi-" Dan said jovially "-I wouldn't miss this bit for the world."

The other members started to plead and beg for their lives, the two figures stood there, soaking it all in. Justin raised a hand, ushering in silence, slowly retracting an aerial from the top of the box he said;

"What hands are here! Ha, they pluck out mine eyes.
Will all great Neptune's ocean wash this blood clean

from my hand? No, this, my hand will rather the multitudinous seas incarnadine, making the green one red."

He pressed a button, simultaneously all of the red lights flickered quickly and a beep emitted. A cascade of muffled bangs rang round the crouched captives, small plumes of black pungent smoke rose from under the chest plates. Rob and his compatriots remained still, their hearts vapourised by a small explosive charge.

"WOAH! Fuck me!" wooted Dan, taking in the scene, breathing in lungful's of burned meat and Kevlar.

"That hit the spot," Justin added, revelling in his handiwork, "Just the way Goldilocks likes it, not too little and not too much," a smile stretched from one side of his face to the other.

"Smells like burnt chicken," commented Dan, still breathing in the loops of smoke.

Justin moved from one body to the next, switching on cameras attached to each helmet, "I want to make sure the kiddies have a good time tonight at their little slumber party. Always good to have something for posterity, they grow up so quick."

Dan held a laptop in the crook of his arm, "Yep, we got clean signals on thirteen of them, the other two are passable," he barked out, jumping out of the back of the lorry.

"Right, let's leave this little shindig, I saw a 4x4 on the way in we can use to get back to Reverend Holier-Than-Thou," Dan stood, savouring the sight once more.

"I'll just get the cargo door, have to make sure our little prides and joy here can get to their supper without any hindrance," Justin added, leaving the fifteen Wolverine inspired zombies to their slumber.

CHAPTER XIX

The four men stood in silence, looking through the metal gateway into the night sky, the crackle of intermittent gunfire, moans and small explosions could be heard nearby. "Didn't we just leave this party?" Philip asked, grasping the fence with his fingers, Jim turned back to the car mumbling to himself.

"Erm guys, look," Jim stopped and pointed to a small wooden shack by the road, the others gathered round and looked inside where two dead soldiers were laying. One had two identical holes in his forehead, caked in blood and soot. Whilst the jaw of the other appeared to be held on through gravity alone, a perfectly circular hole in his temple was crusted over.

"Great, this is just effing great, we get to the end of another trail of breadcrumbs, and aside from Beirut over there, we've got the prospect of some people running around offing soldiers, fan-effing-tastic," Jim rubbed the back of his neck as if he was sanding it.

Philip put a hand on his shoulder, "Dude, look at everything we've gone through and caved the skulls in of today, we have totally *got this*!"

Philip turned back to the car, "Yo Tom-Tom, open the gate up will ya?" Private Thompson eagerly opened the gate, holding it open, "Best close it when we're in too, don't want anything getting in, or out," Philip added.

Jim got back in the passenger's seat, and pointed "Park up by that truck, we can then work out what the hell is going on here, and where Sophie is."

"Who are they?" Sophie's mum asked.

Sophie glowered at her, "Mum, be quiet," she whispered back curtly.

"Well, this cupboard is pretty cramped, I'm pretty sure I've got a broom handle up my foo-foo," her mum replied, shifting in the gloom, making a gentle clanging sound.

Sophie peered through the crack between door and frame again, it all happened so fast, they had only been in the base for half an hour at most before the proverbial had hit the fan. They were shown into a large hanger, rows upon rows of zed-beds greeted them, small foot lockers neatly tucked under each and every one.

They were trying to ascertain what the brown liquid in the mug was that they had been given, when the screaming started. The few soldiers they had seen quickly ran to where the shrieking emanated from, which ceased and was replaced by gunshots and then even more screaming. Not just normal screaming, full on desperate *we are fucked* screaming.

She remembered seeing the first of them come out of the loading bay, the PVC strip curtains parting to reveal figures dressed in body armour and helmets. At first she thought they were just more soldiers, until she saw their hands, or what was on their hands.

A family of five were closest to the bay, they were

kneeling, holding each other's hands and praying. Even over the screaming and gunfire, they never moved, not even when the armoured figure started clawing the girl.

She must've been about six, not much older than that, her brown hair pulled back in a tight ponytail. As she was slashed and stabbed, they kept holding onto each other's hands, still praying amongst her yelps for help. Then the others came and they all abased themselves in front of their god.

"Were they zombies?" her mum asked, shuffling in the cupboard.

"They must've been, only who would do that to them?" Sophie replied, she could hear renewed gunfire, the scraping of metal against concrete, followed by more bawling in pain and agony. Sophie let the door close quietly, it was her mum that had got them in here straight away, it was probably what had saved their lives.

As more of those things staggered into the hangar, more soldiers had arrived, they stood on opposite sides of the vacuous space and looked at each other. As is often the case in times like this, the civilians were in the middle, as the zombies advanced, the panicked soldiers opened fire.

It was a massacre, those not already slain by the upgraded zombies were mown down by the burst of sustained fire.

Then the guns went silent, the undead marched on unperturbed, looking behind her as she fled, she could only see one of the Kevlar encased zombies was down.

They kept on coming, the soldiers were gripped by fear, nothing they did slowed them down, some threw down their weapons and ran, others just stood there, transfixed.

By the time they entered the cupboard, the screaming had started again, the clang of metal on metal provided a steady beat, but it was a faint undercurrent. Sophie pried the door open again and looked, *what are they doing?*

One of the zombies was leaning over a soldier who was pinned to the ground by the finger-knives, every time it moved, he let out a yelp of pain.

Why is he head-butting him?

Looking closer she realised that the zombie was trying to bite the soldier, but with the visor down it was just chewing air.

It pulled its hand back, the blood slick blades slid out slowly. The soldier let out a cached breath, but the respite was only temporary as the zombie then pressed its hand into the soldiers face, slicing through skin and tissue. The soldier gurgled, blood ran down the side of his cheek and he fell still.

Bored by the inability to feed and the meal going slack, the zombie stood up, as he did so, the body still clung onto the blades. It finally let go and slumped to the floor with a wet thump.

"Guys, check this out!" Jay shouted, he was standing at the back of a seven and a half ton lorry, the roll doors gaping open. They ran over to where Jay was shining a torch around the interior.

"What the fuck happened here?" Philip asked, entering the hold and taking in the scene, "And what the hell is that smell? It's like burnt chicken," he added.

A whistle penetrated the still night air, Private Thompson had gone over to the building, "Guys, in here, be ready," he hissed, taking the safety off his rifle and checking the bayonet was firmly fixed.

The others left the lorry and walked over to an open

door leading into the large building, "Look," Tom pointed into the bowels of the building.

"Oh god no," Jim said quietly, he could make out a woman's body lying face down on the floor about twenty feet away from them, even in the twilight, her light floral dress was visibly soaked in blood.

"Let's keep this quiet," Jay cocked his SA-80, "Noise isn't too much of an issue from all the commotion we've heard, but we don't know what we're facing, are they zombies or are they human?"

Philip sniggered, "Or are they dancer?"

The other three shook their heads and crept through the door, into a storage area. Rusting metal shelving units were lined in symmetric rows, Jay gestured to the right "Two go that way, the others go this way," the men nodded in agreement, Philip and Tom sloped off to the right, Jim crouched next to Jay, Wilma already out of her home and ready to strike.

"Seriously Soph, something is right up my...."

Sophie shot her another look, "*Shhhhh*," her mum pushed the broom handle which smacked against the bottom of the metal bucket. A large THUD sounded from within the cupboard and with the aid of crude amplification rang round the hangar, Rob turned his head and walked towards the noise.

They regrouped by a large doorway with a fringe of heavy plastic strips hanging from the entrance, reddish smears halfway up gave a rose tinted view beyond. They nodded and eased the strips aside, taking their turns to sneak into the hangar beyond, "Fuck me," Philip said, astonishment laced his voice.

Inside looked more at home in a book of Genocide than it did to a guide of disused US Air Force bases in the United Kingdom. Bodies were strewn everywhere, a small cluster lay together by the doorway, Jim tried to count how many people were there, but it was impossible to tell with all the blood and torn limbs.

They could see in the middle were more bodies, these appeared to be relatively intact, facing the same way "Poor bastards were running from something," Jay said. A number of well protected soldiers were milling around, they looked lost.

Private Thompson stood up, "Hey! Guys! What the hell has gone on here, do you need any help?" he shouted to them.

The dozen figures stopped as one and turned to face them, Jim, Jay and Philip all stood up, taking in the devastation. "What regiment are you from? Or are you.....are you police? Why are you wearing riot gear?" Tom shouted out, cupping his hands over his eyes to get a better look.

"Tom, shut up, they're not friendlies," Jay said, "Look," he shone his torch at the closest figure, he ran the light up from its feet, untied trainers led to blood stained jeans and then to a bullet proof vest which had buckled at the top, its arms were also clad in armour as was its head.

"Fuck," the torch ran over the gleam of the blades embedded into the glove, Jay shone the torch into its face, skin the colour of ash, eyes white as double cream, it moaned.

"Fuck," Philip shone his torch at another and another, all were the same "Someone has turned them into goddamn zombie terminators!"

The zombies were closing, forming a crescent in front of them. "Suggestions anyone?" Jim pulled out a pistol and checked the safety was off. Tom eased the rifle stock into his shoulder and let off a round, it flew through the air and bounced off the zombie's helmet like an angry wasp.

Philip laughed, "Man, this is *intense*," he took a step forward, checked his rifle and turned to the others. "Follow my lead guys, me Jay and Tom-Tom with the rifles, single shot only, Jimbo, get Wilma ready."

Philip screwed up his face and turned to them, "Listen, and understand guys. Those zombie terminator bastards are out there. They can't be bargained with. They can't be reasoned with. They don't feel pity, or remorse, or fear. And they absolutely will not stop, EVER, until we are all dead!"

Jay looked over to Jim, "Seriously?"

"Philip, that was pretty damn rousing," Tom said beaming with adoration.

Philip ambled to the nearest zombie, clearly a woman, or a cross-dresser, her skirt flowed behind her. "Hey Bunky!" Philip shouted and pointed the rifle down to her foot, a single shot rang out, the bullet shattered the base of the woman's fibula, causing her to crash to the floor in a clatter of armour and plastic.

The others stood gobsmacked, the zombie tried to crawl, its talons scratching against the concrete but unable to pull its body along.

"What?" Philip asked nonchalantly.

"Shoot them in the ankles, they fall down and Jimmy boy here can give them the ole gladiator execution. Or put a round through the base of their skull into the top of the head," Philip beamed.

A moan rumbled behind them, causing them to turn as one, the woman in the floral dress was on her feet, pushing her way through the plastic strips and looking for food.

Jim closed one eye and fired two shots in quick succession, one whizzed past her, whilst the other smacked into her forehead, the moaning ceased and she dropped to the floor like Newton's apple.

The PVC strips swung and ran over her motionless body, Philip sighed, "Okay, *and* take care of the other zombies, man this is getting a bit hectic."

Another shot rang out, another of the armoured zombies collapsed to the floor unceremoniously, "See, piece of piss," he walked on. The others followed his lead, working clockwise they made their way round the room.

They were down to the last half dozen when a scream rang out from the other side of the room, "Jim, you're with me," Philip said, and the pair ran off to the noise.

"Gotta hand it to him, mad as a badger in a traffic jam, but its working," Jay shot another of the hulks in the ankle. Tom kicked the zombie over onto its front, placed a boot on the top of the helmet exposing the nape of its clammy neck, and slammed the bayonet through the base of the skull into the zombie's brain, it twitched, the metal blades tickling the floor before ceasing.

Jim and Philip ran in the direction of the screaming, a short way away they could see a straggler was trying to open a cupboard door.

Philip raised the rifle, "Get away from her you *bitch*!" he shouted and fired a slug into the zombies foot, causing it to fall into the door.

Philip walked up to the side of it and kicked the side of its head, knocking it onto its back, "Fuck, ah well," and walked around to where it's head lay, "Just need to flip Mr Strawberry Blonde here over."

He bent down and grabbed the riot helmet trying to twist the body over, he heaved, nothing.

"Shit."

Two deadly hands started flailing wildly catching Philip on his arm, "OWWWW, fucking hell Beaker," he fell backwards clutching his arm.

"NOOOO," Jim shouted and pulled out the Glock, he stood by its feet and pointed the pistol at its exposed neck.

"Get the fuck off my brother," he growled and emptied the clip into its body.

By the time the last round hit home, the zombie's neck was hanging on by the tiniest of threads. Jim kept pressing the trigger, CLICK-CLICK-CLICK, until he felt a warm hand rest on top of his.

"Sarah Connor?" Philip asked before he passed out on the floor.

"Jay get over here!" Jim shouted, he looked down at

the hand, its familiarity reassured him, "Sophie?"

He turned around, his eyes instantly falling into hers, "Hi Jim."

Silence.

Say something you Muppet, something, ANYTHING!

"Your hair looks nice," he burbled.

I give up on you, I deserve better.

She smiled and gently bit her lip, before looking down to one side, "You better go make sure Phil is okay."

For the briefest of moments he forgot he even had a brother, he gave her a puzzled look before realisation hit and he nodded his head enthusiastically.

Philip opened his eyes wearily and looked up to see Jay examining his arm, "Don't worry, it's nothing serious, just a flesh-wound."

Jay smiled, and suppressed a laugh, "Fine, go on, say it."

Philip smiled back, "Tis but a scratch."

"You're a dick," Jay smiled.

Philip smiled back at him and nodded. "I know, mum always said if you were good at something, keep doing it," his smile receded, eyes reddened.

Jay pulled him to his chest, "It's okay Phil, it's okay."

Tom applied the coup de grace to the last of the reinforced undead, sliding the bayonet from the back of its skull, he looked around the room and shook his head. "It's done guys, everything's……done," he walked to a fold out bed by the gang and sank into it, dropping the rifle to one side.

Jim looked back at Sophie, she looked the same yet different, "I love you," he said, relieved to see her face.

She turned back to him and winked, "I know," and hugged him.

Jim held onto her as if she was the most important thing in the world, "What a day," he mumbled.

She released him and looked up into his eyes again, "Tell me about it."

Her mother clambered out of the cupboard, "Ann Summers could do with a line of those," she said, before looking around, giving Jim a sly knowing wink.

She noticed the two soldiers staring back at her, "Oh, hi, I'm Katherine, Sophie's mother, you two are?"

CHAPTER XX

"Wankers!" Dan shouted, Justin looked across to his colleague and raised an eyebrow, "A group of bastards have just taken care of our little group of attack zombies back at that RAF base," he elaborated.

Justin looked back at the road, "No matter, did we get some good footage?"

Dan grinned inanely, "Oh hell yes! There was one bit where number seven took this family apart, this little girls face man, it just got sliced *off*, it was a work of art," he replied enthusiastically, "FUCK!" he kicked the dashboard in anger.

"Hang on," Justin swerved across the road, the headlights landed on a figure walking across the road. Suddenly half the road went black followed by a loud THUMP as the corner of the 4x4 careened into the figure, sending it cartwheeling through the air and into a road-sign, which bent under the impact.

"SWEET! Good shot Juh, what's the score now?" Dan enquired.

"Humans 1, Zombie Nation 3, the undead seem to be lacking the appropriate defense for this quarter," he replied, veering back into the centre of the road, Dan grinned and tapped away on the laptop.

"Not long now till we're back in Foree my twisted

friend, get on the radio to Reverend Numb-nuts and find out where he wants to meet." Dan nodded and dug the radio handset from his pocket, Justin stared into middle space.

They all speak to me at once, why do they always speak at once? Don't they know that I can't understand them? Surely, for me to hear their valediction they should take it in turns? All they turn into are screams, and then the faces, why do they leer at me like that? Judging. Accusing. I didn't choose them, they were chosen for me. Need more. Need a lot more. I need...

"JUSTIN!" Dan shouted, Justin jerked back into reality and looked across to his passenger, bruised and broken faces were laid over Dan's face, mouths silently moving. The words that came out did not match the shapes the mouths made, he tilted his head sideways as if trying to unlock their secret.

"JUSTIN!" Dan shouted again.

"What?" the ghostly brutalised visages disappeared.

"Did you get any of that?" Dan sighed.

"Reverend Dicknose said that they're just finishing up at the Sports Centre and will be heading over to Portway Junior School after, sounds like the town is asshole deep in the 'Ascended' now," Dan tucked the radio back into his pocket.

Justin sat hunched over the driving wheel, staring into the forbidding skyline. "Get the map, find the quickest way there," he gently accelerated faster, the horizon being hauled towards them like a giant fishing net.

Dan ran his fingers over the map, "I reckon we're only a couple of miles out, ten minutes or so? What you thinking Juh, you've got that mad look in your eye again," he said, smiling with the thought of what was coming.

Justin continued to stare blankly ahead, before saying "We need to take care of those three..."

Dan laughed, "Man, you really did zone out, he said

they lost a man, Frank, got taken out by some kids, it's just him and Billy now."

Justin smiled "Even better, we'll be done within the hour, get ourselves back to the bunker and resupply, it's a brave new world of opportunity brother."

Dan put his hands together mockingly, "Amen brother, for *She* has spoken and all of them have been judged, thou flock hath been foresaketh," the pair of them laughed.

Justin's eyes widened again, "You got the French weekend cabin footage on that?" he enquired, gesticulating towards the laptop.

"I got the best bits, there was a *lot* from that little trip," the pair lapsed into a shared memory.

Justin turned to Dan, smiling menacingly, "Good, I've got an idea…"

The badminton court had a thin layer of watery red liquid on it, a net lay ruffled on the ground, the white top arranged into a makeshift line on the floor, kneeling the other side of the divide were four men.

"What did they say?" asked Billy, he raised the rifle and pulled the trigger, one of the men stopped pleading and was propelled forwards, blood pouring from a wound in his chest, the others sobbed louder whilst Billy reloaded.

The Reverend was counting how many shells he had left, "Not much, said the plan worked as well as they hoped and they were on the way back, said we would meet them at Portway."

Another shot echoed round the hall, behind a set of barred doors the undead banged fists and moaned their displeasure at being denied another meal, another body crumpled on the floor. "Well these poor souls are all that remain here….Reverend?" Billy asked nervously.

The Reverend looked across, "Yes brother Billy?" he snapped open the shotgun, two spent shells ejected onto the floor.

"I still don't trust them, they're not like us, I don't

think they're true believers," Billy loaded another round into the rifle and pulled back on the bolt.

The Reverend loaded his shotgun and raised a hand, "True, but we have need for men like them, what they lack in faith they make up for in conviction. Do not worry brother, when we rendezvous with the others, they will be sent elsewhere."

Billy stood back as the Reverend walked behind the two remaining captives, he pulled out the .22 and placed the barrel against one of the men's back, "May She protect you," and fired point blank, the man arched his back as if electrocuted, before falling to one side. The Reverend stepped over the body and stood in front of the sole survivor.

"Please mate, you don't have to…" he started to plead.

"Shhhhh, do not defile this moment by begging for something that no longer belongs to you," the Reverend replied.

The man stifled his tears, found hidden resolve and straightened his posture. He looked dead into the Reverend's eyes, the only part of his face visible over the wet brown scarf.

He raised his middle finger, "FUCK Y…" he started to shout, his defiance was met by a rifle round through his heart, he remained upright, his body obstinately refusing to move until the internal memo had no reply from his brain, he flopped to the ground.

"Let's go, Her flock is swollen, there is not much left to do," the Reverend walked towards a set of closed fire doors, Billy in close pursuit.

Colin and his chums had been following screams and loud bangs around town all night. Since supper at the supermarket, food seemed to be constantly eluding them, as soon as they reached the sound of the screaming, they met more of their freshly reanimated kin.

They trundled down a deserted car-lined avenue, the

calls to feed were diminishing, but one still carried heavily in the air, they had been lurching towards it for twenty minutes, they were not far now.

"Reverend?" the metallic voice came through the radio handset.

"Yes brother?"

"We're at the school, there's definitely some survivors in here, we've blocked the exits and are waiting for you by the main entrance," came the reply, before descending into squalls of static.

They arrived at the bottom of a short drive, leading up to the staff car park, "Reverend can you hear that?" Billy asked, raising his gun.

The Reverend nodded, "Yes, this is the last bastion of life, the Ascended are being summoned here, we will need to work fast."

In the car park sat a 4x4, it's bonnet buckled and blood stained, the bumper barely clinging to the chassis, Dan and Justin were sat on the roof, they saw the pair and waved, "Yoo-hoo!" they hollered.

As the Reverend and Billy approached, they jumped to the floor and dusted themselves off, Dan greeted them "Evening Reverend, Billy, we reckon they're in one of the classrooms, they sound pretty desperate in there, we might not have long before you know….."

The Reverend nodded and surged towards the main door, his grubby robe flowing behind him, "Her flock will be here soon, let's go."

Justin removed a metal bar he had used to jam the entrance shut, he swung the door open and nodded, the four men entered the school into a long corridor, which had been polished to within an inch of its existence.

Dan pointed into the bowels of the school, pulled a silenced pistol from his belt and started to move down the corridor. They slowly inched their way into the gloom, they got halfway down the corridor when Dan held up a clenched fist, the other men stopped in their tracks and craned their necks.

"Do you hear that?" he hissed, out of nowhere they could hear muffled voices a few doors down, the Reverend nodded and held his shotgun in both hands, they headed towards the sound.

The noise was coming from the last classroom in the corridor, beyond the room was a set of double doors which had been barricaded from the other side, piles of school furniture pressed against the barrier, preventing anyone from entering.

The sound of indistinguishable voices became louder, small squeals of panic could be heard. The Reverend crouched down to one side of the door, motioning for the others to make ready.

Billy stood on the other side of the closed door and raised his rifle, looking down the scope in readiness. Justin and Dan hung back, acting as the vanguard, scanning behind them to make sure they did not become trapped.

The Reverend turned around and gave Billy a curt nod, "Prepare for Ascension!" he shouted and kicked the door with all his might.

Colin heard a loud BOOM, his group had split into smaller factions, some mesmerised by different moans, others by the sound of survivors fumbling around in the dark. Ms Pyjamas had joined him, her foot now completely shorn off, one leg ending in a ragged meaty stump. They turned towards the sound and shuffled after it.

They found a large building with glass running the length of the wall and a firmly shut fire door in one corner. They passed it and walked on, long heavy drapes had been pulled in front of the glass, but they could sense movement from within.

They stomped onwards, reaching a set of double doors leading to a shiny corridor, they banged on the doors but they were firmly braced, *MEAT*.

Colin and Ms Pyjamas retraced their steps, they could hear something inside, but needed to find where it was coming from, they hammered on the glass, cautious to let out moans in case one of their brethren usurped their meal. They heard a constant dull THWACK-THWACK-THWACK, they increased their banging in reply, eager to get inside.

The Reverend awoke to a searing white hot pain in his shoulder, eyes locked open, in his mind he was screaming at the top of his lungs, yet he could not work out why there was no sound. His head was rocked violently to one side, Justin loomed into view, mouthing words he couldn't hear over a loud piercing shriek.

"SHUT THE FUCK UP!" Justin was yelling over and over in the Reverend's face, strands of spit were hitting the red raw skin which now covered eighty percent of his head, he slapped him again.

Dan laughed, "Just, he can't hear you, give it a minute, remember that grenade went off right by his face man, look at him, dude can't even work out what's happened yet!"

The Reverend looked ahead, lying on the floor was a body, face down, it looked familiar, a large pool of blood was spreading from under it. Dan was kneeling over it, holding a large meat cleaver in his hand.

Dan noticed he was looking. "Ha, *do you see who this is?*" he mouthed, pointing the blood drenched cleaver at the lump of meat. The Reverend fought back a lancing pain in his shoulder and looked, the screaming started again in his head.

Dan laughed again and continued chopping, like a butcher he was methodical and completely disengaged from what he was doing. He had already removed both of Billy's arms, the hands lay to one side and he was chopping the arms in two, just above the elbow, his powerful swings cleaved through the meat and bone in one swipe, he seemed to be whistling.

He saw Justin appear in his view again, placing two buckets to one side of Billy's carcass, Dan nodded in thanks, and started throwing the chunks of meat into the receptacles, before loosening Billy's jeans.

The high pitch whine in his ears started to ease, he tried to raise his hands, but realised they were clamped together. He looked down to see the ends of three metal skewers sticking through the skin, bent upwards so they held his hands in place, he felt light-headed.

"Oh no you don't Reverend, look over there," Justin pointed to an object laying on the floor a few feet away from him, Justin bent down and picked it up, pointing it in the direction of what was left of Billy and Dan who had pulled off the dead man's trousers, he waved in Justin's direction.

Justin bounded over to the Reverend, "Say something for the future us's!" he demanded, "Of all the people we meet, you want to make sure you stand out don't you?"

"And you do look so very handsome." Justin flipped the screen round to face the Reverend, he leant in closer and gulped a wad of molten saliva.

He raised his conjoined hands to the side of his face, his scarf and the robes hood had been ripped off, his red fingers touched pus covered skin. It looked like someone had used a potato peeler and shaved off the skin from one side of his face, from forehead all the way down to his jawbone, muscles and tendons grew taut as the pain surged through him, he screamed again.

Justin ran his dry, raspy tongue up the side of the Reverend's ruined face, his spit seemed acidic on the flesh which was bared to the world. Justin made his hand into a rigid claw and stuck prying fingers into the ripped meat, tugging on hanging tendrils, *"Shut up,"* he mouthed, the Reverend suppressed his pain.

"Thank you," Justin released his hold on him and set the camera down on the floor.

Dan threw the jeans to one side, the Reverend watched them land next to another pile of bodies, Justin manifested himself in his eye line once more.

"Them? They *were* here when we got here, we couldn't let them ruin the plan so we took care of them," Justin said slowly, delighting in every syllable.

"Unfortunately we had to deal with them quickly, they felt something you will not-" Justin spat out, licking his teeth slowly, "-our mercy."

"See, it wasn't them you heard, it was the voices of some.....acquaintances we made a few years back, an earlier project of ours, back when we were young and travelled the world," Justin looked off into space again, lost in the moment.

In the background, Dan restarted his macabre activity, hacking into the top of Billy's legs, it took a couple of hefty blows before they separated from the torso. Justin held the Reverend's chin, "Don't worry about him Reverend, he's gone, he survived the blast, but didn't take too kindly to having his throat slit."

He started laughing "NOT NOW," he shouted to something hovering in front of him, he sneered and jolted back to the Reverend.

"I cut him so deep his throat opened up like a yawning Muppet, you should've seen it!," reliving the moment in his mind's eye.

Dan threw the cuts of leg into one of the buckets, and wiped the sweat off his brow with Billy's robe, the sound of glass banging made him look up. "Juh, we best start wrapping it up, the natives are getting restless."

He ripped off Billy's vest and started frantically cleaving the torso, "Always hate this bit, takes ages," he looked across at the Reverend.

Justin disappeared from sight, behind him, he held his breath. Seconds seemed like hours, he exhaled, as he did so, his shoulder was violently pulled from within. Pain receptors in the nerve cluster yelled at his central nervous system, he tried to make a sound, anything, but the pain was so intense it restricted his vocal chords to nothing more than a hoarse wheeze.

"Oh dear Reverend, we will miss you so," he could hear Justin singing through his pain, "But now has come the time for us to goooooooo."

"I look around now and can't see your wooden crook," Justin crooned, his voice still ringing in the Reverend's ear.

"And some little bastard has stolen your big fat leather bound booooooooooooook."

The pain intensified again, "But fear not chum, to make up for your loss, I've got you this big, cold metal hoooooooooooooook."

The Reverend looked to find the source of his agony and could see a butchers hook jutting through his skin. The point, dripping with his own blood broke through the skin just below his collarbone. Justin started laughing hysterically, "It's funny cos it's true!"

At once, the laughing ceased, "Let's go, Billy is nearly prepared and you aren't even ready yet."

The Reverend swallowed again, braced for more pain, it came quickly, he felt himself being pulled from behind and dragged along the floor towards a wooden climbing frame which was built into the wall. It pivoted on a giant hinge which could be swung out into the room when it was needed to be clambered over by the little school urchins.

The Reverend looked around and saw that he was in a large assembly room, where once the sound of children singing hymns filled the room, it was now filled with the sound of his pain. He was hauled over to the frame and unceremoniously dropped by it, the metal stopped grating against the bone and he enjoyed the temporary hiatus from his agony.

"Dan, are you ready?" Dan nodded, picking up the buckets overflowing with human offal.

Pieces of organ slipped out and slopped onto the floor,

"Ha, man, I have enough for seconds."

Justin nodded, "Good, get the attention of our friends outside and prepare the breadcrumbs, I'll finish up here. Oh nearly forgot!"

Justin ran over to the camera and repositioned it, taking in the full picture of the frame and the Reverend slumped in front of it.

Dan walked past, banging on the windows and shouting, "Come on boys, dinner is served," and disappeared into the entrance corridor.

Justin appeared in front of the Reverend, "Now, where were we?" he asked rhetorically, "Ah yes, let's get you ready for your big moment," and turned around.

The Reverend drew from his last reservoirs of strength, "Why?" was all he could muster.

Justin turned around slowly, "Why? Isn't that what the poor bastards ask you? And what did you tell them? Some bullshit about Ascension, or joining her flock, what a load of shit," he pulled in closer.

"Me? I'm honest about what I do, I enjoy this. Actually no, I *love it*. I am broken. I am damaged. I got used to it, I know what I am, I am what they would call evil," he signalled towards the pile of corpses lying in the corner of the room.

"You though, you disgust me. You make it seem like you're doing this for some higher purpose, for meaning. You're not, you're more deluded than me, you are nothing, I think it's time I gave something back to this community."

Justin stared intently into the Reverend's pained eyes, "You."

Dan appeared in the doorway, he was walking backwards and dropping chunks of Billy on the floor. "Just, literally, a minutes time and we have got to be Oscar Mike," he led the chunks towards the climbing frame, threw the bucket on the floor and stood by Justin.

"Showtime Reverend," Justin pulled out another hook from his belt.

The pain was intense, he was on the verge of utter collapse, but was forced back into reality by Justin's fists. "On three, one-two-three," the two men picked him up and hung him on the frame, he kicked out his feet which merely flapped in thin air.

The pain was unbearable. Justin's face appeared in view again "This is *your* Rapture," he laughed and turned around, "Danny-boy, we are leaving," Dan ran into the corridor, and the Reverend heard a loud clang.

The Reverend looked up, and saw both men open a fire door in the corner of the room. As they left, Justin blew him a kiss, he tried to raise his hands to remove himself from the frame.

Colin, Ms Pyjamas and their chums turned, a large piece of walking meat was making noise at them, they turned and lumbered after him, he looked like he could feed all of them for half an hour, teeth ground in anticipation.

They followed him round the side of the building, the barred door was now wide open, eagerly they stamped up the steps. Every other step by Ms Pyjamas left a circular stain on the floor. They staggered into the corridor, *MEAT*, they looked down to see lumps of flesh lying on the floor, bidding them welcome. Some of the followers bent down and shoved the chunks into their mouths, mindlessly chewing on them.

Colin ignored them, he could scent something else, something bigger, something fresher, he followed the giant meal into a large room. He saw a pile of bodies lying to one side, he sniffed the air, *NOT FRESH.*

He cocked his head to one side where the trail of flesh led to the prize, the main course was still alive, pinned and prepared like a spatchcock chicken.

The Reverend couldn't flex his arms enough to raise himself, his hands still pinned together. He tried to swing and see if he could manage to loosen the hold, but the pain made him stop, he heard a low murmur and looked up, knowing what he would see.

Colin stumbled towards the meal, hands outstretched, the Reverend tried one last time, cursing under his breath, before relenting and letting the inevitable happen. Colin stood before the Reverend and stared, a last flash of memory tried to send a text message of recognition, but it was returned to sender.

He took a step forwards, cold, dead digits fumbled through a huge tear in the soiled robes, Colin pressed harder and harder, the skin puckered with the pressure.

The skin broke and puffed out in relief of being breached. Colin pushed his fingers in, eyes still transfixed on the main course, he grabbed hold of a rib and pulled.

Ms Pyjamas had finally made her way in and gouged at the man's thigh, the Reverend gritted his teeth, so much so that his lips started to bleed.

More and more joined in, the Reverend lapsed into unconsciousness saved from the sight of being rent limb from limb until all that remained was bones, flaps of skin and the tatters of his filthy white robe.

CHAPTER XXI

The Foxhound armoured infantry vehicle ground over the gravelled opening to the Bransford Golf Club, its seven and a half tonnes seemed to make the large drive shrink in its company.

"Everyone, we're here," Tom shouted, he swung the vehicle round so it was pointing towards the exit, just in case.

Philip replied with a sulky "Humph."

Jim chuckled, "You're still annoyed that we had to leave Corey aren't you? There was no way all six of us and our gear could've fit. You've seen the roads, they're pretty clogged with traffic in places, we needed something a bit more…..forceful."

Philip pouted some more, Jim looked across, "You know I'm right."

Philip nodded and mumbled something unintelligible. "What was that bro?" Jim asked, suppressing a cheeky grin.

"I said I wanted to drive the fucking Foxyhound thing, only fair."

Tom killed the engine and gave Philip the thumbs up, "Don't worry Phil, I'll make sure you get a go before too long."

"Good work TT, we can camp here for the night, get

some rest and then strike out for Rhayader in the morning, OW!" he clutched his bandaged forearm.

"You alright mate?" Jay asked, Philip winced but nodded in reply.

Jay jumped out of the passenger's seat, stretched and headed towards the rear of the armoured vehicle "This was a bloody good find Tom!," the doors opened.

"Yeah, but a bit on the cramped side," added Jim.

"Hang on," Jay said, pulling the duffel bag along the floor and opening it up, "You got anything you haven't tried out yet Phil?"

Philip looked across, "Good man, give the rounders bats a go if you can, the clay and the wooden ones, the ice-pick is begging for a review too. Also, could you see if the Taser does anything?"

Jay smiled and nodded "My pleasure, Tom, get your arse over here, there's a few budding McIlroys we gotta take care of."

Tom walked round to the rear of the vehicle and looked towards the course. "Ah, no worries, bagsy the ice-pick," Tom said eagerly, Jay nodded, tucked the Taser into his pocket and picked up a rounders bat in each hand.

"Are you alright Philip?" Katherine asked, "You look a bit peaky."

Philip looked at her, "I'm fine," he said through clenched teeth.

"I'd say you could do with a nice cup of tea, but we've got no tea bags," Katherine's motherly instinct kicking in.

Jim smiled and let out a short laugh, "Well, would you believe that we do? Think Jay or Tom has got a little camp stove and kettle, would you mind being mother?"

Katherine beamed, "I'd love to, you two take a moment," gesturing at Sophie.

"Soph?" Jim asked, she nodded, they clambered out of the vehicle and headed towards an ornately wrought iron bench bordering the large car park.

Philip slumped on the floor, resting against one of the

bulky dust covered wheels, "Man, I am knackered, been one long ass day." Katherine looked down at him and then resumed rooting through the bags searching for the stove and kettle.

"I'll take Tiger Woods, you get Ian Poulter," Jay said, Tom looked at him blankly.

Jay sighed, "I got *this* one!" Tom smiled and nodded, swinging the ice-pick through the air, feeling the weight distribution. Still clad in a garish collection of golf clothing, the zombie locked onto Jay, his sun visor positioned at a jaunty cavalier angle, hands outstretched.

Jay sidestepped and swung the wooden rounders bat, smacking the dead golfer on the ear, sending him reeling to one side, he tucked the bat under his arm and pulled out the Taser.

The zombie had his back to him and was wondering where dinner had gone, teeth snapping the air. Jay held the switch down and plunged it onto the golfer's neck.

His arms shot up, as if he was trying to recreate the dance moves from Thriller, a thin rivet of smoke rose from the contact sight. The frigid night air was broken by a fizzing sound and that of teeth chattering against each other.

He released contact and the zombies arms dropped back to their side. Smoke continued to rise from the nape of his neck, he turned around, still as keen to eat Jay as he was beforehand.

"Ah well," Jay stepped backwards and pocketed the Taser, he held both bats out sideways and smacked them both into the skull from opposite sides.

Its head took on the form of a tube of toothpaste which had been grabbed in the middle. Jawbones on either side shattered, and the bats were only separated by an inch thickness of the spinal cord.

The top of its head exploded in a gore filled fireworks display, such was the force that parts of brain were squeezed through the eye sockets. Its eyes swung like pocket watches, in their place ribbed pink chunks of brain looked out.

Jay wiped the back of his hand across his face, removing pieces of brain matter. "Gross," he said, gagging with disgust as the zombie sunk like a brick in a canal.

Tom eyed up his target, he had obviously had his fill during the day as his lips and chin were covered in dried blood, like a child who had stuffed their face with chocolate. A broken golf club stuck out of his shoulder, it moaned towards him.

Tom planted his feet and let it come to him, a few paces out he shouted "FORE!" and slammed the ice-pick into the walking corpses head, eyes rolled up before slipping off the edge and landing in a multi-coloured heap on the floor.

Jay and Tom looked across at each other and nodded, giving each a fist-bump, "Let's have a mosey round, make sure there are no more slack jawed motherfuckers around here," said Jay, he banged the bats together, knocking clumps of cerebral matter onto the manicured fairway.

Sophie and Jim sat on the bench, a foot or so apart, and looked up into the night sky, "Least it doesn't look as though the sky has been stabbed tonight," said Jim, Sophie nodded and laughed, "What?" he asked, almost scared of her reply.

They looked at each other, "Nothing, just weird how much can change in a day or so," she moved a rogue clump of hair from her eyes.

"Listen I…"

"Sophie, I…"

They both said at the same time, looking down at the gravel, nervous laughter broke out. Jim looked up, sitting on his hands and said "No, go on, after you," Sophie looked across at him and took a deep breath in.

"You do know why I broke up with you don't you? I

mean, the reason why."

Jim nodded, "After you said what you did, it was difficult not to see the reasons why, I had become so….caught up in work, in something that I hated but for some reason wanted *so* badly."

She listened intently and then looked down again, her eyes picking out patterns in the stones. "It was just becoming no fun, y'know, one of the things about long term relationships is that you, we, need to constantly work on it, no slacking off. You don't get the benefit of all that lust and energy when you can count the time you've spent with someone in years, instead of months," Philip nodded in agreement, looking sullen.

"I don't know what to say," he said quietly, dreading what Sophie would say next.

She sidled over to him, their legs touching, she put a hand on his knee, the other gently raised his chin up so that his eyes looked into hers. "I'm glad you came after me, you didn't have to, some men wouldn't have bothered," she searched his face for hidden motives.

Jim smiled gently, "Are you kidding? I'd have gone to the ends of the earth to find you, when we got to your house, and saw what was there, I….I thought I lost you," he rested a hand on top of hers.

She smiled back at him, "I thought I had lost you too, don't get me wrong, I meant what I said yesterday, but…with everything that's happened, and after a few truths about my dad, it made me think about everything."

Jim opened his mouth to speak, Sophie placed a finger gently on his lips, "Shh, let me finish."

She moved her hand down to sandwich his hand between hers, "I realised I was just as much to blame as you, just in a different way, you were obviously having a hard time at work, I should've tried to help. I don't know how….but I should've."

Jim gazed deeper into her eyes, "It doesn't matter, none of it does, we've got something that most people on this planet will never get now," he said.

She looked at him quizzically, "Another chance," he added, and placed his spare hand on top of hers.

"One potato-"

She smiled and slapped her bottom hand on top of his "-two potato-"

He did the same "-three potato-" she leant in and kissed him.

She slowly pulled away, "-four," she said softly, they moved into each other, their foreheads resting against one another's. They sat like that for what seemed an eternity, before Jim raised his head and lost himself in her gaze again.

"Nothing quite like a zombie apocalypse and the potential fall of the human race to bring two people back together again huh?" they both laughed and held each other, for the briefest of moments, all the zombies, all the maniacs in the world, mattered not one jot.

"OI! Bumhead! Put her down, the kettles boiled," Philip shouted, Jim and Sophie decoupled themselves from each other, looking sheepish.

"See Phil's still got his way with words then," Jim nodded and held her hand.

"C'mon bumhead, let's get summat to drink and eat."

As they got back to their ride, Jay and Tom appeared out of the murk, "No, I got that last one, you just winged him, who had the shears?" Jay said incredulously.

Tom shook his head "Man, you're lying, I got him, that hoe went straight through, he was dead-dead before you went all Alan Titchmarsh on him."

"Tea's up losers," Philip shouted, Katherine held out a mug, he reached for it, she retracted her offer.

"I'm sorry, was only messing," Philip said disappointedly, Katherine smiled and passed it to him.

Philip flinched as he held the mug, "Hang on a cotton picking moment," and disappeared into the back of the Foxhound.

The group sat down around the back of the vehicle, "All's clear, from what we can see," Jay said, "We managed to get into the clubhouse round back, the internal doors are all sealed up, we should be able to get in there and get some kip tonight," the others murmured their thanks.

Philip appeared, and threw the notebook to Jay, "Could you do the honours please? Much obliged, did the Taser work?" Jay shook his head.

"Balls," replied Philip, "Anyway, get your laughing gear round these," he produced two packets of orange Digestives from behind his back; receiving a muted cheer from everyone.

Under a pitch black night sky, with only a sliver of the moon and a gentle dusting of stars as light, the six survivors sat in the car park of Bransford Golf Club.

"Ahh, for all of life's ills, you can't beat a cup of tea and a biscuit," said Philip, sipping on his tea.

Jim looked across, "Bro, it pains me to say it, but on this you are definitely right."

CHAPTER XXII

Dan peeled his eyes from the road and looked over to Justin, "You watching that *again?*"

Justin turned to him, a grin from ear to ear, "I just love the way that one pulls his appendix out, it's a work of art, shame we didn't get all of it."

Dan turned his concentration back to the road, "Yeah, the range isn't brilliant, no way we were going to stick around, plus, we've got loads of footage from today alone, imagine what we'll have in a few weeks!"

Justin nodded, freeze framing the image, the feral pack picking the Reverend clean, "A work of art," he said to himself. He looked up at the road, "How far out are we?" peering into the gloom.

Dan smiled and replied "Not far, another few minutes, be nice to get back to the bunker, sort some stuff out and re-stock, we got through more than I thought we would to be honest."

The battered 4x4 spluttered up the country road and turned into an unmarked dirt track before stopping just short of a grassy mound. "Home, sweet home," Justin announced and got out of the vehicle. He made his way to the boot and picked up a rucksack bulging with weapons, he tucked the laptop under his arm and slammed the boot shut.

The pair walked towards the mound, the early morning light showed a concealed door built into the hill, Dan removed a padlock and heaved the door open.

Walking into the bunker, Justin flicked a switch, a large room was illuminated in a diffuse yellow glow. Around the room were several large plastic wheeled container trucks, each filled with different items.

There were two large gun cabinets, holding military grade weapons, all pristine and well maintained. Against the far wall were positioned two single beds and a long workbench.

A server rack sat to one side, buzzing with activity, "I'll go upload the footage," said Dan, prying the laptop from Justin and walking over to the bench.

Justin walked to the nearest container, overflowing with pieces of body armour, "Still got enough sets for another twenty I reckon," he shouted, before walking to an unmade bed. He slung the bag on top of an open sleeping bag, made his way to the workbench and sat on a tall stool.

"Beer?" Dan nodded, deep in concentration, Justin reached down to a small fridge under the bench and pulled out two ice cold Estrella's.

He wrenched off the tops and passed one across to Dan, "Skol," they chinked the bottles together and took a large gulp.

Justin looked at the bottle of beer, a stem of white foam rising up the neck, "Aaahhhh, after a busy shift of murder, you can't beat the first ice cold beer of the day."

Dan looked across, "Boom, that's uploading now, your good health my man."

The pair sat in silence for a few minutes, letting the events of the day process, Dan broke the silence, "So, Sickmeister General, what shall we do next?"

Justin took another mouthful and put the bottle down, he scrabbled through piles of paper on the workbench and pulled out a large map.

He laid it down and smoothed out the creases. Dan stood by him, he finished the beer with one large swig, burped and pulled another couple of bottles out of the fridge. Justin examined the map and said "Well, seeing as I'm the kindly sort, I've got two options for you."

"Most of the cities now will have a rather large zombie quota, so no real fun in that, and *way* too much risk involved, we need some easy but larger targets."

Dan nodded in agreement, "Yeah, don't fancy busting my chops getting into somewhere only to have some wannabe body bag chew my balls off."

Justin smiled, "So, option one, is go for one of the larger survivor zones, help the dead get in with some holes in the fence, pop some soldier heads, y'know, general mayhem."

Dan shrugged his shoulders, "Man, that sounds okay, but it's lacking a little pizzazz you know? I wanna do something a little more….out-there, like the ole armoured zombies, but supersized."

Justin nodded eagerly, "I was hoping you would say that Dan-Dan, which brings us neatly to option two. In this we get to carry out a bit of general mayhem as in option one, but the end game gives us something a little bigger."

Justin turned the map over and pointed to an area in Scotland, Dan looked closely, "What the fuck is at Faslane?"

Justin smiled, "Faslane is home to Great Britain's only means of delivering nuclear weapons, Trident, on Vanguard class submarines. One is always out on patrol, another is currently being refitted in Portsmouth and of no use to us, which leaves two tucked up in bed, Vanguard and Victorious."

Dan shook his head, "There's no way on earth those two will still be there, with all this shit going on, they would've recalled the crew and headed off into the deep blue."

Justin nodded, "Yep, this is true, thing is, the crew of Victorious are on extended leave, even if they wanted to, they wouldn't be able to get everyone back from their holidays in time."

He grinned at Dan, "I say we get some more…..volunteers, not many, five will do, send them out front, should keep any remaining guards busy. This time though, we wire the kiddywinks up with as much C4 we can shove into every orifice available, then BOOM! In the ensuing confusion we can do our thing."

Dan looked at Justin with a furrowed brow, "Now, I love offing people as much as you. Well okay, perhaps not as much as you, but there must be hundreds of armed people there."

Justin looked back at the map, "It's a possibility, though one thing we can rely on, peoples need to protect their family in times of catastrophe, they would've heard the stories, seen the pictures, the last thing they would want is for their loved ones to be the latest line of human delicacies."

Dan took another large swig of beer, "Okay, so how many warheads do they carry?"

Justin looked up, "Sixteen Trident II missiles, with an approximate range of seven thousand miles."

Dan raised his eyebrows, "Wow, we could fuck some serious shit up, two things, how we going to target and fire them, and where would we fire them at?"

Justin tapped his fingers against the bottle, "Leave the first part to me, as for where, well, I can think of a few places….." he stared into middle space again.

Dan coughed, "Erm, Juh?" Justin came to and grinned.

"Okay, it's a fair old punt too, so we can have some fun on the way, perhaps see if our little time capsules we buried last week are still breathing," Justin said with a sinister grin.

Dan burst out laughing, "They should be, we buried them deep enough, just whether your filtration and drip system has kept the poor bastards alive this long. Regardless, we can get the video off the local site up there."

They clinked their bottles together, "Cool, we'll pack up after some rest, make sure we take as much as we can, not too sure when we'll be back here."

Dan nodded and said "Never been to Scotland before, we'll have a bonny wee time."

"Oh we will," replied Justin, and sunk back into his thoughts of maleficence.

Colin wretched again, pieces of the Reverend splattered onto the assembly hall floor. Ms Pyjamas was gnawing on a femur, scraping her teeth against it in a desperate attempt to get at the last morsels.

The air was still, their feeding friends who arrived late were spilling out through the open fire door back into the early morning air, Colin followed them.

The near silence made his ears ring, he craned his neck trying to pick up on any sound, he could hear nothing, no screams and no feeding moans, just the muffled strains of a car radio.

He turned towards the road and trudged forwards, Ms Pyjamas was back by his side, clutching the ivory white bone like a club, the end of the pool cue still sticking out from her chest.

They got to the main road and scanned the vicinity, in the sky a bright white disc was slowly being withdrawn, down into the ground.

The two turned their decomposing bodies towards it

and started to move, they walked past a car whose occupants now lay in pieces along the road, the radio still tuned to a golden oldies station.

"Friend, there is a moaning that keeps on calling me, forever calling onwards, it's meant for you and me."

Colin and Ms Pyjamas turned their head to the sound in hope of a snack, disappointed they looked at each other.

"Since the morning we met, we knew we were meant to be, every scrape and trouble we get into, just proves it all to me."

They turned back to the light in the sky and started to meander down the dark street, the radio continued to warble.

"Always onwards, is where we have to be, never stay too long, can't hang around this old city."

The pair kept on walking, Ms Pyjamas still half-stumbling with every other step on her decrepit, gammy stub. Colin still hunched to one side, shattered ribs collapsed but holding firm.

They marched onwards like toy robots, to wherever there was food, onwards, until the end, two more grey faces in the horde.

"One day my friend we'll rest our weary heads, until that day, we'll just march on instead."

CHAPTER XXIII

The Foxhound growled up the road, weaving in-between abandoned vehicles. Where the gap was too small, the mighty beast merely nudged them out of the way.

"When can I read it?" asked Tom eagerly, casting a cautious eye on the road, the moon had bid farewell for another night and the sun was rising from its grave.

Philip glanced up from the notebook, "Later on, got to write this down before I forget, oh and Tom?"

Tom looked in the rear view mirror, "Yes," he answered enthusiastically.

"Are we there yet?" Philip asked jokingly before immersing himself back into his scribbling.

Sophie rested her head on Jim's shoulder, his head was slowly lowering. Eyes closed, his chin touched his chest causing him to wake up with a start, before repeating the process again.

Katherine was cleaning the assortment of weapons they had collected, she was removing some particularly tricky stains from the wooden bats, "Honestly, we'll never get that out," she muttered disapprovingly.

Jay looked into the distance, the journey had been plain sailing since they left Bransgrove, they had met no one, living or dead, he wondered if his family had made it. "Phil?" he asked, turning in his seat to look at Philip sat opposite.

Philip sighed loudly "What is it numbnuts, kinda busy right now."

Jay smiled "You really are one cantankerous bastard aren't you?" Philip laughed and put the notebook down.

"I like you Jay……that's why I'll kill you last," Philip said, straight-faced.

"You kill me in a dream you better wake up and apologise," the two men chuckled.

"Jim only ever quoted Bottom sketches with me, think he lacked the concentration to watch anything over thirty minutes long," Phil looked over to his brother, his head resting uncomfortably to one side, a line of dribble forming a bridge between his mouth and t-shirt.

"Anyway, what's up Jay-ba the Hutt?"

Jay looked down briefly, "I still wanna try and get to my folks, after seeing what happened with……well, you know, I want, no I *need* to at least try, you know?"

Philip nodded, "Of course man, to be honest, I don't even think it's sunk in yet, just been so busy trying to get to Jim, then get to them, and then get here, that I haven't even processed *that* yet."

Jay nodded, "I understand, you guys have done pretty well all things considering to get this far, most people would've cracked up or be one of the not so grateful dead by now. Figure I'll follow you guys to where you set up, and then if you don't mind, I'll borrow this ride and head off."

Philip held the notebook to his chest, thin lines of blood had soaked through the bandages wrapped around his forearms, "Hey, you got red on you," they both laughed.

"It's no bother to me, once we get set up, we should have everything we need relatively close by, if you want, I can come with you, if you need a second pair of hands?" Philip replied.

Jay shook his head, "Thanks Phil, this is something I

gotta do on my own, if things go south, I don't want any one on my conscience, especially when you guys would've found your Eden."

Philip stuck his hand through the hatch into the front cabin, "When you're done, and you find them, get you and your family back to us, we'll front this all out together."

Jay took his hand and gripped it, "Thanks Phil, you're alright, if not a little on the odd side."

Philip gave Jay a huge manic grin with eyes wide open and nostrils flared, "Damn straight, don't forget it soldier boy."

The military vehicle lurched up the road, encroaching into the other lane, it climbed up a tarmacked hill with ease, as it reached the crest, Tom saw a sign at the top. The brakes whistled and the engine let out a low growl as he pulled the Foxhound over to the side of the road.

"Hey guys, take a look," he turned the engine off and jumped out.

RHAYADER 2

One by one they clambered out of the small truck and stood by the bonnet, "Woah, this picture looks a bit familiar Phil, are you sure about this?" Jim asked, his voice laden with uncertainty.

Philip nodded, "Yep, we're not staying in Rhayader though, it was the navigation point only," he pulled a map out of his back pocket, "Look, I'll show you."

He unfolded the map and held it against the monstrous radiator grille, a filthy finger pointed to a place on the map, "We're here, we head down the A470, until we get to this point here, we then get a boat and travel all the way down the river Elan-" he traced the path down the river, which opened up into the Caban-coch reservoir.

"-once we get here, we then head to this peninsula just here, Coed y foel, National Trust area, wooded, there's some wooden lodges there we can hopefully......rent for the season," Philip indicated a green area on the map.

"We will have two reservoirs on our doorstep, and a number of places to get to, in case the local biters get wind of us, plus, Jay, you can still drive to us when you get back."

The others looked at Jay with furrowed brows, "You're……you're going?" Tom asked, crestfallen.

Jay nodded, "I have to, it's day two of this shit, I need to try and get to my folks, get them, and bring them back here."

The group looked at each other, "That's understandable mate, thanks for everything, you get yourself and your family back as soon as possible, take the other radio handset, let us know when you get back," Jim said.

They all looked at each other, "Come on then-" Sophie said, "-group hug," they all embraced, the sound of birds calling the only sound.

They let go, and looked down at Rhayader, it was clear that it too had suffered, with curls of black smoke rising into the sky, which itself was a watercolour red, the sun like a baleful eye looking down on them.

"Red sky in the morning-" Jim started to say.

"Barn on fire!" Philip shouted.

Jim tutted and said, "-shepherds warning."

Philip pointed to a distant fire in the middle of a field and said, "No, genuine barn on fire, anus."

Tom piped up from behind the group;

"Like a red morn that ever yet betokened, wreck to the seaman, tempest to the field, sorrow to the shepherds, woe unto the birds, gusts and foul flaws to herdmen and to herds."

A calm serenity covered the group, Jim squeezed Sophie's hand a little tighter, Jay turned to Tom and nodded his appreciation, whilst Katherine wiped a tear from her eye, "That was beautiful, thank you."

Philip turned to Tom, "What an absolute bell-end."

EPILOGUE

A cloud of breath puffed out in front of his face, the crisp morning air caused his flushed cheeks to add a thin layer of steam to the CO_2 he expelled.

A dirty hand clutched the child to his chest, "Stay quiet Nathan, we don't know what's in there yet," he warned, he felt the child tense slightly, his nod gently butting against his chest.

He tugged the brim of the cap down slightly, securing it firmly on his head, he patted Nathan gently on his shoulders and moved in front of him. The dirty hand which had comforted the child, now reached around to his own back and pulled out a retractable baton from the webbing which held it in place on his backpack.

He ran his eye over the baton, he remembered, as he always did, the day he found it. Running desperately through the streets filled with panic and mayhem, trying to get to the voice which was raised amongst all others.

The policeman had lurched at him from the rear of a parked transit van, he knew what it was before he even had a chance to process all of the information. It had been the eyes that had given it away, large white pearls with a black imperfection at their core.

The bat which had served him with distinction all day gave him one last satisfying crack, the policeman's head burst open like a smashed pinata, candy worm like strands of brain were sent flying from the impact.

The bat though had seen enough, through the combination of his strength and force, the end was nothing more than a collection of splinters, held together through gore alone.

He knelt down by the destroyed zombie constable, and lay the bat at its side, cursing beneath his breath that he was without a sturdy weapon.

The zombie smiting gods were obviously pleased with his work as his annoyance quickly turned to laughter, he noticed the policeman's baton was still hanging from his belt.

By the time he had gotten to the voice, it was too late, he peered in the open car door and saw a lady in her early thirties clutching her throat. Between her white tensed fingers streaked rivulets of blood, at her feet lay a zombie with a wheel lock embedded in its skull.

Her eyes.

It was always her eyes.

Every time he closed his own as he tried to sleep, she would be staring back, the rest of her face indistinct, but those piercing orbs of blue, grey and black stood out. They had burned a hole onto his very being. Throughout that entire wretched first day, he had gone from one request for assistance to another. He had no-one to save. That chance had been denied to him the night before.

NO.

He shook his head clear of *that* memory, in time he would make his peace with it, but not today, not with his burden.

The eyes held him in place, her ashen white face moved gently, he realised she was trying to talk, "I can't hear you," he mumbled.

She nodded.

"NO! DON'T!" he yelled as he realised what her intentions were.

As she pulled her hand from the wound, the blood flow sensed an opportunity, the jugular pulsated and sent a waterfall of red down her neck and onto her pale pink woollen jumper.

The bloody hand pointed to the rear passenger seats, "Nathan," she gargled, blood started to trickle out of the corner of her mouth.

He instinctively moved his hand to her throat, but even in her weakened state, she batted it away.

Her eyes.

"Nathan. Look after him," she commanded, her eyes softened, just for a fraction, before rolling back in her head, her hand fell limp and slapped the side of the driver's seat.

He looked at her, knowing that she was gone, with a gentleness his size belied he rolled her eyelids down, her mortal hold over him extinguished.

He heard a cough from behind the seat, peered over and saw a small boy hunched down in the foot-well staring back at him. His brown hair was gently ruffled, he held his legs to his body and hugged them tightly, a tear formed in the corner of his eye, "Mummy?" he asked softly.

He shook his head, "Sorry kid," the child's solitary tear become a torrent, he tried to quieten him down, but to no avail. He pulled himself out of the vehicle and opened the rear passenger door, the boy revealed to the street, crying and shuddering.

Then he heard the moan.

He grabbed the boy and picked him up as if he was nothing more than a pillow, holding him under his thick, muscly arm. As he stood back from the car, the lady started to thrash around in her seat, still held in place by the seatbelt.

Her eyes had changed, from forceful compassion to cancerous decay. He sat Nathan down on the road, looking away from the car, pulled out the baton and swung….

"Hey, mister!" the child's voice hacked into the recall, jolting him back to the present. Nathan looked at his protector, tracing small grubby fingers over the join from where a previously bushy moustache now bordered a growing beard.

"Call me Francis kid, it's been like nine months, call me Francis," he winked at the kid who returned it with a weird half-blink.

"Ha, right, remember what I told you Nate, stay behind me, we'll go check this cabin out, see if it's got anything we can use, and remember…"

"If anything is in there, I don't run off, I stick behind you and close my eyes," Nathan finished.

Francis ruffled Nathan's hair energetically, "That's right, stick behind me kid." The pair crept through the grey morning murk, towards the log cabin, the morning dew covered it in a shiny, almost artificial looking veneer.

Francis crouched down by the front door, and prodded it with the baton, the door stuck at first, but slowly crept open, beckoning them inside with a hint of menace. Francis looked back at Nathan who was hiding behind him and nodded his head slightly, before edging into the gloomy cabin.

The cabin was one big room, Francis could make out a large stove at one end, with thick wooden worktops running off it, cupboards above and below, some of the doors were wide open, their bowels pitch black. The door opened into the middle of the room, where a large handmade oak table took up residence, detritus was strewn over its top, covering a map which had been opened up.

Francis gestured towards the table, and Nathan scuttled to it and hid underneath, beady eyes busily scanned the interior.

With the kid in relative safety, Francis carefully made his way to the other side of the room, where a camping bed was resting flush against a wall, a bulky sleeping bag lay on top of it.

He pulled a torch from the side of his backpack and shone it over the sleeping bag, his heart skipped a beat as he saw a foot covered in grey, saggy skin protruding from the bottom.

Francis sighed, raised the baton and inched closer to the top of the bed, the sleeping bag had been pulled up, leaving only the decaying foot on show.

Francis slid the baton into a small crease at the top of the sleeping bag, and with the torch still shining on the lump, yanked the bag back.

His gag reflex kicked in, he wretched as he took in the sight of a withered neck ending in half a skull, an avenue of broken teeth were the last things that made up the face.

He kept one hand covering his mouth as he tugged the sleeping bag down, trying to keep bile from being expelled, he saw a shotgun held to the woman's deflated bosom.

"Hey Nate, it's safe, close the door and let's have a look around, I'll get some breakfast," Francis replaced the sleeping bag over the remains of the head and walked to the table.

Setting the bag down he asked, "So do you want tuna or tuna?" Nathan laughed and started rifling through the various items lying on the table.

"Hey Francis, what's this?" Nathan had picked up a booklet, yellowed prematurely with age, held fast with rusting staples.

Francis smoothed out the paper, and read the words on the cover;

PHILIP TAYLOR'S ZOMBIE SURVIVAL GUIDE
FIRST EDITION, PRINTED OCTOBER 2014

NOW DISTRIBUTED TO 34 SAFE ZONES!

He opened the booklet up and read the dedication;

THIS IS FOR MUM AND DAD

THANKS TO JIM, JAY, SOPHIE AND TOM FOR CONTRIBUTING

BIGGEST THANKS GO TO FRANCIS FOR SAVING JIM ON DAY ONE

Nathan started giggling, "That man has the same silly name as you!"

Francis grinned, "Sure does kid, he sure does."

Nathan looked up at him expectantly, Francis nodded, "Fine, you open breakfast up and I'll read you some."

He peeled the pages open and flicked to;

Chapter One - 'The Beginning'

…and begun.

TO BE CONTINUED…

ABOUT THE AUTHOR

Duncan lives in the EPIC county of Wiltshire in Southern England, with his wife Debbie and their two cats, Rafa and Pepe.

Obsessed with zombies, GTA and biscuits, he wiles away his free time writing, playing video games, drinking Guinness and hitting people on the head with a stick.

P.S. Duncan has a Plan B site in mind in case of zombie apocalypse, so if you head to Rhayader, he cannot promise you he will be there with tea and biscuits.

Get in touch with Duncan via;

Facebook –

https://www.facebook.com/duncanpbradshaw

Website –

http://www.duncanpbradshaw.co.uk

OTHER BOOKS
BY THE AUTHOR

What takes your fancy? More zombies? A slice of bizarro weirdness? Some sci-fi/horror nastiness? Maybe…just maybe, a story about an interrupted Inca ritual, the ramifications rumbling through five hundred years of human history?

Whatever it is, why not give one of them a crack? I'm sure I could snag you in the keep net.

It's the thirteenth annual Lou Gehrig awards. Four B-list celebrity virologists vie to claim the Locked In Syndrome cup and get mulched down to form their disease for mass distribution.

A disease hipster takes centre stage on a night when a blast from the past threatens to turn his ordered, pus filled life upside down. In order to blow open a deep rooted conspiracy, he must team up with a disgraced one time child star who wants another shot at the big time, and clear his sullied name.

Together, they're going to show people the real meaning of a meltdown.

"I have never read anything like this, and don't think I'll ever encounter another writer with the ability to write like this. This book is the very definition of the word 'metaphor', is very clever, and totally hilarious."
- Kayleigh Marie Edwards, author of Bitey Bachman

"Remember, you've now willingly plunged yourself into the mind of Duncan P. Bradshaw. You're completely at the mercy of his strange imagination and all the eccentric oddities that his curious mind can conjure up. Indeed, it quickly becomes apparent that the only way you'll be able to wade through the veritable quagmire of lunacy is by simply succumbing to the madness."
- DLS Reviews

heXagrAm

We are all made of stars.

When an ancient Inca ritual is interrupted, it sets in motion a series of events that will echo through five hundred years of human history. Many seek to use the arcane knowledge for their own ends, from a survivor of a shipwreck, through to a suicide cult.

Yet...the most unlikeliest of them all will succeed.

"Hexagram is a visceral journey through the dark nooks and crannies of human history. Lovecraftian terror merges with blood sacrifice, suicide cults and body horror as Bradshaw weaves an intricate plot into an epic tale of apocalyptic dread."
- Rich Hawkins, author of The Last Plague trilogy

"So much more than just a horror novel, this one really makes you think. I like books that make me think, and books that present, and pull off, an original idea. This is that book and it's very much a must-read."
- Castle Macabre

CHUMP

Eight stories which take a different look at these reanimated denizens of death:

CURE WHAT AILS YA - When a snake oil salesman rolls into the Wild West town of Lobo, both he and the inhabitants are unaware of what is about to crawl out of the desert, hungry for brains.

1984 - Finally, after years of being subject to official censure, the true story as to why the Eastern Bloc countries boycotted the 1984 Los Angeles Olympics, is revealed.

RED SABRE ONE - An SAS team are tasked with extracting a high value target from their world famous home.

SENSELESS APPRENTICE - Step inside the mind of one of the undead, unable to do anything but watch on as his body acts on primal instinct.

DEAD DROP - A novella following a courier in the apocalypse. Ceepher's motto is simple; never look inside the package, and always be on time. His latest delivery will put both on the line.

CHARITY BEGINS AT HOME - Whilst out collecting for H.O.A.R.D. (Helping Orphans Affected by the Reanimation Disease), Sadie stumbles upon a middle age couple, who seem to have survived the apocalypse with their pristine house intact.

GONE FISHIN' - Bored, a son pleads with his dad to tell him, again, how his parents got together...one summers day on the lake.

WHACKOS - After 'Reclamation', a radio host and his sound engineer, follow a clean up team, as they confront the after-effects of the zombie apocalypse.